ETERNAL HOPE

LINDA FAUSNET

For all those who suffered in the bondage of slavery, may your struggle, your strength, and your stories never be forgotten. Rest in power.

My books contain steamy sex, bad words, and human beings of all sorts, include gay people. If you're not a fan of those things, you may want to stop reading now. If you're cool with that stuff, come take my hand and join me on this journey...

This book is a work of fiction. References to real people, events, establishments, organizations, or locales are intended only to provide a sense of authenticity and are used fictitiously. All other characters, and all incidents and dialogue, are drawn from the author's imagination and are not to be construed as real.

Published by Wannabe Pride 2020

Editing by Linda Hill

Cover Design by Chuck DeKett

FIRST EDITION.

Library of Congress Control Number: 2020921016

ISBN: 978-1-944043-55-1

❀ Created with Vellum

1

———

A ghost. I got grabbed by a ghost.

Paige trembled as she walked on shaky legs, still reeling from the unseen attack. After a long day of classes, she had been taking a peaceful evening stroll through the historical district of Colonial Williamsburg. One moment she was breathing in the crisp autumn air mixed with the hickory smoke of cooking meat from surrounding taverns, and the next thing she knew *something* had grabbed her ankle. Naturally, she had screamed. Now, she was in the process of being rescued and comforted by the most attractive man she had ever laid eyes on.

Of all people, Orlando Blake had heard her cry out in fear and had come rushing to her aid. Paige had long admired him from afar, but she'd never had the courage to speak to him.

"You all right?" Orlando asked, his hand placed protectively on her back as they walked away from the Peyton Randolph House, where Paige had had her frightening ghostly encounter.

"Y—yes. Yes, I think so," Paige responded in a voice as

shaky as her legs. Her nervousness was due to both the ghost attack and her sudden proximity to such a handsome hero.

"I'm Orlando, by the way. Orlando Blake."

Paige nodded, doing her best to hide that she was well aware of who he was. Orlando's entertaining performances and movie-star good looks made him a wildly popular colonial reenactor.

"I'm Paige Bratton."

"Nice to meet you, Paige," Orlando said, his rich brown eyes filled with concern. Tall and broad-shouldered, he towered over her. Paige fought the urge not to sigh out loud at the way Orlando protected her and calmed her fears. She felt like she was in a romantic movie with the most gorgeous man she'd ever seen in real life. He wore colonial dress, complete with tricorn hat, tan-colored wool button-down coat, and a powdered wig. He managed to make the silly wig look sexy, and Paige was well aware of the alluring, wavy dark brown hair underneath.

They walked in silence for a few minutes.

"I saw her," Paige said at last. "The woman who grabbed me."

She shivered, remembering the vivid apparition. After she felt a cold, unseen hand tightly gripping her ankle, a dark-skinned woman wearing a long-sleeved white shirt and a long gray skirt had appeared out of thin air. Her hair was covered, wrapped in a white cloth.

"Black lady?" Orlando asked.

Paige nodded.

"Yep. I'm pretty sure that was Jackey. People say she haunts the Peyton Randolph House."

"Wow," Paige said, trying to wrap her mind around what she had witnessed. Legs still wobbly, she quickened her pace to get more distance between herself and the ghostly attacker.

"She is not a fan of white people, from what I understand."

"I guess she was a slave?"

"Yeah," Orlando said. "She was owned by Peyton and Betty Randolph."

Paige winced at the word "owned." People owned pets and property, not human beings. She shook her head sadly, knowing it wasn't so long ago that slaves were considered property.

"That's awful," she said.

Orlando seemed surprised by her comment, but then nodded. "Yeah. It is. Can't blame her for not liking white people, I guess."

As Paige's head began to clear, she was able to focus more on her surroundings. She drew in a deep breath that smelled like grass and autumn leaves and gazed across the lush grounds outside the Governor's Palace. The Palace Green, a large, rectangular grassy area edged by trees, was a popular spot for tourists to rest and take refuge on hot days. Late September evenings like this one were cool and comfortable, though. Releasing her breath, Paige felt her body relax. The Palace Green was two streets away from the Peyton Randolph House. Hopefully, that was far enough away to escape that lady's ghostly grasp.

"Do you need to stop for a minute?" Orlando asked, seeming to mistake her deep breath as a sign of distress.

"Oh, no. I'm fine," she assured him with a smile.

"Good." He glanced self-consciously at his hand, still pressed to her back, and dropped it.

Paige felt disappointed that he was no longer touching

her, yet she found the gesture rather sweet. Like he wanted to respect her boundaries.

A group of women in their mid-twenties walked by, openly admiring Orlando's physique. He winked at them, and they giggled like schoolgirls.

They're probably wondering why a hot guy like Orlando is walking with a Plain Jane like me.

She watched the wind ripple through the trees that hadn't begun to lose their leaves. Focusing on nature helped calm her anxiety. At the moment, walking next to an intimidatingly beautiful specimen of a man was scarier than the ghost attack.

"Are you parked at the Visitor Center?" he asked, startling her. "Sorry," he said softly when she jumped at the sound of his voice. She hoped he thought that she was still worked up about the ghost scare.

"No, actually I'm parked at the college."

"You're a student?" he asked, surprise in his voice.

"Yeah. I took a few years off after high school before going to college."

"Cool. What are you studying?"

"I'm a Film and Media Studies major," she said.

Orlando's eyes widened with interest. "No kidding? What do you want to do with your degree?"

"I want to be a film director," Paige said proudly. Though she had little confidence in her looks and her ability to hold her own with a male model like him, she had the utmost confidence in her dreams of the future. She would be a director of movies, documentaries, and maybe television, or she would die trying. Either way, she'd have no regrets on that front.

"Awesome!" Orlando boomed with a deep, sexy voice that matched his perfect exterior. Paige laughed at his enthusiasm. His outburst was unexpected and downright adorable. "I want to be an actor."

"That doesn't surprise me," she blurted out without thinking. Orlando's brow furrowed. "I—I, you know, I've seen you around town performing. You're amazing."

"Thanks," he said with a grateful smile. She could see how much acting meant to him. With his looks, charm, and charisma, Paige found it easy to imagine the name *Orlando Blake* in lights someday. Even his name sounded like a movie star.

"When you're a famous director, maybe you'll cast me in one of your films."

Paige's heart melted at the word *when*. Not if. *When*. It was such a sweet thing to say.

"It's a deal."

"I'm gonna hold you to it," Orlando said with a grin.

They fell into a comfortable silence, and Paige's tense muscles began to relax again. She reminded herself that Orlando was nothing to be afraid of. He was a nice guy, and all she had to do was get through the rest of the walk without saying something stupid.

She glanced to the right side of the road, and her gaze landed on the Bruton Parish Church. She had been inside once. The interior was lovely yet simple, with wooden pews painted white, and soft, velvet cushions. The church was older than the country itself, built more than three hundred years ago. Paige stared at the graveyard that wrapped nearly all the way around the church. She eyed the weathered gravestones and above-ground crypts. Morbid thoughts of the rotting bodies below filled her head.

Dead. Those people are dead. Just like the woman who grabbed me today.

Her knees buckled. Orlando caught her, which made

her knees go weak for a different reason. Holding her tight, he glanced quickly at the graveyard.

"It's okay, Paige."

"I—I'm sorry," she stammered, feeling her face get hot. So much for not acting stupid. "It's just so ..."

"Freaky?" he prompted. She nodded. He gingerly let go of her. "I know this is scary, but I promise Jackey can't hurt you. Well, she did bruise my ankle when she grabbed me before, but that seems to be all the damage she can do. Just stay away from the Peyton Randolph House, and you'll be okay."

Paige shook her head. "I had no idea ghosts could actually touch anything."

"The angry ones can."

She looked at him quizzically.

"That's what I've heard, anyway. Not all ghosts can touch stuff, but the ones with lots of rage can." She continued to stare at him, and he chuckled. "You hear things in my line of work around here."

Paige nodded. After drawing in a deep breath to steady herself, she began walking again. Orlando eyed her carefully.

"I'm fine," she said, feeling self-conscious. She appreciated his concern, but she felt like an idiot. The poor man couldn't even trust her to walk in a straight line.

She breathed a sigh of relief once they made it out of the historical district and into Merchants Square as darkness fell. With the weather pleasant and the historical buildings closed for the night, the shopping area was bustling with tourists buying souvenirs and dining at the local pubs and restaurants. Though Paige normally loved the old-time feel of the Colonial Williamsburg historical district, she was glad to be among modern-day people in an area that was unlikely to be haunted.

As they walked together, people admired Orlando for his authentic colonial costume and likely also for his dashing good looks. *Dashing.* That was the perfect word to describe him.

The College of William and Mary wasn't far past Merchants Square. After walking through the lush grounds of the campus, they arrived at the parking lot where Paige's beat-up 2005 red Buick Century waited for her.

Paige tapped the hood of the car. "She's not much, but she's all mine."

"Nice," Orlando said with a nod of approval. "You gonna be okay?"

"Yeah, I'll be just fine." Her eyes suddenly grew wide. "You're probably parked at the Visitor Center, right?"

"No, I'm in the employee parking lot. It's a little ways past the Visitor Center lot."

"Oh my gosh, I'm so sorry. Now you're gonna have to walk all the way back."

The Visitor Center was in the complete opposite direction of the college. In fact, Orlando would have to walk right past their starting point, the Peyton Randolph House, to get there.

"No big deal. The weather's perfect. Besides, walking helps keep me fit."

With that, he lifted his arms and flexed, his muscles visible even under his wool coat.

"Mmmm." Paige uttered her appreciation without thinking. She couldn't help it. Orlando grinned, and her face heated again. "S—sorry."

He chuckled good-naturedly. "No need to apologize. I enjoy being admired by a beautiful woman."

Paige smiled sadly. They both knew she wasn't beautiful. Still, she appreciated his kindness.

"I'm worried you won't be able to sleep tonight. Do you have roommates? Or do you live alone?"

"I live alone."

"Oh," he said, brow furrowing.

"I'll be fine."

"There's honestly nothing to be afraid of. I promise."

"Thanks. I appreciate all your help. I'd probably still be shivering at the Peyton Randolph House right now if it weren't for you."

He smiled.

He's even more gorgeous when he smiles.

"Take care," he said.

"You too."

Orlando stood by, waiting until she drove off before she saw him in her rearview mirror walking away.

2

Feeling emotionally drained yet rather hungry, Paige stopped at a McDonald's drive-through on her way home. After she ate dinner in the kitchen, she settled down at the desk in her one-bedroom apartment to do some homework. She struggled with her algebra assignment for a half hour before giving up. The material was difficult to understand, and she found it hard to care. Her film classes were fascinating, but she despised the other required courses that had nothing to do with her major.

Grumbling, she glanced up from her work and stared at the black and white photos and classic film posters that adorned the walls of her apartment. At least this semester she had Theories of Film and Media, and World Cinema, in addition to algebra, biology, and Crafting the Essay.

Despite the fairly early hour, Paige was tired. Even so, she feared Orlando was right to worry about her not being able to sleep.

Orlando.

Thoughts of Orlando Blake were a welcome distraction

from both algebra and the day's scary events. She daydreamed of him as she washed her face and brushed her teeth.

Lying in bed, staring at the ceiling, her thoughts filled with visions of his gentle brown eyes and broad shoulders. Many times Paige had stopped to watch him perform for tourists in front of the courthouse or the Governor's Palace in the afternoons when she had a break from classes or on her evening walks. As attractive as he was talented, Orlando always drew large crowds when appearing as a fiery revolutionary soldier, George Washington, Thomas Jefferson, or any other colorful character he inhabited. Though his work schedule varied, Paige familiarized herself with his routine. She frequently picked up the daily program that was printed out for tourists and searched inside for scheduled performances. Like "Resolved. An American Experiment" taking place at the Capitol—a program he was likely to be headlining.

Paige's attraction to him wasn't simply due to his good looks. In fact, the first time she saw him on the historical grounds about a year ago, she had noted his attractiveness in rather a clinical manner, thinking a guy like that should be modeling underwear or something. Then she'd simply gone on with her life.

The next time she'd seen him was different.

Orlando was dressed in the same tricorn hat and woolen coat he usually wore, but this time she was able to observe him in action. She'd stood, mesmerized, as he gave a fiery speech as Patrick Henry speaking against the Stamp Act. By God, he was a good actor. He spoke with intense passion, and he made you believe his basic rights were being trampled on. If there was one thing Paige appreciated, it was talent. As a future director, she liked to believe she had a keen eye for knowing which actor would be right for what role. She'd had physical chills watching his performance. And when he happened to glance her way, it was as if a fire had lit in her belly. Paige had never felt such a strong attraction to a man, not even the famous movie stars she'd been infatuated with over the years.

And he was so *kind.* Paige sighed aloud in bed when she pictured some of Orlando's other performances. One of her favorite acts was when he pulled little kids out of the audience to teach them how to be soldiers. He took such care when choosing a volunteer. He was gentle with the shyer tourists, especially children, and only picked on willing volunteers. It seemed his mission was to make sure everybody had a good time. He would never make anyone uncomfortable.

Then there was the way he had cared for her tonight. She could hardly believe she'd been so close to him and had finally gotten a chance to talk to him. He'd put his arm around her.

She felt a bit silly for having followed him around. Like she was some kind of groupie. However, Orlando wasn't the only reason she strolled around Colonial Williamsburg. She adored the entire area and loved getting fresh air as she walked the grounds that had once been trod upon by the founders of the nation. This evening, her visit had had nothing to do with looking for Orlando. All the historical buildings were closed for the night, and she hadn't expected to see him around.

But she was grateful he had been. Upon hearing her scream, Orlando had bravely rushed to her rescue. There hadn't been any real danger—he had insisted the ghostly woman couldn't hurt her. Still, she could have been held up at gunpoint for all he'd known. Yet, he had come to save her anyway.

Paige also admired that he didn't seem afraid of ghosts. He, too, had been grabbed by this Jackey woman, but it didn't seem to faze him. The man was utterly dreamy all around. She'd had a crush on him for a while, but now the fantasy was more vivid. She'd seen him up close and personal.

And yet, he was still far, far away. A man like Orlando Blake was way out of her league. He could have any woman he wanted. Paige was fairly certain he wasn't married. He didn't wear a wedding ring, even when he wasn't in costume. He might have a steady girlfriend. Or a fiancée, for all she knew. She imagined the kind of woman he might go for. Tall, blond, blue-eyed, perfect body, big breasts, and ultra-feminine.

All the things Paige wasn't. She was no bombshell. Not with her average-sized breasts. And while not exactly a tomboy, she rarely wore dresses. Worst of all was her voice. Other girls had dainty, high-pitched voices. Hers was deeper, and not what you'd expect from a small girl. More than once she'd been mistaken for a man over the phone.

No way was she Orlando's type. He'd probably like a perky girl with perky boobs.

Why do I even care?

It was so unlike Paige to be hung up on a guy. She hadn't been boy crazy in high school, and she sure as hell wasn't the type of girl who always needed a man in her life. Her past was sprinkled with a few steady relationships but nothing too serious. Even though she lived by herself, she wasn't lonely. Right now, she was focused on her schoolwork and her budding film career. Pursuing her dream of becoming a director filled her life with purpose and excitement. Being single hadn't bothered her in the slightest.

And yet, there was something about Orlando that pulled her toward him. She didn't want *a* man. She just wanted *him* for some reason.

The idea filled her with sorrow. Men didn't gravitate to her type, and there was no reason to expect that to change now. Especially with a hunk like Orlando. She wished he *wasn't* quite as handsome as he was. Maybe then she would have a chance with him.

But he was unbelievably gorgeous and unattainable, and that was all there was to it. Best to forget him.

Which left her with nothing but thoughts of the dead woman who had attacked her.

Fear washed over her as she pictured the creepy gravestones outside the old Bruton Parish Church. She felt dizzy again, just as she had when walking past the cemetery. Good thing she was lying in bed, or her legs might have given out again. After breathing in deeply, her head began to clear. She thought back on the time she toured the church. In the graveyard, she had seen a marker for a mother who had died in childbirth. The woman had been buried with the baby, who tragically hadn't survived.

How sad.

Paige supposed it wasn't fair to think of those people as creepy and frightening. They were real human beings who had lived and loved and eventually died. It made her wonder what had happened to Jackey.

She shivered. Orlando had tried to reassure her there was nothing to fear from the ghost of the angry woman, but she was still afraid. The woman had certainly looked like she wanted to hurt her.

She was owned by Peyton and Betty Randolph.

It was hard to fathom what it must have been like to be a slave. Even if a slave was treated reasonably well by the owners, she still had no control over her own life.

Judging by the fury on Jackey's face, it was unlikely she was treated well.

Paige thought back on all the things she had done during the day. She had gone to her classes, some of which she hated, but attending college had been her choice. She had also chosen to eat her lunch at a picnic table on the campus lawn. Later in the evening, she'd strolled freely through the grounds of Colonial Williamsburg. Finally, she'd stopped for food at a drive-through. Her whole life, she'd taken for granted that she was free to do whatever she wanted.

As a slave, Jackey couldn't have done any of those things. She couldn't have attended school. If she'd had a dream like Paige's goal of film directing, there was no hope she could ever pursue it. A slave probably couldn't even choose what, where, or when to eat. Did slaves ever have a day off?

Even though she was excited about her film major, Paige had plenty of days when she felt tired and unmotivated. How could slave men and women bear waking up every day to face a future with absolutely no hope? Forced to work without pay, their every move dictated by somebody else. No way to plan for the future, no choices to make, and no reason to believe life would ever get better.

Does Jackey still see slave owners when she looks at people like me and Orlando?

No wonder she was angry. Jackey's life must have been difficult to say the least, and for some reason she was still trapped here on Earth. Instead of resting in peace, she continued to wander the grounds where she'd suffered in life.

Paige had heard stories of people helping spirits to "go into the light."

Could she do something to help Jackey finally go to her eternal reward?

3

———

Taking her fury out on that Paige girl made Jackey feel better, but only temporarily. She was still mad as hell, and at this late hour there were no tourists around for her to harass. Days like this reminded her why she liked to vanish. Unlike merely becoming invisible to the living, vanishing meant she was unconscious. Like sleep for ghosts, vanishing provided much-needed respite from the earthly world and its ugly inhabitants. Since her death in 1784, Jackey had spent the majority of her time vanishing. She had little use for the outside world anymore.

Watching the slave reenactors at the Peyton Randolph House was one of the few things that gave her any pleasure. For so many years, this damned historical area acted like the colonial times were some kind of party. Williamsburg was a wealthy area back in the 1700s, with huge houses filled with fancy furniture, expensive dishes, and big portraits of rich, white people. Large gardens ripe with vegetables and fancy flowers surrounded the homes. For a long time, tourists were taught that Williamsburg, VA had always been like a playground, where everything was fun and games all the time. Jackey didn't quite remember it that way. Around here, nobody gave a damn how those houses got paid for or how those gardens grew so beautiful.

Even though she'd spent most of her time vanishing—a weird state of limbo where she still existed but didn't see or do anything—she still checked in with the living from time to time. She had seen a lot of people come and go in the last two hundred-plus years since her death. Some had lived to old age, while some suffered from illness and accidents, never making it to adulthood. She'd seen soldiers die in the 1860s when the Civil War raged, and had witnessed, at last, the end of slavery. Yet hate and racism continued to flourish, nonetheless.

In 1926, she had been stunned to see the area where she had lived and died taken over by the rector of the old Bruton Parish Church. That man had gathered investors and transformed the whole place into a crazy tourist spot. Astonished, she had watched as the builders turned back the hands of time. Taverns, homes, and shops were reconstructed to look like they had back in her day.

Jackey had vanished for a long time after that. When she returned to consciousness in 1938, she'd found the builders hard at work restoring the Peyton Randolph House.

She had felt like vomiting at the sight of it, despite her lack of a physical body. Unlike many of the other buildings, the original structure of the property still stood. Jackey watched the men rebuild the overhead passageway that connected the kitchen to the main house, which was a big to-do in the 1700s. Mr. Randolph was proud to have had the first covered walkway in all of Virginia.

Jackey had stared at the huge house in horror, with its dark-red paneled siding and that passageway where she had labored for so long. The house and its surrounding buildings had had several owners over the years, and had even been used as a hospital during wartime. Now it was slowly being transformed back into the nightmarish place she'd been forced to call home for most of her life.

The workers rebuilt the big center section of the house that connected all the rooms, forming a large L shape. Peyton and Betty Randolph slept in the bedrooms upstairs, along with whatever random nieces and nephews happened to be visiting or even living there. The Randolphs had no children of their own. On the first floor were the kitchen, laundry facilities, and the slave quarters.

Renewed sickness had grown in Jackey's ghostly stomach as she entered the slave quarters one night after all the workers had gone home. The bleak rooms looked remarkably similar to the way they had when she was alive. Tiny, wood-paneled rooms painted white, with a fireplace and a window. The first time she had visited the reinvented slave quarters, she sat on the floor and wept.

She'd cried with the loneliness that had consumed her through the years, and she'd sobbed for the friends and family members she hadn't seen in hundreds of years. Jackey also wept for the lost life she had led, spent almost entirely in bondage. She and her mother had been sold to the Randolphs when she was four years old; she had only a few hazy memories of life before this house. After that, her childhood innocence kept her ignorant of the harsh realities of slave life. When those carefree days came to a bitter end, Jackey spent the rest of her life in what was essentially a drab prison cell, with only brief periods of release.

Filled with hopelessness, emptiness, and longing, she couldn't bear to go on. Soon, she'd decided, she would vanish and for a long time. But first, she felt she had to force herself to wander aimlessly through this house of evil. To see and feel all of it.

After mourning in the slave quarters, she'd found the emotional strength to get up and drift through the rest of the house. Her phantom stomach had clenched as she floated past the closet next to the kitchen.

I will not think of that, she willed herself, managing to keep those traumatic memories at bay. For the time being.

Outside, the storehouse, dairy, and smokehouse located behind the main house looked mostly the way she remembered them. She glanced at the ground, all torn up from the construction. Soon, she knew, they would turn it back into the garden that once existed there.

Facing the main building, she had shaken her head.

Why are they doing this?

Jackey had stayed around long enough to see the final completion of the Peyton Randolph House. And to see the tours begin. Proud tour guides greeted guests of Colonial Williamsburg and showed off the authenticity and attention to detail of their latest project.

They boasted about the best-surviving original paneling in the whole district, all the fancy brass hinges and locks, and the cut pine flooring. They showed off all the expensive china, candlesticks, and boy did they ever love those portraits of the Randolphs hanging in the living room. Jackey would have preferred to see the *actual* Randolphs hanging in the living room, but nobody asked her.

Tour guides spoke about the Randolphs like they were royalty. They were, after all, quite high society folks back in that day. In fact, Mr. Peyton Randolph was known as "the father of our county." George Washington himself was the one to call him that. Thomas Jefferson was Peyton's cousin.

The tours tended to harp on the way those great leaders kept Americans from being slaves to the British.

Jackey had nearly shaken with rage as she was forced to relive that particular injustice of her past.

Clearly, as if it were yesterday, she recalled Mr. Randolph getting all high and mighty at dinnertime, shouting about how he wouldn't be a slave to the Crown, all while the enslaved men and women hovered around, pouring his tea and serving his dinner. She recalled how hard it had been to hold her tongue during such incidents. Hell, it was a chore not to whack him upside his head with a copper pot!

As she listened to the tour man drone on about Peyton Randolph's heroics at keeping colonists, *white* ones that is, from being slaves to the British, Jackey had recalled an incident from her past. On one of those nights when she had been particularly tired and beaten, Mr. Randolph had held a meeting at the dining room table with a bunch of lawyers and politicians. She had heard them refer to themselves as slaves one too many times, and she'd nearly snapped. Rather than reaching for the copper pot as she would have liked, she stole a sweet cake as a reward for later. Most nights she went to bed hungry, as the rations for slaves were meager. One of Mrs. Randolph's bratty nieces had seen the theft and tattled on her.

That had been Jackey's first night in the closet.

The horrific memory nearly brought her to her ghostly knees.

The closet.

Dark and small, it had felt like being trapped in a tomb. Truthfully, it wasn't as small as what folks called a broom closet today. The closet was the room that Mrs. Randolph used as an office. Locking slaves in there for the night was one of Mrs. Randolph's favorite forms of punishment. Dear God, it had been terrifying. Gasping for air all night long, Jackey truly feared she would be dead by morning. In fact, she'd rather wished she would be. But she had emerged the next morning, shaking, sweating, yet alive. In reality, there was plenty of air in the closet. But Jackey had a fear of small spaces, which made the punishment more severe. Though Jackey hadn't drawn a breath since 1784, the memory of the closet still made her feel as if she were suffocating.

They surely didn't feature that part on the tour.

In fact, there had been barely a passing mention of the twenty-seven souls held captive day and night at the Peyton Randolph House. Because that would destroy the illusion, now wouldn't it? Much better to make Colonial Williamsburg seem like a fairytale land. Visit the fancy houses, stroll the beautiful grounds, and have dinner at one of the taverns. A good time had by all.

Finally, Jackey had been able to stand it no longer. She had vanished for years after the reconstruction of the Peyton Randolph House.

Modern-day Williamsburg seemed to be slightly better than it had been the last time she had spent any measurable time hanging around. The Peyton Randolph House still stood, and tours were still given, but they had changed a bit.

Now there were people dressed as slaves walking around.

Jackey had nearly suffered a phantom heart attack when she'd come back from her self-imposed exile to see a dark-skinned man wearing a tan waistcoat and breeches, looking much like a personal slave from the 1700s. Did he ever look the part. For just a second, fear had engulfed her. She felt as if she was alive again, and she might be thrust into the closet at any moment for her impertinence.

Eventually, her senses took hold, and Jackey realized this man was a reenactor. A slave reenactor! As she lived and didn't breathe. She never dreamed she would see such a thing. There were others, too. Several men and women walked around dressed like slaves, though none so handsome as the first man she'd seen. They even had a "Peyton" and a "Betty", which was odd. It didn't bother Jackey much, though, as they didn't really resemble the real master and mistress of the house.

For a time, Jackey thought the handsome pretend slave's name was John, because that was what people called him during the day. When a friend stopped by after hours and referred to him as Anthony, the truth dawned on her. He was portraying John Harris, Mr. Randolph's personal manservant. That was why his livery was so much fancier than that of some of the other fake slaves.

Dear, sweet John.

The real John Harris had been like an older brother to Jackey in life. How she'd adored him. He was strong and kind, always doing his best to protect the younger slaves. He held some sway with the master and had even saved her from a night in the closet a few times when her big mouth got her in trouble.

Had tears been physically possible, Jackey would have wept with emotion upon seeing Anthony's lovely tribute to John.

He's not forgotten after all.

For so many years, all the slaves at the Peyton Randolph House had seemingly been completely lost to history. And now, this dear, strikingly handsome Black man named Anthony was paying homage to John Harris. Tourists would know John's name and hear his story.

Certainly, the tours were much better than they'd been

when they'd first begun all those years ago. Still, there were some problems, though not from the tour guides themselves. It was from the tourists.

Like today, for instance.

A group of horrible teenage girls had laughed and joked as they toured the slave quarters. They'd giggled about how the slaves got to live rent-free, and then they'd had the gall to compare the slave rooms to their hotel rooms as they whined about the cost of their vacation.

Jackey had been too angry and stunned to respond at the time. Now, she realized she should have grabbed the ankles of those mean girls, not some random woman who had wandered past the Peyton Randolph House at the wrong time.

Jackey didn't feel too guilty, though. For all she knew, that green-eyed girl hated Black people too. So many white folks did. Gave that girl a good scare, that was for sure.

Then that Orlando character had come to help her, and Jackey found herself chuckling. He was a hoot.

She watched him perform sometimes. He was a sight to see once he got going on his rants about the Crown and all that. Orlando didn't compare the American colonists as slaves to the Brits, so she gave him some propers for that. Like the Randolph impersonators, he didn't look much like the people he portrayed. The real Patrick Henry didn't have quite so many muscles.

Orlando seemed so cocky all the time, that Jackey couldn't resist grabbing him to see what he would do. She was disappointed with his reaction. He showed no fear, only surprise. She'd grabbed him several times, but he hadn't been scared. It was rather annoying.

With all the historical buildings and shops closed for the night, Jackey's anger from the day's events soon faded into boredom. She vanished again until late afternoon the next day. As much as she hated the Peyton Randolph House, there was one thing she loved about it.

Anthony Alick.

Not only was he lovely to look at with his strapping physique and dark, soulful eyes, he was a wonderfully kind man. Jackey's favorite part of the day was just after the historical buildings had closed for the night. When Anthony was working, Jackey followed him to the same spot he always went before he left for the day.

The slave quarters.

Invisible, Jackey gazed upon Anthony as he completed his nightly ritual.

Leaning against the door frame, Anthony quietly said, "Good night, Johnny. Rest well."

In the moment of silence that followed, Jackey could feel the connection between the real John Harris and Anthony.

John would have loved this.

And Jackey loved Anthony.

4

———

Orlando strolled down North England Street as he headed toward the employee parking lot. It was fairly warm for an evening in late September, and he was glad he'd had the chance to change out of his colonial woolen coat and into jeans and T-shirt. He walked past the Peyton Randolph House, then stopped and did a double-take.

What is she doing here?

It was that cute girl, Paige. After what happened yesterday, he didn't think she would ever set foot around here again. Poor thing looked so small, standing there hugging herself as if for protection. She was so still, that Orlando decided he'd better check to make sure she was all right.

"Paige?" he called as he walked toward her.

She whipped around and gasped, her eyes opened wide. Orlando thought she might scream like she had when Jackey had grabbed her.

"Sorry. Sorry! I didn't mean to scare you."

Paige put her hand over her heart. Breathing heavily, she

took several seconds to recover. Orlando walked cautiously closer.

Her fear turned to embarrassment as she recovered from her shock. She blushed deeply, and Orlando fought the urge to smile.

She really is cute.

Not wanting her to feel uncomfortable, he crossed his arms and looked at her approvingly. "I'm kinda impressed you had the guts to come back here."

"I'm still terrified, believe me," she said weakly.

"Then why come back? Plenty of other places to walk around here that aren't quite so creepy."

"I know. I just keep wondering about the woman who grabbed me. The slave." Paige said that last word with a grimace, like she had tasted something awful. "I wonder why she's still hanging around after all this time instead of going wherever she's supposed to go."

He shrugged. "Good question. I never thought about it."

Paige's gaze wandered back to the big, red-paneled house before her.

Turning back, she asked, "Do you know anything about the house and the people who lived there?"

"Sure. I mean, I know *some.* I don't know as much as the people who run the tours there, but you have to know something about all the buildings when you're an employee here."

Paige looked at him with interest.

"Well, let's see. The house was owned most famously by Peyton Randolph, of course. A lot of people don't know who the hell he is, but he was pretty important back in the day. He was kinda one of the founding fathers. He went to the College of William and Mary. Like you."

Her eyes lit up, and she smiled. She seemed pleased that he had remembered. "Nice."

"He's actually buried there. In the college chapel."

"Oh, wow. I'll have to go visit."

"Peyton Randolph was friends with George Washington. He was one of the first to oppose the Stamp Act, and he was elected president of the First and the Second Continental Congress."

Paige listened carefully, but Orlando could see her attention was wandering as she turned to look back at the house. She didn't want a history lesson. She wanted to know about hauntings.

"Peyton and his wife, Betty, owned twenty-seven slaves who lived in the house, plus who knows how many more who worked in the fields."

She nodded sadly.

"They were obviously very wealthy. Owned what was called an urban plantation complex, or a townstead. It was the largest domestic complex in the 18th century. And of course, it was the enslaved people who did all the work."

"Do you know anything specific about Jackey?"

"No, unfortunately, I don't. I know a little about some of the slaves who lived here, but not much. Like John Harris was Peyton's personal manservant who traveled with him all the time. Kind of like a butler, I suppose."

"But an unpaid one," Paige said, a hard edge to her voice.

"Yeah. And then there was an enslaved woman name Eve who was considered especially valuable to Betty. But that's pretty much all I know."

Paige considered his words.

"How did you know her name? Jackey, I mean."

"You hear stuff when you work around here."

I heard it from a guy who heard it from an actual ghost.

It was the truth, but he wasn't about to tell Paige that. She was freaked out enough about ghosts.

As if on cue, Paige's face suddenly went pale. She looked every bit as petrified as she had yesterday.

"Paige?" Orlando asked, alarmed. "Are you all right?"

At first she didn't move. Then she shook her head. She opened her mouth to speak but nothing came out.

"Paige? Paige?" He stepped forward and cupped her face with his hands, trying to get her to focus.

Her eyes drifted down toward her feet. "Sh—she's—She's—grabbing—"

"Dammit, Jackey!" Orlando yelled. Paige grew even more pale, and Orlando was afraid she might pass out. Letting go of her face, he slipped his arm under her knees to pick her up. He was met with some resistance as Jackey must have had a death grip on Paige's ankle. With a little effort, he managed to break Paige free and carry her away from the house.

Across the street, Orlando gingerly set her down underneath a large tree. He leaned her back against the massive trunk and sat facing her.

Gently caressing her face, he looked into her eyes, trying to get her to focus. "It's okay. Everything's okay. There's nothing to be afraid of. I've got you."

Slowly, her breathing steadied and the color returned to her face.

"I—I'm s—sorry," she said.

"Don't be sorry," he said in a soothing voice.

Paige's face reddened, and she lowered her head in shame.

"You must think I'm such an idiot."

"You're not an idiot, Paige. Being attacked by a ghost is scary as hell."

"You're not afraid," she grumbled.

"Well, no. Not really. But being scared is nothing to be ashamed of," he reassured her.

"Ghosts don't bother you at all?" she asked, her green eyes pleading with him to say something to make her feel less humiliated.

"No, they don't. And I'll tell you why."

Paige sat up straighter, eager to hear what he had to say.

"I've had encounters with ghosts before, and they've never been scary. In fact, I'm kind of friends with one."

Orlando didn't want Paige to think he was a nut, but he figured he might as well be honest with her.

"You are?" she asked, eyes wide.

"Yeah. Her name's Rebekah, and she died back in the 1700s. Crazy thing is, when you look at her, you'd never know she was a ghost. She's dressed in old-fashioned clothing, but then so are half the people around here."

Paige nodded slowly, taking it in. Though he didn't mind telling her about his ghostly encounters, he was not about to tell her the whole truth about Rebekah. That the woman had come back from the dead. She wasn't a ghost any longer, but was now a living, breathing woman.

She'd fallen in love with the guy who worked at the cabinetmaker's shop here in Williamsburg, and she was given a second chance to come back to life so she could be with him.

Orlando knew he had to take one careful step at a time with Paige. Too much information would overwhelm her. Hell, it was still hard for him to comprehend sometimes.

"I know it's hard to believe, but it's true. I talked to her a bunch of times on the street, and I had no idea she was dead."

Paige shivered and wrapped her arms around herself.

Orlando wasn't sure if she was cold or if she was creeped out by the word "dead." Just in case, he decided to choose his words more carefully.

"Rebekah's super nice. Not scary at all. The guy who works at Hay's Cabinetmaker's Shop, Gregory, is a friend of mine. He knew I was chummy with her, and he warned me she was a ghost." Orlando chuckled. "Thought the poor guy might be out of his mind at first. Then I asked her if it was true."

"What did she say?" Paige asked, her voice barely a whisper.

"She told me what Gregory said was the truth. And she told me she could prove it. Rebekah said I could reach out and touch her, but my hand would go right through. So I tried it. She wasn't kidding. It felt kinda cold and weird, but not scary. I guess I wasn't afraid because I already knew her as a person. She was always sweet and kind. I knew she wouldn't hurt me."

Paige's brow furrowed as he spoke, likely trying to make sense of it all.

"So I don't blame you for being scared when Jackey grabbed you. You had no warning. At least with Rebekah, I knew what was coming."

"And you said she's nice, right?" Paige asked.

"Oh, yeah. She's a sweetheart."

"What about Jackey?"

"Like I said, I don't know much about her. Gregory is the one who told me her name. Rebekah knows about her. She said Jackey was one of the slaves owned by the Randolphs. She doesn't know her personally, though. I asked her once when Jackey grabbed me. It was weird, because Rebekah couldn't seem to touch anything when she was a— I mean, as a ghost, she can't touch anything. I asked her how Jackey could grab me, and she said it was her anger. Apparently, when ghosts have lots of rage built up, they can touch stuff. Who knew, right?"

Paige's eyes opened wide. "That's kinda freaky. So angry ghosts can do more damage."

"I guess so," Orlando said, treading carefully so as not to alarm her. "But I've never known Jackey, or any other ghost for that matter, to really hurt anyone. Bruised ankles are as bad as it gets, far as I know."

She nodded, still shivering and hugging herself tighter. If he'd still had his wool coat, he would have offered it to her.

Poor girl is terrified.

Though he didn't enjoy her discomfort, he did enjoy coming to her rescue. It made him feel useful and strong.

"Why did you come back here after Jackey attacked you yesterday?"

"I just wanted so much to help her. She was enslaved in life, and now, for some reason, she's still stuck here. I've heard that some people who live in haunted houses are able to help the ghost cross over and find peace. That's what I wanted to do."

Orlando shrugged. "Well, it was nice of you to give it a shot anyway."

Paige fixed her gaze firmly on Orlando, taking him by surprise. "Oh, I'm not giving up," she said, her voice strong and full of determination.

"Really?"

"No. I'm gonna help her," she said with resolve.

Wow.

He was thoroughly impressed with her determination. She had no intention of giving up, even though she was petrified.

Orlando was beginning to see Paige in a new light. More than just cute, she was actually quite pretty. Her dark, shoulder-length hair contrasted with a blouse that matched her deep green eyes, making them stand out. Her tight black jeans showed off her trim, petite figure. He was suddenly very glad he'd changed out of his work costume, especially that goofy wig, so Paige could see what he looked like in normal clothes.

Eying her with respect, he said, "You're a scrappy little thing, aren't you?"

Paige's laugh sounded incredibly sexy. She had a husky, sensual voice you wouldn't expect from such a tiny frame. He could listen to her talk all day.

"I guess," she said modestly.

"It's true. I think it's brave of you to keep coming back here, even though you're scared."

"Oh, I just hate the idea of Jackey being trapped here. She must be so lonely. I don't blame her for being so angry." She glanced across the street and then back at Orlando. An unexpected yet pleasant jittery feeling stirred in his stomach when she looked into his eyes.

"Orlando," she said. The fluttery sensation intensified when she said his name. "Do you think maybe I can get Jackey to talk to me like you did with that other lady?"

"You mean Rebekah?"

"Yeah," Paige said, her eyes flashing with excitement. "Do you think she might appear visible to me again, and this time long enough for me to talk to her?"

Orlando stared at her. Moments ago, she'd been pale, shaky, and on the verge of passing out from fright. Now, she was ready to run right back into battle because she wanted to help a woman she didn't even know.

"What?" Paige asked uncertainly. She smoothed down

her hair self-consciously, as if that was the reason he was staring at her. It was adorable.

"Nothing," he said. "I just think it's cool that you're so hell-bent on helping Jackey."

"Well, if I'm gonna help her, I guess I'll have to get used to her grabbing me," she said, shivering at the thought. "I promise I won't make you come save me again."

"I like saving you."

She smiled shyly. "Thanks. I'll be okay. You said all she can do is grab me, right?"

"Far as I know."

He'd never known her to do anything worse, but he supposed it was possible. He figured he'd better keep a close watch, to make sure Paige wasn't in any danger.

"I better get going. I don't want to keep you any longer," Paige said. She was a little wobbly getting up, and Orlando instinctively reached out to help her.

"Thanks," she said, her eyes filled with gratitude.

"I'll walk you back to your car."

"Oh, you don't have to do that. It's such a long way. Really, I'll be fine."

"I'm making sure you get back safely, Paige," he said firmly. "It's not that far. Besides, I can always take the shuttle bus back to the Visitor Center if I don't feel like walking. Speaking of which, do you want to take the bus back to Merchants Square?"

"I don't have a pass."

"Oh, right," Orlando said. As an employee, he had a pass to take the shuttle bus around the historical district. Though tourists could stroll around the area and shop for free, they needed to pay admission to go inside the historical buildings and to ride the bus.

"I'm fine to walk," she said.

They walked together in silence for a moment, and Orlando began to get the impression Paige was uneasy.

"I'm so sorry to inconvenience you again," she said softly.

"Paige, I don't mind."

"Thanks," she said, briefly meeting his gaze again.

More jitters in his stomach. It was funny. At first glance, Orlando hadn't thought of Paige as exactly his type, but there was no denying he was attracted to her.

"How's school going?" he asked, if for no other reason than to hear her sexy voice again.

"It's going pretty well. Taking a few classes I love along with a few I hate."

"Yeah? What do you hate?"

"Biology for one. I've always hated biology. Not only is it icky, but I always felt like it takes the mystery out of everything, you know?"

Orlando furrowed his brow, not exactly following her logic.

Laughing at his expression, she elaborated. "I have more of an artist's eye, I guess. I'm interested in the beauty and drama of life. Storytelling. Like I said, I want to be a film director, which means being a storyteller. Breaking people down to the cellular level seems like the opposite of what I'm interested in." She scrunched up her cute face. "Does that make any sense?"

"It does, actually," he answered truthfully. He would much rather be out in the open air in Williamsburg, giving performances and feeding off the energy of the crowd, than being trapped inside some lab with a microscope.

"I also hate algebra. I have zero use for it, plus it's incredibly hard. I just don't get it." He could hear the frustration in her voice.

"I could help you with your algebra," Orlando said. "But I won't."

"Why?" she asked, sounding shocked and a little offended.

"Because I'm terrible at math, and you would flunk your class."

Paige's husky laugh sent shivers of delight down his spine.

"Okay, so what classes do you like?" he asked, both because he genuinely wanted to know and because they were walking past the Bruton Parish Church and he wanted to distract her.

Paige glanced at the graveyard, but she didn't seem too upset this time.

"Theories of Film and Media, and World Cinema. I'm loving those classes."

"Oh, very cool. I took a few classes like that in college."

"What was your major?"

"Theater."

"Oh, of course," Paige responded with a smile. He enjoyed the way she said "of course." Acting was a huge part of who he was, and he liked when people acknowledged that about him.

"What kind of movies do you want to make?" he asked.

"I love any kind of movie that has a great story, no matter what the genre. The kind that makes you *feel* something. I want to make the kind of films that inspire people. Give them hope. Or maybe even just make them feel good for a while."

He turned to meet her gaze as they walked side by side. "I understand exactly what you mean. That's what I hope to do with my acting. Make people feel good."

"You do, Orlando. You really do. I've seen the way you

interact with the crowd, and it's fascinating to watch how fired up you get. Makes me feel like I'm watching a real revolutionary colonist."

He grinned, feeling warm all over. Compliments about his acting ability always made him happy, but they sounded even better from Paige's sensual, throaty voice.

"What's your favorite movie?" he asked.

"Gosh, that's tough. There are so many ones I love," she said, pondering the question before giving an answer. "*The Shawshank Redemption* is definitely on the list."

"Oh, *great* movie," Orlando agreed.

"Yeah." Paige shook her head in wonder. "I got to see it for the first time in one of the theaters that shows older movies instead of just catching it on cable. Somehow, I didn't get spoiled about the ending before I saw it. Wow. It just blew me away. Talk about *the feels*. That movie has everything. Drama, moments of comedy, poignancy, tragedy, and inspiration. The cinematography was unreal. Remember that overhead shot the first time you see the prison?"

Orlando nodded, recalling exactly what she was referring to. He could even hear the music in his head. The score and the shot blended perfectly together to form a truly haunting, tragic, emotional impact. When seeing the huge, gray prison for the first time, it was clear Andy Dufresne would spend a long, long time there.

Paige shivered slightly, but not from fear this time. "Still gives me chills, no matter how many times I see it. Simply a gorgeous film all the way around. I'd give anything to be able to create a work of art like that."

She had seemed a tad shy at first, but Paige really got going when she spoke of something she was passionate about.

"Sorry," she said, glancing at him self-consciously. "I'm babbling on."

"No, not at all. That's what I wanted to know. What kind of movies you want to make and why. And you had a damn good answer."

"What about you? What kind of acting career do you want? Theater or movies or TV? Drama? Comedy?"

Orlando smiled, pleased with her questions and with her enthusiasm. She seemed to genuinely want to know about him, rather than just make polite conversation.

"My biggest hope is to become one of those actors who can handle anything, you know? I'd love to be able to do drama and comedy equally well. To be the type where people say that guy can master totally different roles. Like Tom Hanks. He can perform in heavy dramas and goofy comedies, and stuff that's in-between like Forrest Gump. You know what I love best about Tom Hanks?"

She shook her head and smiled, waiting for the answer. He saw a glint of amusement in her eye, and he realized he was just as guilty of rambling on when he was excited about something. She clearly didn't mind.

"I love that when I'm watching him in a movie, I completely forget that I'm watching Tom Hanks. One of the most famous faces in the entire world, and my brain stops recognizing him because he disappears so completely into each role. That's the kind of actor I want to be."

"That's a wonderful ambition." Glancing up, she said. "Wow, we're here already. Time just flew."

"Yeah, it did." Orlando couldn't remember the last time he had enjoyed a conversation so much.

I should probably tell her that.

He couldn't bring himself to do it, though. Give him

lines in a play, and his emotions would spill out all over the stage. In real life he wasn't as good at expressing his feelings.

Paige looked at her car and then back at him.

"Thanks for helping me. Again. I can't believe you had to carry me," she said, a blush blossoming on her face.

"Yeah, I hope that was okay. You looked so upset, I thought you might pass out."

"I certainly might have. Thanks for taking care of me."

"My pleasure," he said as he watched her hair blow gently in the warm breeze. She reminded him of one of those models in a shampoo commercial, except she didn't have their typical "look at how gorgeous I am" expressions. Instead, Paige was more the type of girl who didn't seem to realize how pretty she was.

"Well, I'll see you around."

I hope so.

Orlando watched as she drove away.

5

P aige couldn't stop thinking about Jackey. She also couldn't stop thinking about Orlando, but that was a different story.

Last night, she had lain in bed thinking of all the horrible things about slavery she had learned in school. Specifically, she recalled a drawing of a slave ship her elementary school teacher had shared with the class. Bodies packed so tightly together, there was barely room to move. Each of those "bodies" was a human being. A person. A man or woman who had been brutally kidnapped from their home country and brought to a foreign land, forced to labor endlessly until their death.

Paige had known about this dark period in history but hadn't given it much thought until now. It was simply too dreadful to imagine. Now, she had a face to put with that nightmare. Jackey had appeared so briefly, it was hard to remember exactly what she looked like, except that she was frightening. The woman had been so *angry.* Maybe it made Jackey feel a sense of vengeance to grab people by the ankles as they walked past. In life, she likely had no power over anyone or anything. Perhaps in death she had at least some measure of control.

Scared as she was, Paige was determined not to give up. Whenever she considered simply letting the whole thing go, she remembered that slaving ship.

Throughout the course of the next day, her thoughts kept coming back to slavery. With every class she attended and every meal she ate, she was reminded of her own freedom. Now it was time to help set Jackey free.

After a quick dinner, Paige headed back to the Peyton Randolph House. She sincerely hoped Jackey would appear, yet she had no idea what to do if she did. Her first priority was not passing out. Taking deep breaths, she walked through the historical district, trying to steel her nerves.

She may have died, but she's still a person.

Paige knew she had to get past her fear if she was going to help this poor woman. Slaves were often separated from their families when being sold off, and now all Jackey's family members must be long gone. The only way to reunite them now was in death.

Death.

Feeling woozy already, Paige wondered how the hell she was going to do this. As she got closer to the Peyton Randolph House, she saw a figure standing out front. He was dressed in colonial attire, a tricorn hat, and woolen coat. It looked like Peyton Randolph himself, standing majestically in front of his house. Colonial Williamsburg could be so magical sometimes. Like a movie set.

The man's back was to her, but she knew it was Orlando by the way he stood. She'd have known him even if he wasn't in uniform.

Hiding behind a tree, Paige watched him.

"Jackey," he said firmly. "If you're here, I want you to listen to me. Paige is only trying to help you."

Paige's eyes opened wide at the mention of her name.

"You can do whatever you want to me, but please don't mess with her."

Orlando paused for a moment, looking around. He sighed, turning to walk away.

Then he stumbled awkwardly. His arms flailed as he tried to regain his balance, but he lost the battle and crashed face-first onto the ground. It was a hard hit. Worse, the yard was made of pebbled gravel and dirt, not soft grass.

Paige's hand flew to her face as she watched, her entire body tense, hoping he was all right. She watched him for a moment, ready to rush to his side if he needed help.

Groaning, Orlando rolled onto his back. Then he started laughing.

"Okay, Miss Jackey. That was a good one. I'll give you that."

Oh my God, she tripped him.

Still laughing, Orlando got to his feet and dusted himself off.

"I mean it," he said toward the space before him where Jackey must have been. "Leave Paige alone. *Please.*"

He poked a finger in Jackey's general direction, and then he walked away.

Paige watched until Orlando was completely out of sight before she took a few tentative steps toward the house. Jackey was here, or at least she had been a moment ago. Would she leave Paige alone as Orlando had demanded, or would she retaliate because of his words?

Orlando was gone now. He might not hear Paige if she screamed.

Visualizing the slave ship again, she steeled herself to keep going.

This isn't about you. It's about helping Jackey. Even if she grabs you or pushes you, you'll survive.

On shaky legs, Paige made her way closer. A wave of dizziness washed over her, so she quickly sat down on one of the benches facing the house. Guests sat here while waiting for the house tour to begin or to rest after being on their feet in the Virginia heat all day. Or, in her case, to gear up for a potential ghost attack.

Just as her fear began to subside, Paige worried that Jackey might shove her off the bench. If only there was some way to make Jackey believe she genuinely did want to help her. Then she realized she could simply tell her that.

"J—Jackey? If you're still here, I want to tell you I'm worried about you. I'm just ... Well, I'm sorry that you had to be a slave in life, and I'm sorry you're still stuck here. I just want to h—help you."

Silence.

Paige breathed in and out, doing her best to stay strong while terrified that Jackey might attack her at any moment. How she wished she could react like Orlando. He had *laughed* when Jackey tripped him. A small giggle escaped her lips when she recalled his awkward face-plant.

"That wasn't very nice, what you did to Orlando. But I have to admit, Miss Jackey, it was kind of funny." She looked around the small front yard. Concentrating, she tried to determine if she could feel a presence. Sometimes people said they felt like they were being watched, even when no one was there.

Nothing.

Either Jackey was no longer here, or Paige couldn't sense her presence.

"I just want to talk to you, Jackey. I don't mind telling you, I'm really scared. But I still want to see you."

Muscles tense, Paige waited to see if the woman would appear. Nothing happened.

"It's okay if you're not ready. I can wait for a little while. I just don't want you to be alone."

While she waited, her thoughts drifted back to Orlando and his sweet gesture of showing up to defend her. Shaking her head, she thought back to the way he'd had to help her again yesterday when Jackey had frightened her, and she cringed as she remembered how fear had rendered her speechless and motionless. She'd felt utterly humiliated by her cowardly behavior. At least, she'd felt that way at first.

But he'd taken such good care of her, made her feel so much better. The way he had picked her up and carried her to safety was positively swoon-worthy, as was his tender concern. The way he had spoken gently to her, assuring her she had nothing to be ashamed of. Lots of people would be scared out of their wits by seeing a ghost, let alone being touched by one, but not Orlando. She relaxed against the bench for a little while, reveling in the memory of being held in Orlando's strong arms.

Snapping back to the present, she reminded herself why she was here. Gathering her nerve, she stood, acutely aware that Orlando wasn't here to protect her now. Her body was on high alert and every little sound startled her. The gravel crunching beneath her feet as she walked, the distant shouts of children, a tin whistle being played somewhere across the street. She swallowed hard and walked up the cement stairs leading to the house. The door was likely locked at this hour, so she didn't bother trying to open it. Tentatively, she rested her hand against the dark-red paneling. As she did, she was suddenly struck with a sense of overwhelming sadness.

Perhaps buildings had a memory that held on to the emotions of those who lived there. Paige had heard stories of people who felt an evil presence when they entered a house where a violent murder took place. Maybe Paige could feel the sorrow of the twenty-seven men and women who were enslaved here. Or maybe she just felt sad because slavery was horrible.

She found herself wishing she knew more about what had happened at the Peyton Randolph House. Then she remembered what Orlando had said—that the people who worked in the building would know more about the place than he did.

That's it! I'll take the official tour.

Entering the house as a tourist seemed the perfect way to learn more about Jackey's life. That, and taking a daytime tour with the safety of lots of people around appealed to her.

Besides, aren't ghosts more likely to come out at night?

She shivered violently at the thought, hugging herself. What if the only way to see Jackey was to come back here after dark?

She decided to book the tour first. After that, she'd decide her next move.

Heading down the steps, she stopped to address the front yard where the woman had last made her presence known.

"Good night, Miss Jackey. I hope someday soon you'll let me see you again."

6

———

Paige purchased a three-day pass to visit the historical buildings of Colonial Williamsburg, something she hadn't done since she started college last year. Back then, she had visited several places, including the Raleigh Tavern, the Apothecary, the Silversmith, the Capitol, the Bruton Parish Church, and the Governor's Palace. She hadn't been inside the Peyton Randolph House before.

The first available tour that fit her schedule was on Saturday afternoon. Eager for it to begin, she stood in the front yard, allowing older guests to occupy the benches. Finally, a plump woman in her late 50s emerged from the house and walked down the steps to greet the guests.

"Welcome to the 1pm tour of the Peyton Randolph House! I am Clara, cousin to Betty Randolph," she said, eying the admission badges affixed to each tourist's clothing as she spoke.

Paige smiled as she surveyed the woman's authentic colonial costume; a white cotton dress with a faint, light blue-striped pattern, her hair covered in a simple cotton cap.

Clara may or may not have been the woman's real name, as Paige had no idea if Betty Randolph had had a cousin by that name. At any rate, she was pleased to see the guide was in character, like Orlando frequently was. Though all employees of Colonial Williamsburg who worked in the historical buildings dressed the part, only some played specific historical figures. Some were merely themselves, available to answer questions and give tours. Paige enjoyed the make-believe aspects of Colonial Williamsburg, like being able to have an actual conversation with "George Washington" in front of the courthouse.

"Come along and follow me as we tour the home of one of the wealthiest couples in Williamsburg," Clara chirped as she opened the door to the center of the house, which was flanked by two large buildings.

Paige hung back to allow the older folks and parents with small children to go in first. When she stepped inside, she leaned against the wall of the tiny hallway that connected the two larger parts of the house on the right and left.

Jackey must have walked through this passageway a million times, Paige thought as she surveyed the breezeway with two windows and a spinning wheel resting against the wall in the back of the room.

"Peyton Randolph may not be a household name like many of the other founding fathers," Clara explained, "but he played as big of a part in the birth of the nation as they did. His wife, Betty, also had connections to the new country, as her brother, Benjamin Harrison, signed the Declaration of Independence, and her nephew, William Henry Harrison, would later become President of the United States."

Paige had to work hard to keep her mind from wandering. Though she enjoyed the storytelling aspect of history, she wasn't a fan of dry historical facts. Besides, she was far more interested in the slaves who had worked here than in the people who owned the house.

Clara gestured for the group to follow her as she walked into the next room. "Peyton Randolph was, in fact, a good friend of George Washington and a cousin of Thomas Jefferson. Known as the Father of the Revolution, perhaps Peyton would have been better remembered had he not died before he got the chance to sign the Declaration of Independence. Peyton and Betty Randolph were thought of as a power couple, given Peyton's political standing and their tremendous wealth."

The guide led the tourists into a small room.

"Here we stand in the Randolphs' impressive kitchen," Clara informed the group.

Impressive was not a word Paige would have used to describe the small, rather dingy room. She surveyed the large fireplace surrounded by old wooden barrels and the iron tools hanging on the walls.

"This kitchen is the second-fanciest kitchen in all of Williamsburg. The first being in the Governor's Palace."

Paige nodded, remembering that things were a lot different back in the 1700s. This place might not look like much, but other tour guides she'd encountered said that the average family back then would have had tiny one-room houses with dirt floors. By comparison, the expansive Peyton Randolph complex *was* impressive.

Her ears perked up when Clara mentioned Charlotte, an enslaved woman who had helped cook meals for the Randolphs. Jackey must have known Charlotte. Had they been friends?

As they moved into a tiny room with the sloping roof overhead, Clara again mentioned slaves. She briefly explained that this was the laundry room where they would clean clothes, make candles, and perform other menial tasks.

"Several enslaved men and women also lived in this building, just above where we are now standing," Clara said. Paige leaned forward with interest. She had seen some depressing outdoor shacks at other residences in Williamsburg, and it surprised her to learn that the Randolphs' slaves lived inside the house.

"Two sets of families lived here. Peyton and Betty Randolph, though they had no children of their own, had a number of nieces and nephews who spent a great deal of time on the Randolph property. And then there were slave families who lived where they worked."

Paige shook her head sadly.

There was no escape for those people.

What must it have felt like to live and work in the same place, with your boss's watchful eye on you at all times?

"Twenty-seven of the total one hundred and nine slaves owned by Peyton and Betty lived here."

The sorrow Paige felt turned to anger. More than one hundred people—*human beings*—owned by two people. The inequality was staggering. And how must those enslaved people have felt to be living in such a wealthy house while they lived in squalor? Though Paige had yet to see the slave quarters, she had a feeling they were dingy rooms much like this laundry facility.

"Though those men and women were politely referred to as "servants," make no mistake: they were considered the property of the Randolphs, and nothing more."

Though the idea of people being property infuriated Paige, she was pleased that the tour guide wasn't sugarcoating the past. Sure, these mansions were lovely—so beautiful that many couples had their weddings here—but it was wrong not to look at the whole picture. The truth wasn't pretty, and it needed to be told.

After briefly visiting a room known as the servant hall where the enslaved gathered in the evenings, Clara guided the guests back through the breezeway where they'd first entered and on to the other side of the house.

Paige noticed a marked difference in this side. The paint was a light, cheery blue and everything seemed brighter. No doubt this was the main part of the house where the rich folks lived.

"This room here is Betty's closet. Not the same type of closet we're used to, but instead it was more of a small office. Betty would come in here early in the morning, ready to lord—or lady—over all the functions of the house." Clara gestured to a wooden desk that sat directly in front of a large window. "From that desk, Betty could keep a watchful eye over all the slaves out there in the courtyard laboring in the outbuildings as she tended to her daily work. Here, she would write out food menus for upcoming fancy dinners or list out chores for the servants."

Paige made her way over to the desk for a closer look, easily picturing Betty sitting there like a queen, dreaming up ways to keep her slaves busy. She looked out the window at the row of small buildings.

Jackey probably worked out there.

Clara explained that one door of the closet led to the dining room, one led to a parlor, and another led to Peyton Randolph's office. Paige lifted her head in time to see a dark-skinned woman in a cotton skirt, her head wrapped in a cloth, slip into the room.

Paige's heart seized in her chest.

Jackey.

"This here is Eve, Betty's personal servant."

Upon closer inspection, Paige saw that the woman seemed older than Jackey. That, and she was alive. Paige bit her lip to keep from laughing at her own stupidity. She needed to get a grip.

"Eve is valued at one hundred pounds sterling," Clara said. Paige winced at the notion of putting a price on a human being.

"I'm considered Miss Betty's right-hand woman," the older lady dressed as Eve said. "I travel with her everywhere she goes."

Paige eyed "Eve" with interest, wondering how it must feel for a modern woman to play the part of a slave. It was a tad unsettling, looking at the two women wearing colonial dress, standing in a house that had been here since the 1700s. Paige almost expected Clara to turn to Eve and give her a command. It made her feel slightly sick.

The group moved on to the parlor located next to Betty's office. Clara pointed at the wall where two fancy portraits of Betty and Peyton were proudly displayed. Peyton looked like a slightly chubbier version of George Washington, sporting a fancy waistcoat and a long grayish-white wig. Betty appeared rather stiff in her portrait. Clad in a fancy green-black gown, her features were sharp, and her arms were positioned awkwardly in front of her.

Staring at the portraits, all Paige could think of was that these two genteel-looking people kidnapped human beings and held them here against their will.

Clara went on to describe the opulence of the parlor, which was used to entertain prestigious guests. She pointed out the decorative figurines, the imported carpet, and the gold-trimmed mirror above the fireplace.

Next, they moved to the dining room where the table

was set for six people, complete with linen tablecloth and fancy china.

"In the morning, the dining room was used as an office space," Clara said. "In the afternoon, dinner was served. It was frequently a five- or six-course meal that included salad, soup, hog's head and other meats, vegetables, and dessert. Here, you might find such distinguished guests as Thomas Jefferson, George Washington, and Patrick Henry."

Another "slave" stepped into the room. This time it was a tall, attractive young man with lovely dark eyes. He was dressed in work clothes, yet his outfit was fancier than the woman's. His shoes were polished, and his vest was a shiny silver color.

"My name is John Harris, but you can call me Johnny. I am Peyton Randolph's personal manservant."

Paige made eye contact with him from across the room and smiled. The man bowed his head at her, nodding politely. His gesture made her uneasy, like he was treating her the way a slave might treat a white woman back in the old days. With solemn yet forced respect. The simple nod of deference made her so uncomfortable that it was difficult to understand how anyone could allow slaves to wait on them hand and foot. Still, she knew that was expected back then. Common. People were brought up to believe this was the natural order of things. For all Paige knew, she might have been a slave owner had she been alive in the 18th century.

It was a terrifying thought.

But even during that time there had been abolitionists who opposed slavery. Perhaps she would have been one of those.

"John goes everywhere his master goes and is present during many of Peyton's important dinners. But he is present in the capacity of a servant only and not as a participant."

Paige stared at the fancy table set before her, imagining it piled high with delicious food John Harris couldn't touch. All he could do was stand by in the background, awaiting his next command.

"John Harris was present on the day when the pamphlet authored by Thomas Jefferson was read aloud at this very table, in August 1774. The pamphlet was entitled "A Summary View of the Rights of British America," in which he laid out many grievances against the King. It was common for prominent colonists to refer to themselves as slaves to the British."

Clara fell silent for a moment, allowing her words to sink in. She didn't have to say aloud what everyone must have been thinking. What must it have felt like for real slaves to hear such language coming from slave masters?

They spent a few minutes in the dining room while Clara fielded some questions, then they headed up an ornate wooden staircase to tour the bedrooms where the Randolphs and other relatives slept. Naturally, the bedrooms were the height of elegance for the time, with fancy bedspreads, expensive wooden furniture, and a fireplace in each room.

At last, they got to the part of the tour Paige had been waiting for. The slave quarters. They were located downstairs and far away from the cheery, brightly painted rooms. The group followed Clara back down through the breezeway and then through the first part of the building. Where the slaves slept.

As Paige had suspected, they were plain, dirty rooms, nearly indistinguishable from the laundry facility. The air was musty, and she imagined the smell must have been unpleasant with so many people jammed in there. It was jarring to see the dark spaces with dingy blankets on the floor after seeing the ornate beds with overhead hangings where the white people slept.

This looks like a stable for people.

The reenactors portraying Eve and John were waiting when they arrived. They had not accompanied the rest of the group as they toured the bedroom areas. Paige wondered if slaves were ever allowed up there. She figured they probably were, as they were likely on call day and night.

Unlike the parlor, the dining room, and the bedchambers, it didn't take Clara long to describe the rooms. For enslaved men and women there was no imported carpet, no fancy dishware or figurines, and no gold-plated mirrors.

Paige watched as Clara ushered the group outside to the courtyard. Paige lingered in the doorway, staring at the depressingly empty slave quarters. How could Betty and Peyton rest comfortably upstairs in their elegant bedroom knowing this dark secret of misery existed below the stairs?

But it wasn't a secret, was it? The servants were paraded around proudly before prominent guests. No one was ashamed to own slaves back then.

Though the woman portraying Eve had followed Clara and the guests outside, the man playing John remained behind. She turned to see him standing at attention a few feet away with his hands clasped behind his back, clearly still in character. Even though Paige knew he was an actor, the idea of him being held captive was unbearable. Some of the make-believe aspects of Colonial Williamsburg were too real, too heartbreaking.

"May I ask your real name?" Paige said to the man.

The tall, handsome gentleman smiled, and the warmth

reached all the way to his dark brown eyes. His demeanor changed instantly, and it was rather fascinating to watch him switch from a weary servant to a modern, free man.

"Certainly. It's Anthony. Anthony Alick."

"Paige Bratton," she said, extending her hand. Anthony clasped her hand in both of his. She found the gesture particularly friendly. How strange that such an interaction between a white woman and a Black man would have been unthinkable in colonial times.

Paige wanted to ask him questions, but slavery was an explosive topic. Still, if you couldn't ask questions on a tour about the Randolphs and their slaves, when could you ask? Besides, Anthony's body language and smile were kind and inviting. In fact, he had probably hung back from the rest of the tour in case anyone did have questions for him.

"Is it strange for you? To dress and act as a slave?" she asked nervously.

Anthony nodded pensively, and it seemed as if he appreciated the question.

"It can be, I suppose. We do want to be historically accurate around here, so that means the only parts Black people can play are enslaved men and women. Believe me, it would be fun to play George Washington or Thomas Jefferson once in a while," Anthony said with a grin.

"Like in *Hamilton*."

"Yeah!" Anthony said, his face lighting up. "That was very cool. Seeing people of color playing those founding father roles. But I get why we don't do that around here." He paused to think for a moment. "It definitely can feel strange to play the role of a slave, but I like to think of it as a tribute to my ancestors. Those forgotten men and woman who had their lives stolen from them."

"I think they'd be proud of you and what you're doing."

"I hope so," he responded with a voice full of emotion.

Paige appreciated Anthony's easy nature. He made her more comfortable, and she admired his dedication to his work.

"Do you know anything about a slave named Jackey?"

Anthony's face broke into a wry smile. "Heard some ghost stories, have you?"

Paige laughed. "Sort of."

"Yes, it is true that Jackey is said to haunt the Peyton Randolph House, but I haven't experienced any ghostly sightings myself," he said.

"But do you know anything about the woman herself? What she was like? What she did for the Randolphs?"

Anthony eyed her curiously, as though surprised by the question.

"Well, yes. As best we know, Jackey was born around 1750 and died in 1784. She was born at another plantation in Virginia and was sold away from her father when she was four years old."

"How sad," Paige said.

Anthony nodded, crossing his arms and smiling at her. He seemed impressed that she cared to ask about Jackey. Paige realized people probably asked him questions about hauntings all the time, but it was likely rare that anyone asked anything personal about the slaves.

"Yes, it certainly is. Jackey lived here with her mother and was a personal servant to one of Betty Randolph's nieces in the same way I—or John Harris—was personal servant to Peyton, and Eve was servant to Betty."

"Interesting," Paige said. She wanted to know more but couldn't think of anything specific to ask. Perhaps she should have come more prepared. If nothing else, she knew where to find Anthony again if she thought of anything else.

"Well, I guess I better catch up with the rest of the tour. It was nice meeting you, Anthony."

"Very nice meeting you too, Paige," he said with a smile. It was such a relief to have him treat her as an equal instead of with polite distance as a slave would a white woman. She didn't want to pretend for a moment she was anything like Betty Randolph.

Clara met her gaze as she walked out of the main house and into the courtyard. Paige caught the tail end of her explanation of the outbuildings and listened to her gush about the lovely garden. It *was* beautiful, filled with lush flowers and flourishing vegetables. Yet again, it was another example of something beautiful that had a dark side. Slaves would have tended to the garden, toiling in the hot Virginia sun.

Not anymore, Paige reminded herself. Now paid Colonial Williamsburg employees maintained the garden. Even so, it made her chest ache to look at the garden and the immaculately kept courtyard.

As Clara wrapped up the tour and the guests began to disperse, Paige visited each of the outbuildings, briefly glancing inside each one. They all had signs attached to the front explaining what they were. Storehouse, dairy, smokehouse, and another small kitchen. With each one, Paige tried to look at them from the viewpoint of the people who were forced to work there. Hours and hours of labor, day after day, month after month, year after year with no hope of any respite.

Lingering in the doorway of the outdoor kitchen, Paige's eyes filled with tears.

John, Eve, Charlotte, Jackey, and the rest of you whose names are lost to history.

You are not forgotten.

7

———

Orlando found himself searching for Paige every time he walked by the Peyton Randolph House, even though he knew it was unlikely she would show up there in the middle of the day. Both times he'd rescued her from Jackey at the house were in the evening.

And yet, on Monday afternoon, he spotted her sitting across the street from the house, underneath the tree where he had carried her to safety.

Before he approached her, Orlando took care to compose himself. Namely, he wiped the goofy grin from his face that had appeared the moment he saw her. He couldn't remember the last time a woman had had that kind of effect on him.

"Hey," Paige said, her face lighting up with surprise, and hopefully pleasure, when she saw him coming.

Orlando glanced across the street and then back at her. "Still ghost hunting, are we? This time from a safe distance?"

She smiled. "Yeah. Kinda. Though it's unlikely Jackey will appear in the middle of the day with all these people around."

"You never know," he said, sounding spooky and mysterious. Paige laughed softly. "Not used to seeing you around here during the day."

"I have a break between classes. My next one isn't until 3 o'clock, so I figured I'd come here and have lunch." She balled up the wrappers from her lunch and stuffed them into a paper bag.

"I'm on my lunch break too," he said. "Mind if I sit with you for a few minutes?"

Her eyes opened wide. "No, of course not."

Orlando sat beside her against the huge tree trunk. He suddenly felt self-conscious in his colonial wig getup. He generally enjoyed being in costume, especially while yelling about treason for the benefit of the tourists. But here, sitting with a pretty girl, it felt awkward.

"I took the official Peyton Randolph House tour. To learn more about Jackey and the others."

"Yeah? You find out anything?"

"It was certainly interesting. It's a beautiful house. At least the parts where the white people lived are beautiful."

Orlando nodded, picturing the elegant parlor and fancy dining room. He also pictured the bare, depressing rooms where the slaves lived and worked. Paige's expression fell, and he figured she was probably thinking the same thing.

"I asked the reenactor who plays John Harris if he knew anything about Jackey. He told me Jackey and her mother were sold to the Randolphs when she was little. She was sold away from her father." She paused, and then added in a soft voice, "I wonder if she ever saw him again."

Orlando swallowed against the lump that had formed in his throat. He knew what it felt like to lose a parent when you were just a little kid. Bad enough that Jackey was a slave. He wasn't sure why Paige was so obsessed with helping her, but the part about Jackey grieving the loss of a parent hit home for him.

"He tell you anything else?"

"Not a whole lot. Just that she was personal servant to one of Betty's nieces."

"That must have been fun," Orlando said, shaking his head. "Betty Randolph was a real piece of work from what I hear. No doubt her niece was the same way."

Paige stared at the house across the street, lost in thought. He seized the opportunity to study her. Her expressive green eyes flashed when she got all fired up and softened when she was feeling contemplative. Orlando enjoyed gazing at her as much as he liked hearing her talk.

"You know, they have a slave exhibit set up over at the Raleigh Tavern right now," he told her.

Paige's eyes flashed again when she turned back to him. "They do?"

"Yeah. The bakery is still open as usual on the lower half of the tavern, but right now the main part of the building has the 'Revealing the Priceless' exhibit. They have the names of every slave that was known to have lived in Colonial Williamsburg posted on the wall."

Paige placed her hand over her heart. The gesture reminded him of Rebekah, who often did the same thing when she was feeling emotional. "Oh, that's so lovely. It makes me sad to think of all those people being forgotten. Everybody remembers the big names, the founding fathers and all that, but I'm always afraid nobody remembers the enslaved people."

"Would you like to see the exhibit? I can take you over there."

"That would be wonderful! Are you sure you don't mind?"

"Yeah, I've got time." Orlando stood and offered his hand to help her up. His fingers tingled when he grasped her hand, and he was grateful for the chance to touch her again.

They walked together down Queen Street and past Market Square, which was busy with outdoor shoppers this time of day. Market Square recreated an outdoor market from the 1700s where tourists could buy old-fashioned toys, handmade clothing, and soaps from the era. Paige smiled as she watched two excited kids trying out their new tin whistles.

"Parents are gonna regret that purchase," Orlando said, making Paige laugh.

"No doubt." She drew in a deep breath. "I just love that autumn smell. Smoky, but in a good way. All those fireplaces and wood-smoked food."

"Yeah. Fall in Williamsburg is gorgeous," he said. It was the first week of October, and the leaves were turning orange, yellow, and red. He watched Paige as she gazed at the trees.

"Makes me wish I could shoot a movie here. It's funny, I can't help but look at everything as if from a camera's point of view. I find myself looking at all this beauty around me and mentally figuring out what angles I would use."

"That's cool," he said. "Who knows? Maybe you will shoot a movie here someday."

Paige smiled gratefully at him. "Maybe so."

They turned onto Duke of Gloucester Street and walked for a while.

"I forgot how far down the road the tavern is," she said apologetically. "Hope I'm not taking you too far out of your way."

"Paige," he said stretching his arms out wide, "this whole place is my office."

She smiled, glancing at his colonial outfit. "Right. God, what a fun job you have."

"Right? I'm lucky. Oh, shoot. I just remembered, you need a pass to get in," he said.

"No problem. Mine's still valid," she said, pulling out her three-day pass.

"Good deal."

When they got to the tavern, Orlando waved at the older gentleman who stood at the top of the steps.

"Hey there, Will," he said.

"Good afternoon, Mr. Henry." The man tipped his tricorn hat.

Paige looked at Orlando quizzically.

"I'm Patrick Henry today," he explained with a grin.

"I see," Paige said.

Will glanced at Paige's badge to make sure it was valid. Rules were rules, after all.

"Enjoy your visit to the Raleigh Tavern," Will said as he opened the door for them.

"This was the main dining room back in the 1700s," Orlando explained as he led Paige through a mostly empty room. "They don't keep a table and chairs in here so they can bring in large groups for demonstrations and things like that. The exhibit on slavery is set up in the Daphne Room and the Billiards Room."

As he led her into the Daphne Room, he was tempted to run off at the mouth, telling Paige everything he knew about the Raleigh Tavern. As much as he wanted to impress her with his knowledge, he managed to hold his tongue. She was here because she wanted to learn more about slavery in Colonial Williamsburg, not the history of the tavern itself.

Orlando watched her as she took in the room, with its small fireplace and large windows that let in plenty of light with little need for additional, if discreetly hidden, electric light during the day. She paused to read the information on the wall explaining the "Revealing the Priceless" exhibit, which detailed the efforts of the Colonial Williamsburg Foundation to highlight the issues of slavery. Programming on slavery began in 1979. Prior to then, there had been little mention of the enslaved who had made up half of the entire population of Williamsburg. Orlando mentally kicked himself for not telling Paige that much before she read it on the wall. He could have at least impressed her with *that* knowledge.

Once again, he resisted the temptation to show off everything he knew about slavery. There was something powerful in the way Paige quietly read over the displays, and he didn't want to disturb her.

Music representing the slaves played softly in the background. Quiet chanting filled the room, some in English and others in what sounded like African or Caribbean.

Paige's lovely eyes took on such sadness when she stood back and surveyed the huge display of photographs representing every enslaved person who was known to have lived in Williamsburg. The photographs featured reenactors who worked here as well as other guests brought in to represent enslaved people. At least that's what Orlando figured, since he knew there weren't that many people employed as slave reenactors here.

"So many souls," she said softly.

"Yeah," he whispered as he gazed at the pictures. Orlando felt slightly guilty that he hadn't thought that much about the subject before. Slavery was horrific, but he hadn't ever stopped to contemplate it before he met Paige. The hundreds of photographs all together like this made the issue more real.

A song with the voices of young children began, and Paige groaned.

"I guess I always knew there where child slaves, but I hadn't thought much about it before."

Orlando nodded, sighing softly as he listened to the young voices sing and chant. Child slavery was such a tragic notion, but the voices he heard now weren't real slaves, just modern kids on a digital recording.

The thought didn't make him feel any better. What they represented was real. And not only had there been real child slaves, these modern children were aware of that fact. How must that feel for a young Black child?

Orlando almost voiced that thought out loud when he was distracted by the sight of Jackey's name on the wall.

Seizing the opportunity to touch Paige, he gently placed one hand on her back while gesturing to the photograph with the other.

"Look."

"Oh, yeah," Paige exclaimed as she looked at the photo. She didn't seem to mind his touch, so he kept his hand on her back for as long as he could get away with it. "It doesn't really look like her, does it?"

He inspected the photo of a woman in her forties or so, dressed in typical slave garb.

"I have no idea."

Paige look questioningly at him.

"I've never seen Jackey before. I've felt her, that's for sure. Got the bruises to prove it, but I haven't seen what she looks like."

"Oh," she said. "Well, I only got the quickest glance at her the one time, but I think she was younger than this lady." Paige stared the picture for quite some time. Then she asked, "Do you think I'll be able to help her?"

"Yes," Orlando said firmly and without hesitation.

"What makes you so sure?" she asked, sounding surprised.

"Because you're so damn determined. It's clear you're not gonna give up until you help her."

She smiled proudly. "You're right."

Paige pored over the names and photos some more. "Oh look, there's Anthony! He's the man who plays John Harris." She pointed to a photograph.

"He's so handsome," she said, her husky voice taking on a slightly dreamy quality. "Look at those beautiful eyes."

He had to admit, the man was rather attractive. Orlando couldn't help feeling a tad jealous of the way Paige gazed at the photo.

In an effort to lead her away from the annoyingly handsome reenactor, Orlando walked toward the room next door. "There's more stuff in the Billiards Room."

Paige dutifully followed him.

"Normally, there's a pool table set up in here, but they moved it out for this exhibit. Not sure how long the 'Revealing the Priceless' exhibit will be here."

"Too bad it's not permanent. It should be."

"Yeah. They do other slave stuff, too. Like the reenactors you met, and there's other presentations and stuff similar to what I do. But you're right. They should have a permanent exhibit like this."

With the music playing in the background, Paige and Orlando read over the information in the Billiards Room. More accurately, Orlando pretended to read while watching Paige read intently, not missing a single part of the exhibit. He noticed the way she tucked her dark hair behind her ear when she was really concentrating, and how she bit her lip when she saw something particularly disturbing.

Skimming rather than reading, Orlando got through the exhibits a lot faster than she did. While skipping ahead, Orlando spied something he knew would be of great interest to Paige.

"Oh wow, look at this! It's Betty Randolph's will."

Paige quickly finished reading about slaves working in the fields and came to join him. She smelled faintly like the outdoors. Like the smoky scent of fall she'd said she enjoyed. It was kind of sexy.

She scanned Betty's will and suddenly gasped out loud.

"Oh my gosh, her will mentions Jackey!"

"Yup." Orlando played it cool, as if he'd already noticed that. In truth, he'd stopped scanning the rather dry and detailed last will and testament halfway through before calling it to Paige's attention. He nodded and then discreetly took a closer look.

It started off normal enough. "*IN THE NAME OF GOD AMEN. I Betty Randolph do make my last Will and Testament June 1st 1780. I give to Edmund Randolph Esqr nephew of my dear departed Husband the Family Picture the Silver Chafing Dishes the four New Silver Salt Cellars the Silver Cup and two Silver Waiters I also give him the Suit of Yellow printed Cotton Curtains.*"

Orlando's attention started to wane again, but then Paige read the important part out loud.

"I give to my niece Hannah a Negro woman named Jackey to her use as well as the silver coffee pot and four silver candlesticks."

With that, Paige bit her lip. *Hard.*

"Can you imagine? Lumping a human being in with a coffee pot and some goddamn candlesticks?"

Orlando had never seen Paige so riled up before. Guilt

tore through him, because instead of being enraged along with her, he found her outburst an incredible turn-on.

What the hell is wrong with me? No wonder Jackey hates white people.

It wasn't that Orlando didn't find the institution of slavery revolting. Of course he did. He just found Paige's passion incredibly alluring. The women he usually hung out with—and slept with—were so superficial compared to her.

Paige let out a deep sigh and turned to look at the walls covered with slave imagery. A mix of reenactor photographs and drawings of men and women working in the fields, toiling in kitchens and laundry facilities, and being beaten and tortured for running away.

Her eyes filled with tears, and she softly asked, "How could this have happened?"

Orlando was rather relieved to experience a sickening feeling in his stomach, both at the sight of Paige's tears and at the tragic images surrounding him. Deep down, he cared about the horror of slavery.

"I don't know," he answered quietly.

"Jackey's suffered enough, you know? I can't imagine what she's been through in life, and she shouldn't still be stuck here. She must be so lonely and sad." As if talking more to herself than to him, she repeated, "She shouldn't still be here."

"We can't do anything about this," Orlando said, gesturing to the images of slaves past. "But we can help her."

"You're wrong. We can do something about this," she said, glaring angrily at the exhibit. "We can *remember*."

He admired the strength and power in Paige's trembling voice, and he realized she was right. It was easy to forget about slavery because it happened so long ago, but it was *wrong* to forget. Those men and women deserved to be remembered. Orlando was glad he'd visited the exhibit today, and not just because it meant spending more time with Paige. He was grateful to have the chance to read over all those names and to take a moment to reflect on their lives.

"No matter what it takes, I'm going to help Jackey."

"I know." Orlando had no doubt about it.

He studied her expression carefully. "What's wrong?"

"I'm scared. I know the next step, but I'm terrified."

"What's the next step?"

"I'm gonna have to visit the Peyton Randolph House at night. Not inside, of course. I'm sure there's security and all that. But outside. Where I saw Jackey last. Have you ever heard of Jackey showing up in the daytime?"

Orlando shook his head.

"But Rebekah does?"

Orlando nodded slowly.

Walks around all the time now, since she's no longer dead.

But yes. Even when she was still deceased, she had walked around in the daylight.

"I just get the feeling Jackey wants to be left alone," he said. It was a safe bet, considering she was prone to attacking people who got near her.

"I don't blame her. Still, I don't want her to be alone. She doesn't have to be. Not anymore. I just have to be very patient. I'll go after dark. And wait for her."

Her voice trembled, but Orlando knew her determination remained strong.

"I'll go with you."

"Oh, you don't have to do that. I've bothered you enough already and wasted too much of your time."

Placing his hands firmly on her shoulders, he repeated, "I'm going with you."

Paige smiled, the relief clear in her expression. If she thought he was going out of his way to do her a favor, she had no idea how much he relished the idea of being her protector.

Digging out his cell phone from his pocket, he said, "Here, gimme your number so we can coordinate."

Paige recited the number, and he programmed it into his phone.

"I'll text ya right now so you'll have my number."

She glanced at her phone when it chimed with the notification and laughed.

Give me liberty or give me pizza. Either's good, I'm flexible. Love, Patrick Henry.

8

———

That white girl's never gonna give up.

Jackey watched, invisible, as Paige and Orlando stopped in front of the Peyton Randolph House, hoping to catch a glimpse of her. The question was, did she want to make an appearance?

The girl was forever hanging around this place. Not that it was so uncommon for people to come looking for her. Jackey was no stranger to ghost hunters wandering around in hopes of a supernatural experience. The Peyton Randolph House was said to be the most haunted place in the whole town. Though Jackey loved to grab the ankles of the tourists who particularly annoyed her, she didn't indulge ghost hunters. If you camped out here all night with ghost equipment, you'd go home disappointed. Jackey had no use for ghost-hunting fools.

This time, however, she was tempted to show herself just to find out what the hell Paige wanted with her. And what was Orlando up to? Was he really interested in seeing a ghost or was he just trying to get some loving from that girl?

Knowing him, it was the latter. She'd seen him around town with quite a number of young women.

"You scared?" Orlando asked.

"I am absolutely petrified." She surely was. Shivering awfully hard, and not just because it was nighttime in October. "But I feel a lot better that you're here."

Ain't that sweet, Jackey thought, shaking her head with annoyance.

"It's okay. You're safe with me," Orlando said, putting his arm around her.

Jackey scoffed out loud, but since she was still invisible, they couldn't hear her.

Yep. Definitely trying to get some from that girl. Playin' the hero like that.

"I don't think I could have tried this without you. I thought I could, but it's scary here at night."

Jackey circled the two, still debating whether or not to show herself. She took the opportunity to look at Orlando's cute little bottom. He was pretty fine for a white man, she had to admit.

"Maybe I should try talking to her," Paige said. She swallowed hard and then called out, "Jackey? If you're here, I'd like to talk to you."

Jackey walked around to face Orlando and Paige.

"I don't like the idea that you're stuck here all alone. I would just like, you know, to be your friend."

"You *got* to be kidding me," Jackey yelled. That girl didn't even flinch, nor did Orlando. Some folks could feel the presence of spirits, especially upset or angry ones. These two idiots couldn't sense a damn thing.

Her eyes flashed with fury. "You wanna be my friend, do you? One thing I've learned, is you never trust a white person when they say they wanna be your *friend!*" Jackey's voice grew louder, but of course it made no difference. There was only one way to make her fury known.

Jackey faded into view.

Paige gasped sharply.

"You wanna be my *friend*, do ya, li'l white girl?"

Orlando stepped in front of Paige to protect her.

"It's okay," he said in a firm but soothing voice. "It's all right. She can't hurt you."

"You sure 'bout that, Orlando?"

He blinked, surprised that she knew his name.

"Yes. I'm sure," he said, though he sounded uncertain.

Looking him up and down, she laughed bitterly. "You know I can just walk through you to get to her."

With that, she charged forward straight through Orlando's body. He shuddered from the freezing sensation while Paige screamed and threw her arms in the air to shield herself. Recovering from his cold shock, he grabbed Paige and pulled her close. The girl went whiter than she already was.

"Stop scaring her," Orlando roared. "She only wants to help you!"

He's pretty brave, I'll give him that. Nothing I do seems to rattle him.

Jackey got right in Paige's face. "You scared of me?"

"Y—yes. Yes, ma'am, I'm very, very scared of you."

Good.

She enjoyed seeing Paige frightened out of her wits. It was also amusing to hear a white girl call her "ma'am." Orlando pulled her tighter against his body.

"I—I'm scared you're gonna grab me again, but I hope you won't," she managed to say. "I never knew ghosts could touch anybody before, and that's frightening. B—b—but I have to admit. It—it was kinda funny when you tripped Orlando."

Jackey's face broke into a tiny smile in spite of herself. That *had* been funny.

Orlando whipped his head around. "You saw that?" he asked, looking horrified.

A shy smile crossed Paige's face, and she nodded. Orlando actually looked embarrassed, which was refreshing to see. He was usually such a cocky bastard, being so good-looking at all. He must really like this girl.

Remembering herself, Jackey fixed a hard glare back on Paige. "Now what in hell do you want from me?"

She flinched, and it took her a moment to recover. "I want to know why you're stuck here. Why you haven't, you know, crossed over to Heaven where you belong?"

"How do you know I belong in Heaven?" Jackey snapped angrily. The girl didn't flinch this time.

"I'm sure that's where you belong. You've suffered here on Earth long enough."

Jackey wasn't sure what to say to that.

With one last look at Orlando and then at Paige, she turned and walked away. Then she disappeared.

Paige let out a shaky breath. Jackey reckoned the girl was grateful she didn't grab her. Yet. She could still do it if she chose to. After all, she was invisible most of the times she reached out and grabbed folks.

"It was nice seeing you, Miss Jackey. I hope to be able to talk to you again soon."

Jackey floated toward the girl and got right in her face. If Paige sensed her presence at all, she didn't show it. Glancing at the girl's ankle, she thought long and hard about giving her a good scare as punishment for bothering her.

Instead, she turned and floated away from the Peyton Randolph House.

"You did it!" Orlando exclaimed proudly.

"Yeah," Paige said, doing her best to come down from the adrenaline high. She'd been so frightened the entire time Jackey was there. "Yeah, I guess I did."

He engulfed her in a warm, friendly hug, startling her, but in a good way. She felt safe in his arms, protected against the October chill and the creepiness of speaking with a dead person.

"And she didn't even try to kill me," she said once Orlando had released her and she regained the power of speech.

"She's a tough broad for sure, but I think you're gonna be able to wear her down."

"I hope so. It won't be easy to get her to trust me, that's for sure. But it'll be worth it if I can help her." She wrapped her jacket tighter around her body.

"Come on. Let's get you back to your car. It's freezing out here," he said.

Paige fought the urge to sigh audibly. Orlando was always so protective of her. As much as she would have loved to believe it was because he was interested in her romantically, she was pretty sure he was just being a nice guy.

The logical part of her brain told her that while a nice guy might walk a girl to her car occasionally, they didn't often come out late at night to freeze their butts off at their workplace just to keep a girl company. Had it been any other man, she might have suspected he had feelings for her. But

Orlando? Impossible. He was ridiculously out of her league, with his supermodel good looks and charisma. She couldn't afford to get caught up in romantic fantasies of Orlando Blake. It wasn't gonna happen. Besides, helping Jackey was far more important.

On their way to the car, they chatted about Jackey and how exciting it was that she had actually made an appearance. Paige tried not to get caught up in the warm glow of Orlando's larger-than-life presence beside her.

It wasn't easy.

9

———————

Late into the night, Jackey wandered the empty streets of Williamsburg. She didn't bother to turn invisible since there was no one around to hide from. After hours of pondering, she still couldn't understand why Paige had shown up tonight, especially since she was quaking in her boots the whole damned time.

Being alone for so long, Jackey didn't relish the idea of having people follow her around like those two twits had been lately. She could always vanish if she wanted to. That would take care of the problem. Hell, she could vanish for a hundred years and not come back until Orlando and Paige had died.

The thought of them dying saddened Jackey for some reason.

Not like I care one whit about them, but I'm not a monster. I don't wish them any harm. Just want them to leave me alone.

She pondered the question Paige had posed: why Jackey was stuck here after all this time.

Most earthbound spirits knew why they were still here. Might be something bad they'd done in their life and they felt too guilty to pass on to the other side. Or something violent or tragic happened to them that they couldn't get past. Most living people didn't understand that ghosts were most likely to be haunted, not the other way around.

Jackey's whole life had been difficult. Not like one instance of tragedy and violence kept her here. She had plenty of bad memories, but who didn't?

After more than two hundred and thirty years of her existence after death, she could honestly say she hadn't a damned clue.

As much as she hated to admit it, Jackey needed help crossing over. She was no closer to escaping this existence than she was the day she'd dropped dead. Granted, it didn't help that the vast majority of that time was spent vanishing, existing in a state of being, yet not doing anything, feeling anything, or learning anything new.

For the first few years after her death, Jackey had actively tried to cross over. She truly had made an effort understand what was wrong with her and why her spirit remained trapped between worlds. During that time, she'd spoken to other spirits and had seen many of them make it to the other side. But they'd known why they were still here. They might have resisted facing their problem for a while, but eventually they'd attacked it head on and had the breakthrough they needed.

But if you didn't know what the problem was, how could you possibly fix it?

Was that persistent girl the answer? She'd never tried talking to the living about her troubles. Paige seemed sincere on the surface, but Jackey knew better than to trust her. She'd made that mistake before. Her heart had been deeply, permanently scarred by trusting the wrong person. Though nothing physical could hurt her anymore, she could still be emotionally wounded, which would only add to the burden of her existence.

What if this whole thing was some kind of stupid game? Paige and Orlando could be laughing at her behind her back. As a ghost, she was no stranger to being used as a cheap party trick. Like those damned teenagers and their Ouija boards who set up camp outside the Peyton Randolph House trying to conjure up the tortured spirits who haunted the place.

If Paige and Orlando betrayed her, she would feel that devastation long after they were both dead and buried. She would live—exist, rather—with that pain.

They claimed to want to help her. Jackey was pretty sure Orlando was along for the ride so he could eventually go along for the ride with Paige. But Paige sure acted like she cared.

What if she really could help her? What if trusting her was the only hope left for escaping the eternal misery of existence?

That little white girl was terrified of Jackey because she was a ghost. She didn't know Jackey was even more frightened of Paige.

10

Orlando sat as close to Paige as possible without touching her as they waited on the bench outside the Peyton Randolph House the next evening. He was grateful to have ditched his goofy wig and custom getup for a normal shirt and jeans.

"I'm glad there aren't too many people here," Paige said, scanning the area for any sign of Jackey. "She might not show up if there's a bunch of tourists wandering around."

"She might not show up at all, you know," Orlando suggested as gently as he could. For Paige's sake, he hoped they would see Jackey again. If she showed up, he'd have an excuse to keep hanging around with Paige. If she didn't, Orlando would have to man up and ask Paige out already.

He was usually pretty smooth around women, but there was something about Paige that kept him off-balance. She was different from the women he was usually with. Smarter, more caring, more passionate, more *everything*. Though he'd certainly enjoyed the company of women for the night, he never dated anyone seriously. For the first time, he wondered what a committed relationship would be like.

He wasn't used to wanting any woman this much. It wasn't particularly difficult to casually ask someone out on a date. Most of the time they said yes, occasionally they would say no; he'd get over his bruised ego and just go on with his life. He knew he wouldn't recover so easily if Paige turned him down, so he found himself putting off asking her out. Orlando was falling hard for Paige, and it was oddly unsettling. Helping her with this Jackey project was the perfect way to give her a chance to get to know him, and hopefully like him, before he made his move.

Without warning, Jackey appeared before them. Paige gasped, and Orlando put his arm around her and gently massaged her back. She didn't seem particularly scared, just startled. Still, he enjoyed touching her and found it hard to stop. She didn't seem to mind. Well, she didn't seem to *notice*, but he figured it was all the same.

"Hello, Miss Jackey."

"It's just Jackey. I don't need the pretense of the 'miss.'"

"Yes, ma'am," Paige said nervously.

Jackey rolled her eyes, and Orlando chuckled. He liked her spunk.

"Why do you keep showing up here disturbing my eternal rest?"

"Somehow I don't think you're resting much," Paige ventured carefully. "And that's not fair to you. Like I told you before, I just want to see if we can help you go to Heaven."

"What makes you so smart you think you can help with that?"

"I don't *think* I can. I just hope I can."

Paige sounded so earnest. Orlando hoped Jackey would believe her sincerity. She stared at Paige for a moment, then walked one step closer. Paige drew in a sharp breath, her body tense.

"I ain't gonna hurt you," Jackey said wearily. "Let's just talk and get this over with."

Jackey crossed her arms and waited for her to begin. Her movements were fascinatingly lifelike. If you hadn't seen her appear out of nowhere, you'd never know she was dead.

"Ah, w—well ... I guess I should start by asking if you know why you're still here. Why you haven't been able to move on."

"I don't know," Jackey responded flatly.

Orlando tried to read her expression, wondering if she really didn't know or if she was simply refusing to tell them. He wasn't sure. Paige seemed uncertain of what to say next, so he stepped in.

"You know, I have another ghost friend, who—"

"*Another* ghost friend? You think we're friends?" she snapped.

"Clearly not yet. But I think we can win you over," he said with a wink.

A subtle hint of amusement flashed in her eyes. She even stared unabashedly at his body, raising an eyebrow in what looked like approval. He was tempted to flirt with her further, but he didn't want to piss her off.

"Anyway, I'm friends with this other ghost," he said, though it felt strange to refer to Rebekah as a ghost since she was very much alive now. "And she's always known exactly why she's been stuck here since her death. In life, she made a mistake that had tragic consequences, and she didn't think she deserved to cross over. She's known as the Weeping Woman, because sometimes she cries when she gets lost in her memories."

"Wow. That's really sad. Maybe someday we can try to help her, too."

Paige's worried expression made Orlando's heart melt.

She was such a sweetheart. She could probably handle Rebekah's story since she was getting used to the whole ghost thing. But now wasn't the time.

"You don't have any idea why you've been here all this time?" Paige asked.

"No. I wish I did."

Jackey's expression was so somber that Orlando decided she was probably telling the truth. She had the weary and exhausted face of a woman who had tried and failed for more than two hundred years to figure out what the hell was wrong.

"I went on a guided tour of the Peyton Randolph House to learn more about the enslaved people who lived there," Paige told her. Jackey eyed her with interest.

"Yeah? Ya learn anything?"

"I did. I saw all the places where they lived and worked. It looked just awful. Jackey, I'm so sorry that happened to you. You didn't deserve that. None of those people did. As long as I live, I can't understand how people like Peyton and Betty Randolph could live with themselves knowing what they did to you all. How on earth could they sleep at night in those fancy beds upstairs knowing they had human beings held captive downstairs?" Paige's voice rose in anger as she spoke.

Jackey's expression softened as she listened, and Orlando's heart went out to her. After what had happened to her in life, it couldn't be easy for her to even attempt to trust a white person.

How lonely she must be. Orlando had started on this little adventure hoping to play the hero for Paige, but now he genuinely wanted to help Jackey, too. No one should have to suffer the way she had in life, and for her to continue suffering in death was beyond horrific.

They had to help her.

"I'm sorry too, Jackey. For everything you've endured." His own words sounded so weak. He had no idea how to express how bad he felt.

Jackey didn't seem particularly touched by his words. Maybe she thought he was just echoing what Paige said.

"I spoke to one of the slave reenactors there," Paige said.

"Which one?"

"A guy named Anthony. He plays John Harris."

"Damn, that man is *fine*," Jackey said, fanning her ghostly face with her hand.

"I know, right?" Paige said enthusiastically.

The two women shared a laugh. Paige met Orlando's gaze briefly, and he smiled and nodded. Getting Jackey to laugh was a breakthrough.

"He has the most beautiful eyes," Paige said wistfully.

Jackey nodded. "That he does."

"I asked him if he knew anything about you."

"And what did you find out?" The hard edge was back in Jackey's voice.

Paige smiled softly, taking her time to answer the question.

"He said he didn't know a lot about your life. He said you were born in 1750 and died in 1784. Is that right?"

"Yes."

"Can I ... May I ask how you died?"

She thought for a moment. "Was real strange when I died. It was confusing at first. Happened so fast. I was alive one minute and dead the next. I'd been sick for a while. Fever, coughing, and my chest hurt so much. Lungs not working right. Still had work to do. Nobody cared if you were sick. Well, at least no white folks cared. Anyway, I was working in the yard at the time. Last thing I remember was a bad coughing fit, and it was real tough to breathe. And then I guess it was over. Took a bit for me to understand what happened."

Orlando watched Jackey as she spoke. She seemed so lost.

"I was talking to people, and then I realized they couldn't hear me." Her voice dropped to a whisper. "It was frightening."

Paige gazed at Jackey sorrowfully, so Orlando began rubbing her back again. She turned to face him and smiled gratefully. When it was clear Jackey was done talking about her death, Paige spoke again.

"Anthony said you were servant to one of Betty's nieces."

Jackey's expression hardened at that, and she looked away. Paige fell silent again, not wanting to press too hard.

Though Orlando was also concerned about pushing Jackey too far in case they scared her off, he was overwhelmed with sorrow at her plight. He felt he had to speak.

"Paige told me you were sold away from your father at a very young age," he said.

Jackey turned back toward the two. She nodded.

"Did you ever see your father again?"

"No," she said quietly.

Orlando's heart squeezed in his chest, understanding that particular pain all too well. It felt like "I'm sorry" would lose its meaning if he kept saying it about every tragic thing that had happened to Jackey, so he kept quiet. But he looked into her eyes and he saw a glimpse of gratitude. Like she understood that he was genuinely sad for her loss.

"Being a slave your entire life, there could be any number of things keeping you here," Paige said, her voice earnest yet cautious. "You must have a lot of terrible memories. Can you think of anything specific that you think might be why you're still here?"

"No!" she shouted. "I told you, I don't know!"

Paige swallowed hard, and Orlando tightened his grip around her. The two kept silent for a moment, and their patience paid off.

"All this time," Jackey began, "I tried to see what went wrong. People die all day, every day, year 'round, but there's only a few that stay as spirits. I don't know why I'm one of them."

Orlando felt Paige relax beneath his arm. They had to tread carefully, but they were already making some progress.

"I was a good person," she said, despair in her voice. "I wasn't perfect, but God knows I did the best I could. I don't understand why I'm being punished."

"It doesn't make any sense, does it?" Paige said.

"No, it sure doesn't. I mean, you don't see Betty Randolph 'round here, do you?"

Paige leaned forward and, unfortunately for him, out of Orlando's grasp. He felt empty without her warmth.

"Yeah, you're right. How can that be? I don't know of any slave owner ghosts, do you?" Paige said angrily.

"Well ..." Orlando said. "Actually, Rebekah was a slave owner. At least her family was."

"They were?" Paige said, sounding shocked and offended that he could be friends with someone like that.

"Yeah. And Jackey, for what it's worth, she is sorry about owning slaves."

Jackey scoffed at that, and Orlando didn't blame her one bit.

"I know. I'm not saying it's an excuse, but she was brought up to believe that it was okay to have slaves. She died around the 1760s I think, and she's had a lot of time to think about it. She feels awful about it now."

"Well, that don't help the slaves she owned, now does it?" Jackey said.

"No, it doesn't," he said.

Jackey turned to face the Peyton Randolph House.

"I hate this place," she said. "Gave me nothing but oppression and suffering and fear. Yet, it's the only home I ever knew. There were people I loved in there. Family. Friends who might well have been family, they were so dear."

Looking at Paige, she said, "I knew the real John Harris. The man Anthony plays on the tours. He was a good man. Like a big brother to me. Looked out for me like he was my own kin."

"That's lovely," Paige said. "Were you ever married, Jackey? Did you have children?"

"Oh, no. I refused to get married, and I didn't want no children. You bear children and there's a good chance they would be ripped right from your arms."

The heavy weight of that truth settled upon them. The unbearable horror of it.

"Lucky I never have kids. Was rather a miracle. I 'spect I was barren," she said matter-of-factly. "Must have been, because I did have my fun with men."

"Is that so?" Orlando said, fascinated by this unexpected information.

Jackey chuckled. "I mighta known that'd get your interest."

She glanced at Paige and then back at him. It felt as if she could see right through him and his feelings for Paige. Would she call him out on it? Jackey was not one to mince words.

"Bein' with a lotta men was my way of rebelling, I guess. Didn't have much control over my own life, but I could control my sex life. I enjoyed the company of several men, which would have shocked Miss Betty. That's why I did it. That, and it was one hell of a lot of fun."

"Good for you," Paige said, defiance in her voice. "That's incredible. Sometimes I wish I could be that brave."

Orlando wondered exactly what she meant by that. Did she mean she wished she could sleep with a lot of men too?

She could start with me.

Casual sex wasn't what he wanted with Paige, though. That would never be enough.

"Have you ever been in love?" she asked.

Jackey made a motion with her chest like she was sighing, but naturally there was no breath. She took a long time to answer that question, which was answer enough for Orlando. It wouldn't take that long to say no.

"Yes," she said at last. "But it happened too late."

Orlando wondered if perhaps the man she loved was already married, even if it wasn't recognized legally. He knew it was commonplace for slaves to marry back then. Perhaps the love of Jackey's life had a wife and children. Could that be the regret that had kept her here after death? He was about to ask her, but she spoke first.

"A wonderful, caring man," she said in a faraway voice. "With a smile so sweet. Kind of a half-smile, but it still made his eyes crinkle up in the corners of 'em."

Paige placed her hand over her heart again. The gentle yet powerful way Jackey spoke of this man made it clear how deeply she had loved him.

"I'm tired of talking," she said abruptly. Perhaps Jackey was uncomfortable with how personal the conversation had become.

"That's okay," Paige said. "We can stop for now, but I hope we can meet again."

Jackey didn't respond right away. But she didn't say no, either.

"It doesn't have to be here. I understand being near this house makes you unhappy. Maybe we could get together somewhere else?"

After a long pause, Jackey said, "Maybe."

Paige's face broke into the cutest smile, her eyes full of optimism. "Where do want to meet?"

"Can't be too far from here. I'm not able to wander a long ways from where I died," she said, shooting a look of disgust at the Peyton Randolph House. "But I don't wanna meet where its crowded in town. I got no choice but to wear these damned rags I had on my whole life. Can't stand it when people think I'm play-acting here and they ask me a bunch of dumb questions about slavery."

"Wow, I hadn't thought of that," Paige said. "That would be annoying. Orlando, where's a good place to meet that's not too far away and not crowded?"

"There's a big grassy area around the old Public Gaol. Way down the end of Nicholson Street. Should be pretty empty, especially after the buildings close for the night."

"That sounds perfect. What do you think, Miss— I mean, Jackey? Would you be willing to talk with me again?"

Jackey looked into Paige's eyes, filled with such hope. She laughed.

"Sayin' no to her is like kickin' a puppy dog, ain't it?"

"Tell me about it," Orlando agreed. He couldn't refuse her anything when she looked into his eyes.

"Fine," Jackey said, sounding unenthused. "Tomorrow evening after five at the Public Gaol."

Without another word, Jackey walked away. After several steps, she disappeared into thin air.

Orlando and Paige sat together on the bench for a moment in silence. At last, Paige let out a deep breath.

"That was incredible. I can't believe I actually got a chance to talk to her," she said. "And that she's willing to meet up again."

She turned to look at Orlando, and his stomach did somersaults. God, she made him crazy. In a good way.

"You don't have to come with me to meet with her. I'm not scared anymore."

He felt guilty about it, but he wanted her to be scared. He wanted her to need him.

"I don't mind. Honestly, I want to help Jackey too."

As soon as the words left his mouth, he realized how much he genuinely meant them. Talking with Jackey tonight made everything real to him. Colonial Williamsburg had always been like an elaborate set where he could act out different characters. He'd seen the slave quarters and places where slaves had worked, but he hadn't thought much about it. Until now. The woman he had spent the evening talking to had been held captive and forced to work in the dark recesses of a house owned by one of the wealthy and powerful in town. He felt terrible for thinking of this whole thing as "this Jackey project." She wasn't a project, nor was she just an excuse for him to get close to another girl. Jackey was a woman who had been horribly oppressed. She deserved to be set free, and he was more than happy to help in any way he could.

Still gazing into his eyes, Paige said, "That's so sweet of you to care so much."

Orlando experienced a flood of emotions. He wanted to tell Paige how amazing she was for facing her fears and trying to help Jackey, and that she was one of the coolest people he had ever met. As usual, he couldn't find the words or the courage to say what he felt.

"I'd like to help," he said instead. "I mean, if you're okay with my tagging along."

"Of course," she said softly.

Fighting the urge to lean down and kiss her, Orlando stood and offered his hand instead.

"Come on. Let's get you out of the cold."

11

———

Paige made her way through town toward the Public Gaol just before 5pm. There wasn't much to the place as far as Williamsburg attractions went. The two-story brick building had a bunch of cell blocks inside and not much else. She recalled wandering through there once, since the doors were left open to the public. It wasn't even manned by any employees. Located at the far end of Nicholson Street, it was part of the historical district's larger tours as opposed to a major attraction on its own. The spacious area surrounding the old gaol was ideal to meet with Jackey. With no shops or taverns nearby, there was little reason for tourists to be around after hours. Mostly just trees and grass.

After sitting in the grass a few feet from the gaol, Paige's heart leapt in her chest when she saw Orlando, all broad-shouldered and masculine, walking her way. She allowed herself an audible, dreamy sigh while he was still out of earshot, then she turned away, pretending not to have seen him.

"Hey," he called softly when he got near. She figured he

spoke quietly so as not to startle her. He was thoughtful like that.

"Hey," Paige said, turning to face him. He had changed out of his work clothes and was wearing blue jeans and a button-down black shirt that complemented his longish dark brown hair and brown eyes. She had to look up, and up to meet his gaze. He was so *tall.* She stifled another sigh.

Orlando took a seat next to her.

"I hope she shows up," Paige said. "I'm afraid she might change her mind."

"I doubt it. She's still kind of wary of us, but I get the feeling she does want our help." He laughed. "I feel like I gotta be careful about what I say. For all we know, Jackey's here now and we just can't see her."

"That's true. I hadn't thought of that."

Paige and Orlando looked around as if expecting her to appear at any time. Paige laughed awkwardly, and he joined in. This was a strange situation to be in for sure.

"There she is," Orlando said, and Paige followed his gaze. Sure enough, Jackey was walking down Nicholson Street in the distance.

"She's so lifelike," Paige remarked.

"Yeah. It's crazy."

Jackey walked up to where the two were sitting.

"Hello," she said stiffly.

"Hi, Jackey," Paige responded. "It's good to see you."

Jackey looked at Orlando. Specifically, she looked him up and down. It wasn't the first time Paige had seen her check him out.

Something we have in common. We both think Orlando is hot.

As a free living woman and a deceased former slave, she

and Jackey couldn't have been more different. But they were still women.

"Do you want to sit down?" Paige asked.

"Don't make no difference. I can't feel anything anyway," Jackey said. She did sit down in the grass, but not too close to them. Once again, Paige marveled at her lifelike motions.

"So now what?" Jackey asked. "I'm just supposed to sit here and tell you my life story?"

"Well," Paige said, not sure what to say next. She did want Jackey to tell her everything about her life, but it was a lot to ask. After all, Jackey barely knew them.

"Why don't we talk about your life? So far, I'm the only one spilling all my stories."

"That's fair. What do you want to know?" Paige asked.

"You got a boyfriend?"

"No."

"What about you?" she asked, turning to Orlando. "You got a girlfriend?"

Paige tensed, afraid to hear the answer.

"Nope."

Thank God.

Paige knew she didn't stand a chance with a man like Orlando, but thinking about him with another woman was still painful.

"Why?" Orlando teased. "You interested, good-lookin'?"

Jackey's face edged slightly into a smile.

"Boy, I'm too much woman for you to handle."

His face turned glum. "I know," he grumbled.

Paige laughed, and she saw unmistakable amusement in Jackey's eyes.

"You got a job?" Jackey asked Paige.

"Not at the moment. I'm a student at the College of William and Mary. I took a few years off after high school to work and save up money so when I went to school, I could just concentrate on my studies. That, and my parents helped out with tuition, so I don't have to work right now. I'm very lucky that way."

Jackey nodded, and Paige felt like "lucky" was a vast understatement. Especially considering who she was talking to.

"And I know what you do for a living," she said to Orlando. "You're a slave owner reenactor."

"Of sorts, I guess. I never thought of it that way," he said. "I mean, the founding fathers did a lot of things, but you're right. Being slaveholders was one of them."

Jackey nodded. The sadness in her eyes replaced some of the anger. Paige was grateful for Orlando's answer. He could have gone on to defend people like Thomas Jefferson and George Washington for all their great deeds, but this was not the time or place for that.

"They do acknowledge the fact that the founders of the country were slave owners, but maybe not as much as they should," he admitted.

"Never seen you give any performances as a slave master," Jackey said, the edge back in her voice.

"That's true. I don't get to decide what and where I perform. I can improv some stuff, but not which presentations to give. I'm gonna level with you, Jackey. Even if I could choose to do a show as Thomas Jefferson as a slave owner, I wouldn't. It would be awkward and uncomfortable, and I wouldn't want to do it."

Orlando's eyes never left Jackey's as he spoke. She gazed at him for a bit, and then she nodded.

"I guess we got to talk about me now," she said.

"When you're ready," Paige said gently.

"I'm not sure where to begin."

"At the beginning. What's your earliest memory?"

"I was born at the Berkeley plantation in Charles City, Virginia." Jackey laughed. "That ain't my first memory, though. I don't remember *that* far back. But I got a few memories of that place here and there. And memories of my father."

She looked so sad as she spoke.

"I only saw him in the evening time. I didn't know it then, but he was working in the fields during the day. My mama worked in the kitchen. My parents were good about keepin' the truth from me. For as long as possible, they kept the whole idea of slavery from me. I was so little then. I didn't understand that it wasn't our house and it wasn't our kitchen. I hadn't seen the owners' fancy bedrooms, so I didn't think nothing about the small room we slept in."

With a heavy heart, Paige thought about what it must have been like for slaves to have children. The burden they carried, fully aware of the hopeless future for their sons and daughters. No wonder Jackey didn't want children of her own.

"I don't remember a whole lot about my papa, but I remember he was kind. Used to play with me, toss me up in the air to make me laugh. Things like that."

Orlando stared at the ground as Jackey spoke. Paige had never seen him look so unhappy.

"Then when I was four years old, we moved— No. We didn't move," she said angrily. "We were *sold* to the Randolphs. Least me and my mama were. My papa had to stay behind. I remember coming to live at the Randolph house and askin' and askin' where my papa was. I guess eventually I quit askin'."

"That must have been so hard for your mother," Paige said.

"You cannot imagine the pain she suffered," Jackey said in a voice so cold, it chilled Paige's blood.

No. She couldn't imagine.

"I was confused when we got brought to the Randolph house, but I wasn't really frightened. As always, my mama protected me. Kept me from knowin' the truth. There were more children here than at our old home. Things weren't so bad because I had kids to play with. Children of slaves and lots of child relatives of Betty and Peyton. We had a grand old time. For a while. I even made friends with a li'l ol' white girl. She was four years old too."

Jackey gazed into the distance. The sun had slowly begun to set behind the trees, and the air had grown colder.

"She was my best friend," Jackey said in a sorrowful voice. Paige's heart sank. It was all too common back in those days for children to die of any number of illnesses. Clearly, something terrible had happened to the little girl.

"We played together all day long, her and me. She had such lovely toys. Beautiful dolls, wagons, balls, every kind of plaything you could want. But that wasn't the only reason we were friends. It was so much more than that. There's somethin' so special about childhood friends, you know what I mean?"

Paige smiled and nodded, recalling her own childhood. Those warm summer nights when she played with the neighborhood kids until the streetlights came on and she had to go home.

"We laughed together all the time. Had so many jokes between us that only we understood. We even came up with a secret code when we wanted to talk about cute boys. White boys," Jackey said, raising an approving eyebrow at Orlando. "Black boys, it didn't matter. We liked 'em all."

"Never really outgrew that did you, Jackey?" Paige said.

That got a laugh out of her, which made Paige feel warm all over.

"No, ma'am. I guess I didn't."

"Good for you," Paige said.

All too soon, the spark of amusement was gone from Jackey's eyes as the memories took over.

"We was as close as sisters. I didn't have sisters, but I figure that's what it would have been like if I did. That girl was my best friend in the world for years and years. Then we turned ten years old."

Jackey's eyes took on a hardened, cold look.

"Ten years old. That was the end, the way I see it. The end of my childhood. The end of my life as I knew it."

Paige shot a concerned look in Orlando's direction. He looked worried too. Neither one of them really wanted to know what terrible thing happened next in Jackey's life.

"My li'l best friend was Miss Betty Randolph's niece, and on my tenth birthday, Miss Betty informed her that she was now my owner. Course she wasn't my legal owner. Miss Betty still was, but Hannah—that was her name—might as well have been my official mistress."

A cold chill went through Paige as she suddenly recalled Betty Randolph's will.

I give to my niece Hannah a Negro woman named Jackey to her use.

"At first, my friend didn't know what to think. Up to then, we were both just kids. We saw the Black people working in the house and the white people eating in the fancy dining room and all that, but we never thought nothing of it."

Jackey closed her eyes for a moment. How weary she was, and yet as a ghost, she couldn't sleep like a living person could. Paige was more determined than ever to help her find eternal rest.

"It was a shock to us both at first, but it sure didn't take long for Hannah to come around and like the idea. Oh, she got used to it right quick. I was like a little toy for her to play with."

Storm clouds gathered in Jackey's eyes as she spoke of the heartbreaking betrayal of her childhood friend.

"That little bitch," she said, her ghostly form trembling with anger. "Everybody's perfect little princess. Had her li'l dainty tea parties for all her *real* friends. I couldn't play with her no more. Oh, no. I was there to serve. She was like a little girl copy of Betty Randolph. Oh, she *loved* to follow her lead. Screaming at the servants, ordering them around."

Jackey's expression grew so cold that it frightened Paige. She found herself wishing she had Orlando's arm wrapped around her like he'd done on the bench at the Peyton Randolph House. She knew Jackey couldn't hurt her—much. But who knew what would happen if she flew into a rage. As a white woman, Paige might well be the target.

"Soon enough, everything became clear to me. Mama and me weren't a part of the household. Betty wasn't friends with Mama, she was her owner. White people had all the power, and the Black people had none and they never would. I stopped my mama in her tracks and insisted she tell me about what happened with my papa, and she finally did."

Jackey suddenly let out a loud shriek of pure, unrelenting grief and agony. Gasping, Paige covered her mouth. She hadn't ever seen anyone in such pain before, and she hoped she never would again. Tears filled her eyes as she witnessed the horror of Jackey reliving her nightmare.

A warm arm wrapped around her waist. She hadn't noticed Orlando slide closer. His touch provided immediate comfort.

But no one could hold and comfort Jackey. How empty and lonely that must feel.

"Everything I thought I knew about my life was a lie. Betty, Peyton, and Hannah weren't my friends. They were my enemies. My tormentors. And they would be for the rest of my life. The Randolphs had *bought* me and my mama and tore us away from my papa without a second thought. All these people I had trusted. And loved. I had *loved* Hannah. Turned out they were all nothing but pure evil." Her voice dropped to a whisper. "I was scared to death."

"From that day on, a sense of hopelessness hung over my head. What was the point of doing anythin'? I would never get to go to school," she said with a pointed glance at Paige. "I had no dreams of what I would do when I grew up. I knew what I would be. A slave. Just like my mama and my papa." Her voice broke with emotion, sending a searing pain through Paige's heart. "Like an animal, I was born in captivity and I would die there. Why bother getting married and having children? So many times I didn't want to even get outta bed."

Jackey's phantom fists trembled with rage as she spoke. "But you didn't have no choice. Didn't matter if you were tired or sick or just weary from being alive. You had to get up early anyway and work for your master and mistress."

Jackey stopped speaking for a while, and Paige and Orlando sat motionless. What words of comfort could they possibly provide after hearing such a tale? Her trauma cut so deep that Paige felt stupid for even thinking she could help Jackey. What the hell did she know about suffering?

"Out of all of 'em, Hannah was the worst tormentor. After a while, I didn't even recognize her anymore. Was like all those years of being friends was just a dream. Real life with her was a nightmare." Renewed fury flashed in Jackey's eyes. "I wanted to kill her. Honest to God, some days I wanted to kill her. I *hate* her for that."

"What do you mean?"

Jackey blinked. So caught up in her pain, she looked at Paige as if she had forgotten she was there. Her expression crumpled, and she cried without tears. "I was a good person. I didn't want to hate anybody, and I sure as hell didn't want to wish nobody no harm."

"I know you're a good person," Paige said. "But there's only so much abuse *anyone* can take without wanting to resort to violence. It's only natural."

"That's exactly right," Orlando agreed. "Wanting to harm somebody who spent their life traumatizing you is not the same as wanting to hurt somebody just for the hell of it."

"I suppose," she said uncertainly. "Wanting to kill somebody, even for a minute, that's not who I wanted to be."

"You didn't get much choice about who you wanted to be, did you?" Paige said. "There are people out there with all the freedom in the world, and they still choose to harm others because it suits them. You are not that kind of person, Jackey. Sounds like you spent your entire life in survival mode, just trying to get through each day as best you could."

Jackey smiled sadly. "Yes. That's it. There were times when I tried to fight back and other times, I just couldn't. I was too tired to fight, so I gave up. So many times. I felt like a failure when I gave in." The hard edge in her eyes returned. "Hannah's favorite game was making me dance for her li'l friends."

Orlando let out a noise of utter disgust, mirroring Paige's thoughts exactly. What a horrid person Hannah had been.

"Wasn't enough to force you to work," Orlando said angrily. "She had to try to break your spirit, too."

"Yes," she said. "That's 'zactly right. Sometimes I would

just do it because I didn't have it in me to fight no more. I'll never forget the laughter from her and her snooty friends." Her voice quaked with rage.

Paige's entire body tensed, understanding completely how Jackey could have easily snapped one day and killed Hannah. She wasn't sure what she would have done in the same place.

"Days when I just couldn't take it no more, I'd refuse to dance. I remember the first time I did," she said, pride in her eyes. "Hannah didn't know *what* to think. Flat out told her no, I did. 'I will not dance for you and your damn friends, little Missy!' Then I said she might wanna cut back on them tea and cake parties 'cuz she was gettin' a little portly around her middle!"

Paige and Orlando laughed at that, and Jackey's eyes brimmed with satisfaction.

"That was probably the proudest and happiest moment of my life. That look on her face. After all this time, I can still see it in my mind clear as day." She mimicked a shocked look, which got them laughing all over again. "Oh, she was so embarrassed in front of her friends. It was *glorious.*"

All too soon, the beaten-down look on Jackey's face was back. "Of course, there was a reckonin'. She tattled to Miss Betty about what I did."

The silence hung heavy in the air.

"Betty locked me in the closet overnight," Jackey said, shuddering at the memory. "That was Betty's office, what they called the closet."

"Yes," Paige said. "I saw it when I went on the house tour."

"Might not seem so bad to be stuck in there overnight. But it was. I was always fearful of small spaces. Don't know why, but they make me feel like I'm in a tomb. Like I can't breathe."

"Sounds like you're claustrophobic," Orlando said. She looked at him, confused. "That just means you're afraid of small spaces. It's not uncommon. My dad is like that. Hates to feel too cramped. Avoids elevators, and he won't fly on airplanes. Being in small places won't really hurt you, but the fear is quite real. That must have been awful for you."

"It was," she said. Her eyes clouded over as she remembered. "It was dark in there. So dark. Truly did feel like a grave. I couldn't see anything, and I was all alone. Couldn't barely sleep in there, and when I did, I woke up screamin' because I didn't know where I was. My friends and family heard me screamin' but there was nothing they could do. If Mr. and Mrs. Randolph heard me all the way upstairs, they didn't pay me no mind."

"I'm so sorry, Jackey," Paige said.

"I still fought Hannah once in a while after that, but it wasn't worth it. Most of the time ... I just danced." She lowered her head in shame.

Fresh tears filled Paige's eyes when she saw how broken Jackey was. God, it was infuriating. Not enough they had to steal your family and your life. They had to steal your dignity too.

Orlando massaged her back. He always seemed to notice when she was upset.

"That little girl," Jackey continued in a faraway voice. "Same one I played with and laughed with and even cried with. *I trusted her,*" she roared, startling Paige. "I thought she was my friend." In a trembling voice now, she said to Paige, "All this time ... I don't know why I'm still here, and I don't know how to go home. I don't want to trust you. But I don't know what else to do."

"I promise I will never betray your trust, Jackey."

"I hope not," she said, eyes full of fear. "I don't want to talk no more."

Jackey got up, and Paige began to get up too. Orlando jumped to his feet first and held out a hand to help her. She hadn't realized how much she'd needed that, but she was physically and emotionally shaken by Jackey's terrible stories.

Paige opened her mouth to call after Jackey, but the woman disappeared after walking a few steps. Paige let out a long, shuddering breath.

"Wow," she said.

"Yeah," Orlando said grimly.

"What she's been through," Paige said, shaking her head. "It's so much worse than I could have imagined. I feel so out of my element. Like, who am I to presume I could possibly help her?"

"But you are helping her. You should be proud of yourself for what you're doing. I know I'm proud of you."

"You are?" she asked.

"Yeah," Orlando said with uncharacteristic tenderness. Paige held his gaze, acutely aware that it was the longest time she had ever done so. She didn't want the blissful moment to end. "It's not easy to earn her trust, but you're doing it. Probably the only one in hundreds of years. That's, well, it's an incredible thing."

"I guess so," Paige said, her eyes still lingering on his. "Thank you so much for all of your help with this."

"I'm not doing all that much," he said with a shrug. "Mostly here just for moral support. You're the one who's making all the difference. I knew you could do it. Right from the start."

"How did you know?"

Orlando's lips slid into the most adorable smirk. "I knew that day when Jackey scared you so bad I had to pick you up and carry you to safety. You'd barely caught your breath before you told me you had no intention of giving up. I'll never forget that fiery determination in your eye. *Damn.* I wouldn't be able to deny you anything if you gave me that look."

"Is that so?" Paige said flirtatiously. Feeling daring and impetuous, she seriously considered shooting him that fierce look and asking him to kiss her. Heart pounding, she hesitated just a second too long.

Orlando reached over and took her hand and kissed it. Paige let out an involuntary dreamy sigh. His warm lips on her hand were nearly as exciting as a kiss on her mouth would have been.

"You did great tonight, Paige. You really did."

He smiled at her, then held his arms open for a hug, which she gratefully accepted. She melted into his body, feeling safe and warm in his arms.

"We're gonna help her find peace somehow. I promise."

Paige nodded into his chest, holding on to him as long as she could before letting go.

12

Jackey might have hated the Peyton Randolph House, but she couldn't stay away from the place entirely. Not on days when she knew Anthony would be working, anyway. The day after speaking with Paige and Orlando, she lingered at the house all day, even though rehashing all those memories had made it even more difficult to be there. She hadn't spoken about Hannah for so long, and sharing those painful memories had brought forth a lot of unpleasant feelings.

Even so, it did seem like Paige really cared. She hadn't struck Jackey as a melodramatic, attention-seeking kind of girl. But she'd cried, seeming genuinely upset. Strange to have a white girl feel bad about what had happened to her. Jackey had seen that kind of thing before, though. Sure, once in a while loudmouthed tourists said ignorant and racist things about slaves, but plenty of other visitors seemed regretful when they heard about how the slaves were treated here back in the old days.

Yes, Paige seemed sincere, but so had Hannah. As a child, Betty's little niece was sweet and kind. Generous with her toys, and loving and dear. Who could ever have imagined she would grow up to be such a monster? Certainly not Jackey. Trusting Paige was dangerous. She could change too. Or she might be a terrific actor like Orlando. Even though it seemed like Orlando cared too, she'd seen him in action many times and knew what he was capable of. Funny, charming, and a highly talented performer. He could easily put on an act, pretending to care, and not actually give a damn about her troubles, and she'd never know. He was that good.

Even if Paige didn't turn out to be evil or be putting on an act, she might grow bored with trying to help Jackey cross over. It had been centuries since she had died, and she had little reason to believe Paige could do much in a hurry to help her. Would Paige still be hanging around six months from now? Or in a year? Odds were pretty good Paige would eventually stop coming around, and Jackey would be left all alone again.

Though anger was a constant, speaking with Paige and Orlando had brought out a feeling she hadn't experienced in quite some time.

Fear.

The threat of physical harm was centuries past, so she feared no one living or dead. Until now, she'd only interacted with the living to frighten the tourists when she was in a bad mood. But Jackey felt herself beginning to care for Paige and Orlando, and it terrified her. She felt particularly close to Paige, and she could hardly believe she'd told her about Hannah. Not that she regretted telling her about her ordeal, exactly. It had felt good to talk about the trauma she'd held onto for so long. Only time would tell if it would turn out to be a mistake.

The tense knot of fear and worry in Jackey's ghostly

mind and heart began to ease instantly the moment Anthony walked by her, heading into the Peyton Randolph House. He shut the door behind him, and Jackey eagerly went through it to follow him inside. She always remained invisible when she was around a lot of people. Not only did she hate having to answer intrusive questions from people thinking she was an employee of the historical district, it was too much effort to avoid physical contact with living people. Much better to remain invisible and go where she pleased.

Best of all, she could stare at Anthony's heavenly body, and he was none the wiser.

Such a fine-looking man. How handsome he was when dressed up as John Harris in his fancy livery. Anthony didn't resemble the real man, thank goodness. Since Johnny had been like a big brother to her in life, that would have been too strange. Jackey saw Anthony in quite a different way, with her vivid fantasies of what the broad-shouldered, strapping man looked like under his clothes.

Good thing Anthony didn't change out of his clothes at the end of the work day—she might not have been able to resist taking a peek. She didn't want to violate his privacy, but she had so few pleasures in her spiritual existence. Surely, she could be forgiven such a tiny indiscretion.

Anthony headed to the dining room where his part of the tour would begin. Jackey stayed with the rest of the group for a while, but she quickly grew bored, wishing they could skip the parts about Betty and Peyton. She did appreciate the references to slavery, though, remembering all too well when they ignored that part altogether. She scanned the group to see if anyone sensed her presence, but nobody seemed to. Sometimes one or two individuals would look in her direction, even when she was invisible. They'd seem confused, unsure why they were feeling uneasy all of a sudden. Some people were naturally attuned to the supernatural, whether they knew it or not. Of those sensitive individuals, some embraced their abilities and actively sought out spirits to attempt to communicate with them. Others were afraid and tried to ignore what they were experiencing.

Sometimes it seemed Anthony might sense her presence. She knew he cared deeply about the slaves who lived here so long ago. He made that clear by the reverence he showed when speaking of them, and the tender way he said good night to Johnny every evening before he left work. Being Black himself, he seemed to feel a kinship with the men and women who had been enslaved in the house. But even beyond that, once in a while he would look around when she was there, as if sensing her.

Times like that, it was all too tempting to show herself to him. She wouldn't appear out of thin air, though. The last thing she wanted was to terrorize him. She could turn visible elsewhere and then approach him carefully, just to say hello. If only she wasn't forced to appear in her wretched old slave clothes. Oh, how she wanted to be beautiful for him. Bad enough she'd had to wear such rags in life, and now it seemed she was damned to all eternity to be dressed like this.

Familiar rage shook her, and she tried to fight it. She didn't want to be angry. Not today. Not when she had a chance to at least see Anthony and be in his presence.

But Jackey had never seriously considered talking to Anthony. Not only could she not bear to have him see her in these clothes, the idea of him knowing she was dead was unthinkable. People reacted to her in one of two ways. Either they teased her, trying to get her to make a ghostly appearance for their own perverse pleasure, or they ran away from her. She'd heard far too many screams over the years. The idea of Anthony's voice being one of them was too much to bear.

No. She wouldn't ever allow Anthony to see her or even know she existed. A possible vague awareness of her presence was the closest she would ever get to him.

At last, the tour group slowly made its way toward the dining room. Jackey had seen the tour so many times, she could have given it herself. Now, wouldn't that be something? She'd mention slavery, too, all right. Give those tourists more truth than they could handle.

The youngsters served as a reminder to Jackey of why the presentation wasn't any harsher than it was. There were three children on today's tour, ranging in ages from around seven to ten years old or so. Even she could appreciate that too much information would be upsetting to little ones.

She watched them carefully, touched when she saw how somber they looked when hearing about the slaves who lived here. That they cared gave her a much-needed sense of hope. Things weren't near as bad as they used to be, and praise God, she hoped they never would be so awful again.

At last, they reached the dining room where Anthony stood tall, hands clasped behind his back. The tour guide introduced him as John Harris and talked a bit about his duties as Peyton Randolph's right-hand man. Anthony spoke about his, or John's, life and what it was like to work for Mr. Randolph. Jackey adored the sound of his deep, sensual voice.

Being in Anthony's magnificent presence sparked delicious erotic fantasies. Jackey could swear that man's voice turned her on more than anything else in the world. Though she'd been intimate with several men, she hadn't desired them the way she did Anthony. Nor did she love them. They were merely a way to pass the time, to provide her with physical pleasure to blot out the pain of living, if only for a short while. With Anthony, things would have been different. Yes, she longed to have sex with him, but more important, she longed to be with him in every way a wife would be with a husband. She wanted to be by his side. To laugh, to love, to fight, to make up.

The whole idea was preposterous. Never mind the fact she was *dead.* Why on earth would he want her?

She shrugged off the sad thought and instead returned to her favorite fantasy of all. The one where Anthony made passionate love to her.

In Mrs. Betty Randolph's bed.

That fantasy was positively delectable. Betty would turn 'round three times in her grave at the thought of Black people defiling her precious bed like that.

How pleasurable it would be. Anthony would be an exceptionally skilled lover. She was sure of it. His body was strong and muscular, his disposition gentle and kind.

Perfect.

As the tourists began to shuffle out of the dining room, Jackey's attention came back to reality. Too bad Anthony didn't go upstairs when the tour visited the bedrooms. Seeing him in Betty's bed chamber would make her fantasy all the more realistic.

Instead of walking up the stairs, the three children lingered behind with their parents. Jackey watched as the mother gently prodded the youngest one to approach Anthony. The little girl was shy, so her mother spoke up.

"Sir? She wanted to ask you a question if that's okay," she said.

"Of course," Anthony said, his expression softening. He

smiled warmly at the little girl, nodding at her encouragingly.

"Were the slaves really sad?"

Jackey's heart melted at the question, and she could see Anthony felt the same way. It meant so much that at least some people cared.

"Yes, I think they were sad sometimes. They didn't get to do a lot of the things they wanted to do because they had to work a lot."

The little girl nodded somberly.

"But they had friends and family of their own, and the hardships of slavery brought them closer together. They supported each other. And they fought with each other, just like you probably argue with your parents sometimes."

"Mmm hmm," the mother agreed, and the girl smiled.

"Did the slaves ever have days off?"

"Yes, they did," Anthony said. "They had Sundays off. On Saturday nights they would get together and sing and dance. Sometimes they would travel to see other friends and family members."

"That's good," the girl said.

"It was good. It gave them a least a little bit of freedom and some time away from work."

Jackey admired the compassion in Anthony's eyes. The way he answered the child's questions honestly but took care not to upset her too much.

Such a dear man.

It would be wonderful to speak with him, to have those gentle brown eyes gazing at her. He always displayed deep compassion for the slaves, and she had no doubt he would have treated her with kindness and concern if given the chance. But it was not to be.

Jackey was comforted by his presence, so she stayed at

the Peyton Randolph House all day until it was time for the building to close. Somehow, she felt less lonely with him near. Even the anger and hatred she felt in the house faded when Anthony was there.

Jackey followed Anthony to the slave quarters just after 5pm when the house closed to the public. He did look around briefly and look in her direction as if he sensed her. Then he turned back to lean against the door frame, to complete his nightly ritual.

"Good night, Johnny," he said.

"Good night, Anthony," she said.

After pausing just one moment, Anthony left.

13

Orlando slowed his pace as he neared the gaol the next evening, not wanting to appear too eager. Drawing in a deep breath to steady his nerves, he took in the scent of October in Williamsburg. The air was crisp with a hint of cinnamon and pumpkin spice. That was nice and all, but his favorite scent these days was Paige; sweet and slightly floral. He didn't know if it was perfume or her shampoo or what, but he loved it. Damn, he really was far gone on this woman. He couldn't remember the last time he'd noticed what a woman smelled like.

He had changed out of his costume as quickly as possible after work. As much as he hoped Jackey would make an appearance, he wanted a little alone time with Paige first. He still wasn't willing to risk screwing up their new friendship by asking her out in case she said no, but he figured spending more time with her might move things in the right direction. He hadn't gauged yet whether she had any romantic interest in him.

Orlando took it as a good omen when her pretty face lit up with a sweet smile at the sight of him.

"No Jackey?" he asked.

"Not yet."

He sat down next to her on the grass. The air was noticeably chillier than it had been the night before. He watched her carefully, eager for her to show signs of being cold so he could offer her his jacket. Then, not wanting her to catch him staring at her, he looked around for Jackey.

I want you to make an appearance, Jackey. But gimme a few minutes, would ya?

"How's school?" he asked.

"It's okay," she said, distractedly searching for any sign of her favorite ghost.

"I mean, in general," he prompted. "Do you like college?"

"I like college overall, I guess. And the College of William and Mary is a good school. I just wish I could get out in the real world already. Maybe I'd feel differently if I could have gone to film school out in Los Angeles. I'd still be in college, but at least I'd be in the middle of where all the film action happens, you know?"

"Oh, I know. Believe me, I know."

"Do plan on moving out there sometime?"

"Not sure yet. Either Los Angeles or New York. Depends on where I can get acting work first. It sucks that you couldn't have gone to school out there, but if you had, we never would have met."

"Yeah," she said softly.

Saying out loud that he was glad they'd met made him feel exposed, and he wondered if it had been a mistake. But then she gazed into his eyes for a bit. Hadn't she done the same thing the other night when he'd dared to kiss her hand?

Orlando nearly laughed out loud at the notion of hand-kissing as a daring move. He'd done some seriously x-rated things on first dates before, but this was *Paige.* Everything felt new and exciting and scary with her.

Paige let out a soft gasp. Orlando followed her gaze and saw Jackey approaching in the distance.

"I'm so happy to see you, Jackey," Paige said.

"Me too," Orlando said. Though he'd wanted more alone time with Paige, he felt honored that Jackey trusted them enough to return.

The ghost woman nodded uncertainly, looking down at them where they sat on the grass. "Not exactly sure what the plan is here. Every time we meet, I'm expected to tell you more 'bout my personal affairs?"

She sounded defensive, and Orlando couldn't blame her. Paige bit her lip uncertainly, so he stepped in.

"I know it must feel pretty one-sided for you to be telling us all this stuff about your life. For a while now, I've been wanting to tell you ... Look, I won't say I know how you feel, because I don't. The way you were treated and everything that was taken away from you. My God, I can't imagine. But I do understand what it's like to lose a parent when you're just a kid."

Jackey dropped her defensive stance a little, and she took a seat in the grass across from Paige and Orlando. She still kept a bit of distance from them as if to protect herself.

"I lost my mother when I was seven years old."

He was aware of Paige watching him. Without looking, he knew her expression; that familiar, compassionate sadness on her face when she learned of somebody's else's suffering. He could feel how much she cared.

"What happened to her?" Jackey asked.

"Car accident. She was hit by a drunk driver and died instantly."

"Orlando, I'm so sorry," Paige said softly.

"Thanks," he said with a weary sigh. "Scary, you know? How everything can change in the span of a few seconds' time. You're here one minute, gone the next."

"Makes you realize how precious life is," Paige said.

"I guess," Jackey said, the hard edge in her voice muted by the glimmer of compassion in her eyes. "Hard for me to think of life being precious. A lot of times it wasn't. It was just hard."

"I get that," he said. "Life is supposed to be about finding your purpose, figuring out what you're supposed to do. Pursuing your dreams, maybe having a family of your own. You weren't allowed to do any of that."

Jackey eyed him curiously and then nodded. "Don't think I would have minded dyin' young like that. Then again, a lot of good droppin' dead did me anyhow. Just got a different kind of shackles now."

It was hard to know what to say. After a brief silence, Orlando spoke again.

"When I was born, my mother wanted to name me Orlando, but my dad didn't like the name. He thought it was too flashy and unusual. After she died, I insisted people start calling me Orlando because it was what she wanted. I guess I felt like I had to do something to honor her memory. When I got old enough, I had it legally changed."

"That's lovely," Paige said. "Orlando suits you so perfectly! Hard to imagine you being called anything else."

"Yeah, it always felt right to me, too."

"What was your real name?" Jackey asked. The question irritated him. He wanted to explain that Orlando *was* his real name. It was like asking a kid who was adopted *Yeah, but who's your real mom?*

"Orlando *is* his real name," Paige responded, reaching over to squeeze his hand. He grinned at her.

"Come on. Fess up. What is it?" Jackey asked, amusement in her voice.

"I don't wanna tell you," he whined. "You're just gonna tease me about it."

"Quite likely," she said. "Spill it."

"It's Gordon."

Jackey cackled wildly, and it was impossible not to join her. Paige laughed too, shaking her head at Jackey's fit of laughter.

"You are *not* a Gordon."

"Told ya," he said after their laughter had subsided.

"Were you close with your mother?" Paige asked Jackey after they finally stopped laughing.

"I was," Jackey said. "She was a good woman. Always took care of me. Somehow, she always made me feel safe. Shieldin' me from the slave life as long as she could and comfortin' me when it became impossible to hide the truth. Had such a *strength* about her. Always did what she was told by Betty and the other white folks. If she didn't, she might be locked in the closet and away from me, and she wasn't 'bout to let that happen. Some other slaves fought back sometimes. Some of them ran away. I used to wonder if my mama didn't have me to look after, maybe she'd have run. Maybe I held her back."

"Or maybe you gave her a reason to live," Paige said. "A purpose in a life that felt like it had no purpose sometimes."

Jackey smiled at her. "Maybe so."

Paige briefly met Orlando's gaze, and he gave a quick nod. This was progress, and they both knew it.

"Once in a while I'd ask her why we didn't just run away. 'Specially on those days where Hannah was giving me a rough go of it. I'd ask why we couldn't just run away and never look back. Mama told me that here at least we had food and a roof over our head. We were safe," she said, then repeated softly, "We were safe. As I got older, I understood a little more what she meant. We didn't get beat by our owners. And some other masters, they would get to foolin' around with some of the women slaves."

"Rape," Paige said angrily. "They would rape them."

"Yeah, you right," Jackey said. "That's the word for it. But far as I knew, that never happened at our house, thank the Lord. I guess we were supposed to feel lucky. We had it good," she scoffed. "But it was liked being locked in a jail cell. Yeah, nobody gonna hurt you. Yeah, you got food and water, but who cares? If you don't have your freedom, you got nothin.'"

Orlando found himself overwhelmed, humbled by Jackey's words. Like Paige had said before, who the hell were they to presume they could possibly help her?

"What would you have done with freedom if you'd had it while you were alive?" Paige asked.

Orlando was surprised by Jackey's reaction to her question. She stared at Paige in astonishment for a few seconds.

"Nobody ... Nobody's asked me that before," she choked out. "That's one of the reasons I don't like people seein' me. They look at me and see a slave. It's no different than when I was alive. Back then I was a plaything to be owned by a master and a mistress. Nowadays, people just see a victim, even when they think I'm just pretendin' to be one. Nobody treats me like an individual. A person. Until now."

Jackey's eyes were filled with wonder and gratitude as she spoke.

Good job, Paige. Orlando wanted to hug her, knowing how elated she must be feeling. He kept still, though.

Asking Jackey questions wasn't enough. It was important to listen, and really hear her answers.

"I loved to draw and paint. That was my passion. Something that was just mine. We were allowed to have our own little garden, my mama and me, and so we had something to barter with. We went to the market to trade up, and my mama was able to get me paper and paint and brushes. Stuff like that wasn't always easy to come by in those days, but Mama managed to get them for me. And they were *mine*. Back in the old days when I played with Hannah's toys, I knew they were all hers. But the pretty paper and paints belonged to me."

"What did you draw?" Paige asked.

"Started out drawing nature. Trees and flowers. The sunset. And I started drawing the people I loved. I drew a picture of my mother, and she cried when she saw it. I didn't just draw her likeness, I drew *her*. The way she actually was. Strong, lovin', beautiful, scared. A proud but quiet fighter. I could do that, you know? I knew how to draw people like they really were."

"You knew how to capture their essence," Paige said. "You have the soul of an artist."

"Maybe so. I loved that picture of my mama. Was 'specially precious to me after she died."

"How old were you when she died?" Paige asked. That look of concern was back.

"Sixteen."

Paige drew in a breath and let it out.

"Don't matter how old you are. You ain't the same person when your mother dies. Changes you."

Orlando's chest ached at those words.

I know, Jackey. I know.

If you were lucky enough to have a good mother, she

was your protector, your biggest champion. Losing her left a huge hole in your life and in your heart. Orlando's eyes filled with tears, and he wiped them quickly, hoping Paige wouldn't see. He knew a man shouldn't be ashamed to shed tears of grief, but he still didn't want her to see him like that.

Speaking up to let Jackey know what he was feeling was the right thing to do. It wasn't fair to expect her to spill her guts while he took the easy way out and kept his mouth shut. As usual, he couldn't find the right words to express his emotions. With no stage, no script, no fictional character to embody, he felt lost.

He composed himself and glanced at Jackey. Her expression was soft and kind. Maybe he didn't have to say what he was feeling, Maybe, through their shared grief, she already knew.

"After my mama died, I took comfort in that picture I drew. When my heart was heavy, I'd pull it out and look at her face. Remember her strength and her courage. Most of all, I'd remember her love. Looking into her face in the picture, I just knew she still loved me. I could feel it. In my heart, I knew her spirit hadn't died. She was still out there somewhere. She still existed. Out of my reach, maybe, but still here. And she still loved me."

"And she still does," Paige said.

Jackey nodded. "Yes. Made me feel good, too, to see how my drawin' could have that kind of powerful effect. Brought me peace and comfort and helped me remember her face. You think you never forget, but your memory fades over time. Can be hard to remember the specific lines and features, even in a face you loved so much," she said in a faraway voice. "I loved that picture. 'Til I sassed Hannah on the wrong day, and she tore the picture into pieces right in front of me."

"You've got to be fucking kidding me!" Orlando roared, frightening both women. "I'm sorry. I didn't mean—"

"No, you right," Jackey said with a bitter laugh. "I'm right there with you. Some days I can only get through by imaginin' Hannah burnin' in hell. Since she ain't a ghost like me, I can only hope that's where she ended up. I know it ain't right for a Christian woman like me to be thinkin' such, but I don't care."

"I can't believe she did that," he said, literally shaking with rage. To have lost both parents and be treated with such cruelty. It was unthinkable.

"Jackey, I—" Paige began sorrowfully.

"I know, I know. You're sorry," Jackey said. She didn't sound angry, just tired.

"I don't mean to treat you like a victim. I hope you know that. I just feel terrible about everything that you've had to endure."

"I know, honey. Let's just say I know you're sorry 'bout everything I been through, so you don't have to say it again."

Paige smiled. "Fair enough."

Jackey smiled back, and Orlando's rage subsided slightly.

"Does it help for you to know that they do exhibits on slavery in Colonial Williamsburg? Orlando and I just visited one recently where they listed all the names of the enslaved men and women. I found your name."

"Did you now?" she said, looking amused. "Yes. I will say it helps. They didn't used to talk about slavery at all. Just made believe it never happened. When they first restored the Peyton Randolph House back in 1938 and started tours, there wasn't any mention of slaves at all."

"Wow," Paige said, eyes wide. "Sometimes I forget how

long you've been around. You must have seen so much during all that time."

"Well, kinda yes and kinda no. I died in 1784, so I been around since then. But that doesn't mean I've been awake and conscious since then. Being a spirit, I can be alert when I want to be, but I can also fade away for a time if I choose. We ghosts call it vanishin'. It's like being asleep. You still exist, but you're not aware of anythin' going on around you."

"Fascinating," Paige said.

The notion of vanishing wasn't new information to Orlando. He'd learned about the concept of vanishing from Rebekah.

"Gives me a break at least," Jackey said. "Think I'd have gone mad by now if I had to be around all the time, day and night, with no end. Anyhow, when they first restored the Peyton Randolph House, you best believe they made no mention of people like me. Instead, they just showed off the fancy house and all the trimmings. Like it was some kind of castle for King Peyton and Queen Betty.

"So it does make me feel better that they talk about slavery now on the tours. Know what else helps?" Jackey asked, and Paige shook her head. "Anthony Alick, that's what!"

She grinned, and Paige giggled.

"Much as I do hate that house, I still spend quite some time there. Least on days when that fine-assed man is workin'."

"I don't blame you," Paige said.

"He's a wonderful man," Jackey said with obvious fondness in her tone.

"Seein' Anthony and the others honoring my friends and my family is lovely. The way they're keepin' their memory alive. Helps to see they ain't forgotten," Jackey said, her voice thick with emotion. "I spent a lot of time vanishing over the years. Seein' Anthony and his good work gives me somethin' to look forward to. A reason to keep showing up 'round here. In the beginning, after I died, I stayed 'round all the time. Wanted so badly to escape this lonely existence. Did all I could to figure why the hell I was still here and how to fix it so I could escape. After a while, I couldn't bear it. I didn't see any point in tryin' anymore, so I vanished for a long spell. Just gave up. But maybe it's time to try again."

"Do you think you're ready to give it another shot?" Paige asked.

"I'm here, ain't I?"

"Yes, and I'm so grateful." Paige's lovely smile lit up her whole face. The sweet girl was happiest when she was helping somebody else.

"I don't mind telling you, it's nice to have you all sit and listen. Don't see what good it will do overall in getting me outta here, but it's nice."

"We're not exactly sure how it'll help, either," Orlando said. "But I promise you, we won't stop 'til we figure this out."

"It's getting late," Jackey said. "I'm sure you're tired after workin' all day and then sitting with me. You all go on home now."

"Same time tomorrow?" Paige ventured hopefully.

Jackey nodded. She got up, and Paige and Orlando did the same.

After walking away a few paces, Jackey turned around and looked into Orlando's eyes.

"I'm real sorry 'bout your mama," she said.

With that, she turned and disappeared.

14

———

Paige stared into the distance where Jackey had disappeared, feeling emotionally overwhelmed but also cautiously optimistic. She had opened up a lot tonight, which was a huge deal. Paige couldn't imagine how lonely she must be, and she could only hope being her friend would help.

She was so preoccupied by her own thoughts that she hadn't noticed she was shivering in the cold night air. Orlando had, though.

"Here. Take this," he said, shrugging off his jacket and putting it around her shoulders.

"Thanks," she said quietly. Orlando's shoulders drooped and she saw deep grief in his eyes. She wondered why she hadn't noticed it before. Tonight must have triggered some painful memories for him. That, and Orlando was a terrific actor. If anyone could hide pain convincingly, it was him.

"You're doing great with Jackey," he said, making it clear he didn't want to talk about his mother. He started walking and she fell into step beside him. "She seems to be letting her guard down more."

"I know. I feel like she is starting to trust us a little, and I love talking with her. I'm just not sure where to go from here. Why *is* she still here? What if she's still holding on to all that pain and suffering she endured in life and that's why she's trapped? What do we say to that—get over it? I still feel so presumptuous trying to help her. As if I could ever really understand the hell she's been through. I'm white. How could I possibly know how she's feeling and what it's like to endure such racism, and—"

Paige's eyes suddenly opened wide.

"What?" Orlando asked.

"I just got a great idea. Why don't we ask Anthony for help? To put it bluntly, not only is he Black, but he's a slave reenactor. It's kind of ridiculous for a couple of white people like us to think we know what to do to help, but I'm sure that he's has endured lots of racism in his life. And he's obviously interested in honoring the memories of all the people who were enslaved at the Peyton Randolph House. He would probably welcome the chance to help Jackey."

Orlando laughed. "And wouldn't Jackey love a chance to talk to him. She thinks he's sexy."

"He *is* sexy," Paige agreed enthusiastically, picturing his broad shoulders and sensual brown eyes. "And you're right. She would probably love to get to know him better."

In her excitement, she walked faster toward her car. She slowed her pace when she realized she was making Orlando practically run to keep up with her.

"The hard part is explaining the whole 'talking to the dead' thing to him. Do you think he'll freak out?" Paige asked.

"No idea. I don't really know the guy. Some people are terrified of ghosts and some aren't."

"Tell me about it. You're never scared, while I've been a complete wuss this whole time."

"No, you haven't."

"Perhaps you've forgotten about having to scoop me up off the ground and carry me to safety," she said, feeling embarrassed at the memory.

"I haven't forgotten," Orlando said. The tenderness in his voice surprised her. It also made her feel less ashamed at having been so scared. "Paige, the definition of being brave isn't lack of fear. It's being afraid and going forward anyway. You were scared to death, and yet you kept coming back to see Jackey. That's what I call brave."

"That's very sweet," Paige said.

Orlando shrugged. "It's true."

When they reached Paige's car, she took off his jacket and handed it back to him.

"I have to remember to dress warmer. Weather might be comfortable enough during the day, but it gets cold after dark."

"Yeah, it does."

Orlando gazed at her, hesitating, as if he wanted to say something but wasn't sure. Paige held her breath for a moment. A light breeze chilled her, making her wish he would wrap his arms around her. Everything was silent as she waited for him to say something.

Maybe he's trying to get the courage to ask me out.

"You're ... ah ... doing great things for Jackey," he said. "You should be proud."

"Thanks."

After another moment of awkward silence, it became clear Paige had completely misread the situation. She felt stupid for even thinking Orlando might have romantic feelings for her. As if a guy like him would be nervous about asking out a girl like her.

The more she got to know Orlando, the more she liked him. It wasn't going to be easy seeing him all the time and knowing they would only have friendship between them. He simply didn't see her that way.

Impulsively, she reached out and hugged him. He hugged her back enthusiastically, thank God.

"Thanks again for everything," she said, squeezing tight before reluctantly letting him go.

"My pleasure," he said. "Believe me."

PAIGE'S STOMACH tingled with excitement when Orlando called out to her as she walked down Nicholson Street toward the Public Gaol the next evening. She stopped to let him catch up. As much as she hoped and prayed that they could somehow help set Jackey free, Paige wondered if she would ever see Orlando again afterwards. Would their friendship survive, or was it entirely based on their mutual desire to help Jackey? Did Paige even want their friendship to last? If she and Orlando kept hanging out together, he'd inevitably start dating someone else. What a nightmare it would be to smile and nod at his new love and pretend a knife wasn't twisting in her heart.

"Hey there," he said with a friendly grin when he reached her side.

"Hey."

Just focus on Jackey. She needs to be the number one priority right now.

They chatted about their day as they strolled together.

Orlando asked about her classes, and she asked him about the characters he'd played in town today.

"Well, look at that," he said, his smile broadening once they got within sight of the Public Gaol. Jackey was already there, waiting for them. "That's a good sign, right?"

Paige smiled. "I think so."

"Hello there, Gordon," Jackey said with a wry grin as the two approached her.

"Hello, Jackey," Orlando said.

"I'm only teasin' ya. I ain't gonna call you that. Orlando is to honor your mama, and that's as it should be."

"Thanks," he said.

"Sit down. Make yourself comfortable," she said, gesturing toward the grass. "If that's even possible sittin' on the ground."

Paige and Orlando sat down in the grass and Jackey took a seat across from them, closer than usual, which Paige took as another good sign.

"It's cold out, isn't it?" Jackey asked, looking at Paige's heavy jacket. As much as she loved the chivalrous way Orlando gave her his jacket, she didn't want him to be cold, so she'd dressed warmly tonight.

"Yeah, kind of. I guess you can't feel anything like that anymore?" she noted sadly.

Jackey shook her head. "No. It's not all bad, though. I didn't like the cold anyway, and I sure as hell got my fill of Virginia heat in the summer when I was alive. So that part of being a ghost suits me just fine."

"Good," Paige said. She bit her lip nervously, unsure how to broach the subject of speaking to Anthony.

"What's wrong with you?" Jackey asked, clearly picking up on her nervousness.

"Um, nothing. I'm okay. I—I just wanted to talk to you about something. But I'm not sure, you know, how."

"You're still afraid of me, aren't you?"

"Yes, but not because you're dead. I want to help you so much, but I feel like I don't know how to help, and I'm scared of saying or doing the wrong thing."

"I don't want you bein' scared of me, Paige. I know I can be intense sometimes, but I don't mean to be."

"You have every right to be intense. And angry. And, well, anything else you might be feeling."

"Out with it already. I won't bite. I *can't* bite. I promise I won't even grab your ankle," she said with a grin.

Paige drew in a shaky breath. "Well, Orlando and I were talking. And, well, we're white."

"What?" Jackey said, eyes wide in mock outrage. "How come you never told me that before? I can't believe you kept something like that a secret from me!"

Orlando laughed, and Jackey joined in, her brown eyes sparkling with amusement. Paige laughed too, but it was nervous laughter.

"I just mean, since we're white, we can't possibly understand what you've been through no matter how hard we try. We've never had to experience racism at all, let alone the kind of awful suffering you've had to endure. We just feel we're very limited in what we can do."

"Oh, I see," she said, her voice rising. Though it was physically impossible, it looked as if her muscles were tense. "You're quittin' on me already."

"No, not at all! I promised I wasn't gonna give up on you, and I meant it. I swear. It's just that we were thinking maybe we could bring in somebody else you could talk to. You could still talk to us, of course. I still want you to talk to us.

But there's another person who could maybe help in a way we can't."

"And who might that be?" Jackey asked, looking unsure.

"Anthony. From the Peyton Randolph House."

"No," she said flatly. "Not him."

"B—but I thought you liked him," Paige said.

"I do like him. Who doesn't? But that doesn't mean I want to talk to him 'bout all this," Jackey said, casting her eyes downward.

"I know it must be difficult to talk about such personal things. I feel honored that you've told us a lot already," Paige said softly. "It's just that I want to help you so badly, but sometimes I don't know how. I don't know what to say or what to do to make things better. As a white woman, it's the height of arrogance to think I would have anything to say that could help you."

"I suppose," Jackey said. "But not him. I don't want to talk to Anthony. I just can't."

Paige nodded, dejected but trying not to show it.

"Can I ask you something?" Orlando said. Paige's stomach tightened.

Please don't make this worse. Tread carefully.

"If you had the chance to live again, this time as a free woman, would you want to do it? Or would you rather just go to, you know, eternal rest I guess you'd call it?"

"Hmm." After a pause, she added, "Don't matter what I want. I'm dead."

"Well, yes, but ..." Orlando eyed Jackey, then looked over at Paige. "There's something I never told you about my friend, Rebekah."

Jackey furrowed her brow.

"I didn't want to say anything because I was afraid you'd think I was nuts," he said to Paige. He sighed heavily. "Look,

I'm gonna tell you both something that you're gonna think is totally insane, but all I can do is swear to you that it's God's honest truth."

"Well you got my attention," Jackey said with a wink. "You ain't lied to me before, far as I know, so spill it."

"I didn't know Rebekah was a ghost when I met her. She just looked like a normal person. Anyway, she became friendly with a buddy of mine who works here in Colonial Williamsburg. At Hay's Cabinetmaker's Shop. Name's Gregory. Do you know who I'm talking about?"

Jackey shook her head. "Don't think so."

"Pretty sure I haven't met him, either," Paige said. "You've told me about him before, but I don't think I've visited the cabinetmaker's shop."

"He's a good guy. I started seeing him with Rebekah a lot. They'd sit under a tree across from Market Square on his lunch break, and they'd be walking around town and stuff like that. I had no idea she was, you know, dearly departed. She dressed in 18th century clothing, but so does Gregory. So do I, so I figured she worked here. Gregory was obviously crazy about her, but he kept saying they could never be together. I thought she might be married or something. Then one day he finally broke down and told me the truth. She had died a long time ago, and what I was seeing was her ghost, not her body. He told me they were in love, but they couldn't ever be together because she was dead and he was alive."

Paige sighed. "You mentioned them before, but I didn't know they were in love. How sad."

"Yeah, that's what I thought. Here he finally found this perfect woman for him, and she wasn't alive anymore. Talk about soulmates," Orlando said with a rueful laugh. "Her situation was different from yours, Jackey, because she understood exactly why she was stuck here. Gregory helped her work through her issues. He helped set her free."

"Did she cross over?" Paige asked, unsure of what to hope for. She hoped Orlando's dear friend was at peace, but her heart hurt for Gregory being left behind.

"Rebekah knew it was finally her time. She felt compelled to return to the river where she died. She and Gregory said their goodbyes and she left."

Paige held her breath. Orlando glanced at her and then at Jackey.

"Well?" Jackey asked impatiently. "Did she cross over or not?"

Orlando shook his head slowly. "No. She didn't. She came back ... *To life.*"

The women stared at him. He laughed.

"Aaaand now we're at the part where you think I'm nuts."

"What are you talking about?" Jackey demanded.

"I mean, Rebekah was dead and existed as a ghost. And then she came back to life. She's flesh and blood now. A living woman," Orlando explained. Turning toward Paige with a smile, he added, "And I'm happy to report that she and Gregory are currently living happily ever after."

"Wow," Paige said, trying to wrap her mind around the incredible story.

"That's why I asked if you would live over again if you could, Jackey. I don't know if Rebekah coming back to life was like a one-time thing, or if it could happen again, or what. She and Gregory were in love, and I think that was the reason she was able to come back now. There were reasons ... Well, I don't want to tell too much personal stuff about her without her permission, but let's just say due to the events of her life, she was supposed to come back and live again. There were things she hadn't done in life that she was supposed to do. Her younger brother came to greet her that day at the river, and he told her that normally she would be born again as an infant. In her case, because of Gregory, she could return to life as she was."

Jackey nodded slowly, taking it all in.

"That's the great thing, Jackey. When it's your time, it will probably be loved ones who come to get you. Maybe it will be your mother and your father."

"I hope so," she whispered.

"What do you think?" Paige asked Jackey. "If you had the chance to live again now, knowing things would be different than the first time you were alive, would you want to do it?"

"No. No, I sure wouldn't. I'm tired, Paige. I'm so tired."

"I understand," she said.

"Then we'll just have to keep the focus on helping you cross over," Orlando said. "Listen, I know you must have your reasons for not wanting to talk to Anthony."

He paused for a moment, giving her a chance to explain her objections to meeting with the man. Her expression stiffened, making it clear she would offer no explanation.

"But would you maybe be willing to talk with somebody else?"

"Who?" she demanded.

"Rebekah."

"Why, because she used to be a ghost, too?"

"No. Because she was a slave owner."

Paige's body tensed, terrified that Jackey would fly into a rage at the idea. Her expression remained neutral, unreadable. The only sound was the whisper of the wind through the trees.

"I mean, if she were willing to meet with you, would you want to talk to her?"

"What good would that do?" Jackey asked.

"I'm not entirely sure, to tell you the truth. I just figure you never got a chance to confront Betty or Hannah for what they did. Maybe talking to Rebekah could give you some sense of closure. Some healing," Orlando said. "I know the Randolphs didn't express any remorse for owning slaves, but Rebekah truly is sorry for having slaves when she was alive. I was thinking it might help to hear that from her."

"Maybe," Jackey said flatly.

Hope soared in Paige's heart as she watched Jackey think it over. She didn't seem angry, just thoughtful.

"If we ask Rebekah and she agrees, will you talk with her?" Orlando leaned forward and batted his eyes. "Pretty please? For me?"

Jackey laughed so loudly that it caught Paige off guard.

"You're an idiot," Jackey said playfully.

"That is very true."

"Handsome man like you is used to gettin' your way, ain't you?"

"I use all my charms when it comes to convincing beautiful women to do what I want," Orlando said. Leaning toward Jackey, he said in a husky voice, "So what do you say, gorgeous?"

Jackey laughed again. "Fine, fine. Who I am to resist?"

"Yay!" he said, clapping his hands like an eager child, making Paige laugh.

If anyone could work their charms on Jackey, it was him.

"I think it might really help, Jackey," Orlando said.

"I hope so."

Me too, Jackey. Me too.

15

Paige insisted on going with Orlando to talk to Rebekah the next day, and he was grateful. Not only would he get to spend extra time with her, but she would meet his friends and see for herself that he wasn't totally insane. Neither Jackey nor Paige had expressed any doubts about his story of Rebekah coming back to life, but he was still eager to show some proof.

He led her around the back of Hay's Cabinetmaker's Shop rather than entering through the front door like tourists would. Gregory was expecting him because he'd texted him earlier, asking if he could talk to him and Rebekah about helping Jackey. They weren't expecting Paige because Orlando hadn't known she would be with him.

"Wow, it's so pretty back here," Paige said, looking around the area behind the shop, with its quaint wooden bridge and trickling stream.

"Yeah, it is. It's nice in the shade during the blazing hot summer," Orlando said. He opened the door to the shop so Paige could go in first.

They were greeted with festive harpsichord music upon

entering. Fortunately, there were no tourists around at the moment. Gregory, clad in his colonial black button-down vest and white shirt, sat on a wooden bench playing his heart out on the instrument. Upon hearing the door open, he looked up and gave a nod and a smile. Rebekah stood just behind him, proudly watching him play. Gregory's brown eyes flashed, and his dark brown hair whipped all over the place as he finished his song with a flourish.

Rebekah looked different than she had when she was a ghost. With her light brown hair cut to shoulder length and her face sporting light makeup, she affected a more modern look. Orlando had never seen her wear pants or shorts, though. Today she looked lovely in her long-sleeved dark blue dress.

Paige applauded when Gregory finished playing, and Rebekah joined in.

"That was beautiful," Paige said.

"Thanks," Gregory said with a smile.

"Gregory, this is Paige Bratton," Orlando said.

"Very nice to meet you," he said warmly. He and Rebekah exchanged a quick glance as if to say *So we finally get to meet Paige.* Though Orlando hadn't confessed his feelings for her to either of them, they weren't stupid. He talked about her all the time, so it was pretty obvious.

"You too," Paige said. Her eyes grew wider when she turned to Rebekah. "And you must be the one who ..."

Rebekah laughed. "The one that came back from the dead. Yes, that would be me."

"Wow," she whispered.

"I know," Rebekah said with another laugh. "Rebekah Jennings. I'm so happy to meet you."

Paige shook her hand, still awestruck.

"I'm glad to meet you too. I'm so happy everything

worked out for you and Gregory. Such a beautiful love story," she said.

"Thank you." Rebekah's soft gray eyes turned to Orlando and then back to Paige.

Rebekah was always saying she wished Orlando would find a nice girl to settle down with, and he knew she hoped the two of them would get together.

Paige looked around at the woodworking projects and tools on display. "This place is really cool. I can't believe I haven't visited before."

"A lot of people miss the shop when they visit Williamsburg, since it's not located on the main street," Gregory said. "Not everybody knows it's here."

"This is gorgeous," Paige said, examining the harpsichord.

"Gregory made it," Rebekah said proudly.

"Are you serious?"

"Well, I helped make it. Me and some other guys," Gregory said modestly.

"And he plays it so beautifully," Rebekah gushed.

"And Rebekah sings beautifully," Gregory said, wrapping his arm around her.

Orlando pretended to stick his finger down his throat and made a loud gagging noise, making Rebekah and Gregory laugh.

Paige punched him in the arm. "Oh, stop it. I think they're sweet together."

It was true, and Orlando couldn't help feeling a tad jealous. They were always touching, since they'd likely never forget how it felt when physical touch was impossible. How great it would be if he and Paige could have that kind of relationship someday. To be able to pull her close whenever he wanted instead of needing an excuse to touch her, like when she was upset or cold or afraid.

"What can we do to help?" Gregory asked. "Everything okay?"

"Oh, yeah. Everything's fine. So," he said to Paige, "they know all about Jackey and how we're trying to help her and all that."

"That's good," she said.

Orlando turned to Rebekah. "We were hoping that maybe you might be able to help us, Rebekah."

"I would love to help! Anything you need. What can I do?" she asked, her pretty eyes lighting up.

"The thing is, what we want you to do ... Well, it won't be easy," he warned.

"What exactly do you want her to do?" Gregory asked, sounding defensive, his arm still protectively wrapped around Rebekah's waist.

"We would like you to have a talk with Jackey," Orlando said.

"Okay," Rebekah said, nodding.

He glanced at Paige, and she smiled weakly. He knew she understood how awkward this was for him, and he was glad she was here for moral support.

"We want you to talk to her about owning slaves."

Rebekah's expression fell, and it hurt to look at her. In his heart, Orlando knew that asking this of her was the right thing to do. Yet, he felt like he was shoving his sweet friend into the line of fire.

"I see," she said softly.

"I know it's a lot to ask," Paige said. "But Jackey never got a chance to confront Betty or Peyton Randolph, or any of the other slave owners. We don't really understand why she's still trapped here as a ghost, but we're hoping that talking to you might help."

After a moment, Rebekah said, "That makes sense."

"It won't be the easiest conversation you've ever had," Orlando warned. "Jackey's a good person. She really is. But you can't imagine how much she's suffered. She can get pretty angry, and you need to be prepared for that. But I think this could help her immensely."

"I don't know about this," Gregory said, his forehead creased with lines of worry.

"I understand. I'm nervous about getting her involved in this too," Orlando said. Rebekah seemed so delicate, fragile. It was hard to reconcile that she'd been a slave owner just like Hannah. Except for one critical thing Rebekah had that Hannah hadn't. Remorse.

"I want to do this," Rebekah said, her voice shaky yet determined. "It's silly for us to sit around discussing how hard this will be for me. My discomfort is *nothing* compared to what Jackey and all those other people endured. To say this is the least I can do is a vast understatement."

Gregory sighed heavily, but it was tough to argue with that point.

"You just tell me where and when. I'll be there." Rebekah sounded resolved in her decision but there was no mistaking the fear in her eyes.

16

Paige and Orlando met up at Jennings Tavern before sunset as they'd arranged. They figured it would be best to confront Rebekah's slaveholder past directly by having them all meet where she and her family—and their slaves—had lived.

The reconstructed building was located on Duke of Gloucester Street, the main road where tourists traveled all day long. Fortunately, there were no restaurants or shops down this way. With nothing open at night, they'd only have to worry about a few stragglers wandering down the road.

"You okay?" Orlando asked.

"Not really," Paige responded, her stomach clenching with anxiety. "I hope this works, but I'm scared it might make things worse. You just never know how Jackey will respond to anything."

"I know. Sometimes she laughs when I think she'll get mad, and then she gets upset when I least expect it."

Paige bit her lip. "And Rebekah is so sweet. I feel like I'm leading her to slaughter."

"I am worried about her. But as tough as this is, it might

actually be healing for her, too. She's distraught about having been a slave owner, and maybe this will give her a chance to atone in a small way."

Paige spotted Gregory and Rebekah walking down Duke of Gloucester Street toward them. Gregory held her close to his side. As they neared, Paige's face contorted with lines of concern.

"This is gonna be tough on Gregory, too," Paige said quietly, and Orlando nodded.

"Thank you so much for coming." Paige met Rebekah's gaze. "Are you nervous?"

"I'm absolutely petrified," she said. She wasn't kidding. Her body trembled, but her voice remained steady.

"We're all gonna be right here by your side the whole time," Orlando reassured her.

Rebekah squeezed Gregory tight, but then she let go of him. She looked first at Gregory and then at Paige and Orlando.

"I'm so glad you're all here with me, and that I don't have to face this difficult experience alone. But we need to have some ground rules. Remember, tonight is all about Jackey. She has every right to be angry and to say absolutely anything that she's feeling."

With a loving gaze at Gregory, she said, "I know it will be hard, but I need you to be still while she's here. However she reacts, believe me I've got this coming to me and then some. I can't have you defending me tonight. There is no defense for owning slaves. It doesn't matter that it was common at the time or that the founding fathers of our country owned slaves. That doesn't make it okay. Gregory, my darling, you must hold your tongue when Jackey speaks."

One look at Gregory's expression and Paige knew it

would be one of the hardest things he would ever have to do. His eyes full of sorrow, he nodded.

"There she is," Paige said as gently as she could.

Rebekah gasped. She turned to see Jackey approaching them.

"It's gonna be okay," Orlando said. He looked nearly as worried as Gregory.

"Hi, Jackey," Paige said with a nervous smile once Jackey had stopped in front of her. "I'd like you to meet Gregory Markham and Rebekah Jennings."

She nodded wordlessly. Perhaps it was good that shaking hands was physically impossible. It would have been awkward anyway.

"I wanted to ask you guys," Paige began, "were you two alive at the same time? Might your paths have crossed at some point?"

"When did you die?" Jackey asked Rebekah pointedly.

"1762."

"Hmm. I would have been about eleven years old then. Don't think I ever saw you."

"No," Rebekah said. "Probably not."

"How did you die?"

"I drowned. I drowned ... myself," Rebekah answered.

Paige gasped involuntarily.

That poor woman.

"Oh," Jackey said with a slight flicker of compassion in her eyes. "I never heard nothing 'bout that at the time. But my mama usually tried to protect me from stuff like that. Things were hard enough for us."

"Yes, I'm sure they were." Still trembling, Rebekah charged forward. "My family owned this tavern. Have you ever been inside?"

"Not in life. Been pretty much everywhere around this town since I died. So yes, I've seen the inside of it."

"I didn't see you around much when I was—" She scanned quickly for nearby tourists and whispered, "dead."

"I vanished for most of the time since I died. Didn't see much point in hanging 'round here."

"Oh, I see. Jackey, I want you to know I understand how lonely it is to be a spirit. And I know you probably feel you can't escape this existence, but you will. It happened for me, and it'll happen for you, too."

That was met with stony silence. Jackey stared at Rebekah for a second and then turned toward Gregory.

"You the cabinetmaker man?"

"Yes. Yes, I am."

Jackey took a moment to look him up and down, inspecting his physique. Paige and Orlando exchanged an amused look. Typical Jackey. The woman never missed an opportunity to ogle a handsome man, which Gregory certainly was.

"Not bad," she said.

"Thank you." Gregory's response sounded like a question.

"But not better looking than me, right?" Orlando asked.

Jackey looked at him and then back at Gregory.

"Hard to say."

"Dammit," Orlando muttered. Jackey tried but couldn't suppress her smile.

Addressing Jackey, Rebekah said, "Is there anything in particular you'd like to ask me?"

Jackey stared at her, eyes cold, for an uncomfortably long time.

"Not just yet," she answered at last.

"Okay," Rebekah said. "We can't go inside, but let's walk around back."

She started toward the side of the tavern and the others followed.

Gesturing toward the main building, she said nervously, "As you know, my family owned Jennings Tavern. There was a public dining room and a meeting room downstairs, and there were places to sleep upstairs for guests and for my family. But that's not important. What matters is what happened here."

Sorrow clouded Rebekah's eyes as she gazed at the outbuildings behind the tavern.

"This was the kitchen," she said, glancing at Paige.

At first, Paige wasn't sure why she was being singled out. Then it occurred to her that Jackey probably knew every inch of Colonial Williamsburg after being here for so long, and Orlando and Gregory were knowledgeable of the place because of their jobs. Paige was the only one who wasn't familiar with the details of the place.

It was beginning to get dark, and the streetlights cast a slightly eerie glow in the yard. Jackey stalked over to the kitchen and peered inside. Darkness clouded her features. Perhaps seeing the building brought back bad memories of her days at the Peyton Randolph House.

"I used to enjoy baking," Rebekah said in a shaky voice. "Because I had the luxury of baking as a form of leisure. The slaves were the ones who had to cook the meals during the awful summer heat and the cold of winter."

"Bet you ain't never come out here when the weather was bad," Jackey snapped.

"No, I didn't."

"Didn't you ever feel bad eating all the good food cooked

and served by your slaves when they barely had enough to eat at all?" Jackey asked, eyes ablaze with fury.

"At the time, no. I should have. Looking back, I can't imagine why I didn't feel bad. At dinner, I was happy to be with my family, and I enjoyed eating the food. I remember thanking God at each meal for the bounty before us. I don't ever remember thinking of the slaves and what they endured. At least, not back then I didn't. In the hundreds of years that have passed since then, I've thought about it many times."

Rebekah's eyes teared up, and Paige saw Gregory's body stiffen. Jackey shook her head, eying Rebekah with utter contempt. And who could blame her? After everything she'd been through in life, she had no reason to believe Rebekah was sincere. No doubt Hannah's betrayal still weighed heavily in her mind and heart.

"How many slaves did you own to use and abuse on this property?"

"We owned twelve slaves," Rebekah said with a wince.

"Did you know all their names?"

"Yes."

"What about their spouses and children? Did you know all their names?"

"No, I did not," she answered, her voice trembling.

"Because you didn't care about their personal lives, did you?"

"I gave no thought to their lives outside of what they did in the tavern. In some ways, I think that's one of the greater sins of mine. Indifference." She wiped her tears quickly. As painful as it was to face her past, Rebekah was doing her absolute best not to garner sympathy. She'd obviously meant it when she'd said tonight needed to be all about Jackey.

"I got a question for you," Jackey said, her voice rising.

Rebekah's muscles visibly tightened. "By all means, ask me anything."

"What in hell made you think it was all right to hold human beings hostage and force them to work against their will?"

Rebekah swallowed hard. She took a moment to consider the question.

"I was taught from a very young age that it was the way of things. The natural order. My parents told me that people with dark skin were not like us. They weren't ..." She drew in a deep breath, struggling to continue. "I'm s—sorry. It's h—h—ard to talk about this. About things I no longer believe. You deserve to know the truth, so I'm not going to try to make it sound nice. I was taught that Black people were not intelligent like us. They were more like animals."

As much as she tried to fight it, Rebekah began to cry.

"I know, I know," Orlando said softly. Paige glanced over at him and realized he was talking to Gregory, who looked positively grief-stricken. Not being allowed to comfort the woman he loved was killing him.

Rebekah let out a sharp, irritable sigh as she roughly rubbed her tears away.

Jackey's steely glare never wavered from Rebekah.

"We were told that Black people couldn't take care of themselves. That they needed us to provide food and shelter for them. I let myself believe that when I was alive, because it was easier."

Crossing her arms, Jackey turned her head away from Rebekah's words in disgust.

Paige felt terrible that her heart ached for Rebekah. It felt disloyal to Jackey, and it shocked her to her core. She never could have imagined she would have sympathy for a slave owner. It felt wrong. And it made her face an uncomfortable truth.

"Listening to you speak, Rebekah, is kind of frightening," Paige said. "I'm a modern woman, and the idea of slavery is horrifying to the 21st-century me. I'd like to think if I'd lived back then, I would have been against slavery. Would have fought it with everything I had. But hearing you talk, it makes me wonder. What if my mother and father, the people who I trusted most in the whole world, taught me what your parents taught you? Would I have believed them too?"

She chanced a look at Jackey. Her eyes still blazed in anger, but she appeared interested in what Paige was saying. She believed what Jackey needed most from her, from all of them, was the truth.

"It's a terrifying thought, but I can't honestly stand here and say for sure that I wouldn't have been like you, Rebekah. I just don't know."

Rebekah soft gray eyes were filled with gratitude for Paige's words.

"Why did you kill yourself?" Jackey asked bluntly.

A strangled cry escaped Gregory's throat, and Paige gazed at him sorrowfully.

Jackey was nowhere near ready to forgive Rebekah, which was totally understandable. She had no reason to forgive her if she didn't want to. But her question was clearly intended to hurt Rebekah as much as possible. She was lashing out in pain and anger again. And it was hard to blame her for that.

Weariness filled Rebekah's eyes. It took her a moment to gather the emotional strength to answer the question.

"I was responsible for the death of my little brother," she said, her voice catching. After all these years, the grief still seemed fresh. "I was supposed to be looking after him and ... I got distracted. H—he drowned in the James River."

Rebekah wiped tears with her quivering hand. Jackey's face remained hard, but a glimmer of softness shone in her eyes. A harsh life of suffering had made her tough and angry, but she was a goodhearted woman who couldn't help caring about others.

"I couldn't bear the pain. That, and it didn't feel right to live anymore after I'd killed ... A—after the accident."

Jackey glanced over at Gregory. A single tear fell from his cheek. The sorrow in her eyes deepened. Though she'd wanted to wound Rebekah, doing so clearly brought her no pleasure.

"So I suppose your family was quite wealthy," Jackey said.

Rebekah breathed in deeply twice before answering.

"Yes, we most certainly were," she said.

"Did you ever taunt your servants? Make them dance or do silly things for your entertainment?"

"Absolutely not. My brother and sister and I were told we were never to do that." Rebekah laughed bitterly. "That kind of thing was considered cruel. I've thought a lot about that over the years. It was forbidden to tease those Black men and women, but somehow it was all right to keep them as slaves? Looking back, I don't understand how slave owners like my parents could be aware their servants had feelings when it came to things like mockery, but not when it came to being owned."

Taking a risk, Rebekah walked closer to Jackey and stood before her.

"I wish I had more answers for you," she said softly. "Why this happened. How anyone could have ever thought it was all right to treat human beings like that. The only thing I can say now is how sorry I am for my part in this." Tears welled in her eyes as she whispered, "I'm sorry, I'm sorry, I'm *sorry*."

Jackey whipped her head around so fast it made everyone gasp. The fire in her eyes looked lethal.

"I don't care what your parents taught you. I don't care that pretty much every wealthy white person in this town owned slaves. That ain't no excuse for believing in what you did and doing what you did. My God, what you did to people like me. And to my papa. And to my mama."

The heart-wrenching grief in Jackey's voice nearly brought Paige to her knees. No history lesson she'd ever learned in school about the institution of slavery could possibly show the human cost, the devastation, the *horror* of what those people went through.

While Jackey's ghostly form shook with rage and sorrow and anguish, no one else moved. After all, what could anyone possibly do at a moment like this?

Then Rebekah said something unexpected. "I know why you're still here."

Jackey's eyes grew wide. "What?"

Rebekah hesitated, looking terrified to speak again.

A spark of panic went through Paige.

You can't quit on us now, Rebekah.

Paige walked over and stood next to her. "It's okay. Please tell us what you know."

She nodded. Turning to face Jackey, she said, "It's your anger."

"What do you mean, it's my *anger*?" she shot back.

"Strong emotion is always what keeps a ghost earthbound. For me, it was guilt over my brother's death. After I died, I still couldn't—*wouldn't* let go of the pain I felt over my mistake. It was as if I was physically holding on to it."

Rebekah held up a tight fist as she spoke. "Gripping that regret and refusing to let go of it. In my case, what happened was my fault."

Gregory made another anguished sound, struggling mightily not to rush to her rescue.

"It was an accident," Rebekah said, smiling sadly at Gregory. "But it was still my fault. I had to learn to forgive myself. With Gregory's help, I was able to do that. I should have been paying attention that day. I loved my brother." Her voice broke, but she went on. "I would never have hurt him intentionally. When I was able to let go of my literal death grip on my guilt, I was set free."

Rebekah put a hand over her heart. "But oh, Jackey. In your case, your anger is entirely justified. You have every right to be filled with rage at what you had to endure in your life. None of it was your fault. And yet ... Your anger ties you here like a rope wrapped around a huge boulder. If you can let go of it, somehow, you'll be free too."

Jackey turned away, staring off into the distance. No one spoke, out of respect and to give her time to process this revelation. After a time, she turned back to Rebekah. Instead of rage, Jackey's expression was empty. Lost. And it was so much worse than witnessing her anger and grief.

"I had my whole life stolen from me. Torn apart. I was kidnapped away from my papa when I was four years old, and then I watched my mama suffer every day until she died from some illness they'd probably have cured if she'd been white. I lived my life in bondage. Nothing but pain and oppression. And now I'm doomed to eternal suffering unless I stop being angry about all the sins committed against me by other people."

Everyone stared at Rebekah, willing her to say it wasn't true.

Instead, she nodded slowly.

My God, there really is no justice in this world.

Hopelessness consumed Paige in that moment. Yet, it was nothing compared to the way Jackey must have felt.

Jackey stared at Rebekah for another long moment, and then she turned and walked away. Once she got halfway down Duke of Gloucester Street, she disappeared.

Only after Jackey was gone did Rebekah allow Gregory to pull her into his arms to comfort her. Holding her tight, he rubbed her back as she sobbed uncontrollably.

Wordlessly, Orlando walked over to Paige and pulled her into an embrace.

"It's okay," he murmured in her ear. "Everything's gonna be okay."

Paige wanted to believe him, but she didn't.

Orlando tightened his grip around her as she started to cry.

17

———

Paige found it nearly impossible to concentrate in class. Yesterday's talk with Rebekah had been devastating on so many levels.

Jackey was supposed to let go of her anger in order to cross over—what kind of cosmic joke was that? Paige wouldn't blame Jackey if she gave up on ever escaping her lonely existence.

Paige had been so obsessed with thinking about Jackey all morning that she thought she was hallucinating when she saw the woman walking across the campus lawn toward her. She shielded her eyes from the sun to get a better look.

It couldn't be. Could it?

"There you are," Jackey said with a smile. "I been wandering 'round all day looking for ya. I was invisible most of the time. Only showed up like this once I saw you."

Seeing Jackey out in the open in broad daylight felt surreal. And with a smile on her face.

"Can we go talk somewhere?" she asked, glancing around self-consciously. Being so close to the historical district, nobody batted an eye at a woman dressed as an

18th-century slave, but Paige knew how much she hated being seen.

"Yes, of course," Paige said enthusiastically. She led Jackey to a more secluded area behind one of the large school buildings, and they sat together under a tree.

Paige looked at her expectantly, hardly believing she'd showed up.

"So I got a temper, and that's why I'm still here," she said wryly, making Paige laugh.

"That's not exactly true. Saying it like that makes it sound like it's your fault when it clearly isn't."

Nodding, Jackey said, "Hannah, Betty, and Peyton are the ones who did me wrong, and now I got to be the one to fix it."

She sounded more tired than ever before, which was saying a lot.

"I can't even begin to tell you how—"

"I know, I know," Jackey said, waving her off. She didn't sound mad, just too weary to hear how sorry Paige was.

Paige fell silent, feeling more helpless than ever.

"I know doing all that yesterday wasn't easy for any of you. I still ain't sure what to think of that Rebekah girl," Jackey said with a spark of anger in her eyes. "But she's sorry, and that's more than I can say of most people like her. Doesn't fix what she did. Doesn't make it go away, but hearin' her say she was sorry ... It helped. It truly did."

Relief swept over Paige to hear that introducing her to Rebekah hadn't been a huge mistake.

"With your permission, I'd like to tell Rebekah you said that."

Jackey laughed. "Yeah, yeah. Go on and tell her."

She gazed around at the campus for a moment, watching the students mill around. When she finally spoke, it sounded as if she was talking more to herself than to Paige. "All those years of suffering. Just thinkin' about it gets me riled up. I can't help it. It's how I feel. That's why I vanish so much. I'm tired of being hurt and sad and angry as hell." She turned to face Paige. "I'm just supposed to forgive them? Just like that? Stop being mad? Get over it?" The barely suppressed rage was clear in her voice.

Paige gazed at her friend with sympathy. "I've been thinking a lot about that since yesterday. Thinking about everything Rebekah said. She managed to finally forgive herself for what happened with her brother, but hearing her talk, you can tell she still feels terrible. She found some measure of peace or she wouldn't have escaped her life as a spirit, but she obviously hasn't completely gotten over it, if that makes any sense."

"What's your point?" Jackey asked. For once, she didn't sound angry or accusatory. Just inquisitive.

"I mean, she didn't let go of *all* her guilt to be set free. It would be ridiculous to expect you to forgive your captors and go on your merry way. Maybe you just have to let go of *some* of your anger. You don't have to stop being angry altogether. Maybe you just need to find some sense of peace with what happened."

Jackey nodded thoughtfully, and fresh hope bloomed in Paige's heart.

"If nothing else, at least we have some idea of what we're dealing with now. Some clue in how to move forward."

"I suppose." She shook her head as if ridding her mind of bad thoughts. "I'm sick to death, so to speak, of talking 'bout this. Let's talk about somethin' else."

"Okay, sure."

"What's the story with you and Orlando?" she asked with a sly smile.

"W—what do you mean?"

"Don't you act all innocent with me. You shared a bed with him yet?"

"No!" Paige said, feeling her face get hot.

"But you'd like to."

More than anything, Paige wanted to confide in her. She was tired of keeping her feelings bottled up, and it was only fair to share personal things with Jackey. After all, Jackey had bared her soul many times.

Glancing around as if Orlando might somehow over-hear, she said quietly, "If we talk about this, you have to swear you won't say anything to him. You don't have much of a filter, you know."

Jackey laughed heartily. "You're not wrong about that." Holding up her hand, she said, "I swear I won't breathe a word and not just because I can't breathe."

Paige stared at her, worried about trusting her.

More solemnly, she said, "I swear on my mama's grave. And on Orlando's mama's grave. I won't do you like that, Paige. This is just between us."

"Okay." She let out a sigh of relief.

"Now you tell me the truth, young lady. You want that man's body."

"Yes," she confessed. "His body and every other part of him."

Jackey smiled and nodded. "So there ain't ever been anything between you two? You ain't ever fooled around or nothin'?"

Shaking her head, she said, "Nope. He's never made a move on me. Not that I expected him to. He just seems so far out of my league. I don't think he would ever go for a girl like me."

"Why not?"

"You know how he is. He's so handsome and sexy. And funny, talented, outgoing. He's just so *everything*, you know what I mean?"

Paige felt a little silly gushing about Orlando. But Jackey nodded thoughtfully, making Paige feel like she understood.

"I feel so plain next to him. I'm not funny and dynamic like him. I'm not pretty."

"Of course you're pretty. You're a lovely girl."

Somehow, hearing Jackey say that meant more than if Orlando himself had said it. Their relationship had been so combative. For the first time, it felt like Jackey was her friend.

"That's so sweet of you to say. I think if he was interested in me, he would have said so by now."

"Maybe he's just shy."

"Oh yeah. He's a real shrinking violet, that one."

Jackey laughed. "Okay, fair enough. He ain't shy. But he does touch you an awful lot. He's always putting his arm around you every time you get all upset over something."

"You noticed that too?"

"Definitely. It's like he's always lookin' for a reason to touch you. I think he might be sweet on you. Want me to ask him for you?"

"No!"

Jackey laughed again.

Paige's stomach fluttered just picturing Orlando's masculine jaw and sensual brown eyes.

"Orlando's just so sweet and caring," she said with a sigh. "He's been protective of me since the beginning when I was still scared of you. He never left my side. And now, he seems interested in helping you. I find that so ..."

"Sexy?"

"Yes," Paige said, giggling. "I never understood why some

girls have a thing for bad boys. Not me. Give me a handsome hero any day."

Jackey nodded, looking thoughtful.

"What's your perfect type of man?" Paige asked.

"I agree with you about the hero thing. I suppose my perfect man would be tall and strong. A nice guy like Orlando. Brave. The type of man who's kind to children. Smart. A man with kind eyes."

Paige watched her carefully as she spoke. She got the distinct impression Jackey was talking about a specific man.

"You mentioned you've been in love before," Paige said.

"Yes. I don't want to talk about it, Paige." There was no anger in her refusal to talk. Just deep sadness.

"Okay. I want you to know you can tell me anything, Jackey. But only if you want to."

She nodded gratefully and smiled.

She's so beautiful when she smiles.

"Don't give up on Orlando, honey. You two might wind up together in the end."

"Do you think so?"

"Well, I do think he's being kind and tryin' to help me. But I don't think I'm the reason he shows up night after night," Jackey said, her eyes filled with warmth. She was clearly rooting for she and Orlando to be together.

"Hard to say," Paige said wistfully. As much as she loved to picture herself as Orlando's girlfriend, it seemed so unlikely. "Sorry to get so off track. My love life is unimportant compared to what you're dealing with."

"Don't you worry about that. I'm glad to talk about somethin' else for once."

"Maybe distracting you with other stuff can help with making you less angry."

Jackey shrugged. "Maybe."

"I hate to go, but unfortunately I have a class to get to."

"That's all right. You go on ahead."

"This was nice, Jackey. Talking, you know, just us girls. We'll have to do this more often."

"I'd like that," she said with another lovely smile.

PAIGE FELT giddy for the rest of the afternoon. She couldn't wait to tell Orlando how she had sat and talked with Jackey. But she certainly wouldn't tell him what they'd discussed.

Oh, you know. I told Jackey all about how crazy I am about you.

They'd had plans to meet up at the gaol at the usual time, but of course Jackey would be there. Paige decided to call Orlando on the phone instead of trying to track him down somewhere in the historical district.

"Hey, Paige. Everything all right?"

"Oh, yeah. Everything is fine. Are you busy? Do you have a minute?"

"I always have time for you," he said.

He's so sweet.

Orlando was probably still in costume, which meant he had to be discreet about using his cell phone. Reenactors weren't supposed to be seen using modern technology since it spoiled the illusion.

"I had the most wonderful talk with Jackey this afternoon. She came to see me on campus. How great is that?"

"Are you serious? She actually showed herself on campus to come and find you?"

Paige grinned widely at the enthusiasm in Orlando's voice. She'd known he would understand that this was a big deal.

"Yes. I could hardly believe it when I saw her. We sat together under a tree and just talked for a while. It was nice. Like talking with an old friend."

"What did you guys talk about?"

You. We talked about you being a dreamy, magnificent, hunk of a man.

"You know. Girl talk," she said, trying to sound mysterious. He laughed. "It seemed to help her to sit and talk about different stuff with me. And you know what else she said?"

"What?"

"She said that talking with Rebekah made her feel better."

"She actually said that?"

"Yes! I was so afraid meeting Rebekah might have scared her off or made her so angry she'd never speak to me again."

"I was worried about that too," Orlando said.

"I've been thinking that since talking to us and then to Rebekah seemed to help her, maybe speaking with Anthony might be the best thing for her right now."

"We floated that idea before, remember? It didn't go so well. She made it clear she didn't like the idea."

"I know. But I was thinking it can't hurt to go ask him if he's willing to help. He might think we're crazy and tell us to leave him alone."

Paige pictured Anthony's warm smile, and she knew that was unlikely to happen. If he did think they were crazy for believing in ghosts, he would be polite about it.

"Besides, Jackey enjoys flirting with you, and I think she might really like talking to Anthony. If nothing else, he'll be something pretty for her to look at while she's trying to figure all this out."

Orlando laughed. "She does seem to enjoy the company

of men. I guess we could at least talk to Anthony about Jackey."

"Do you think you could find out when he's working? Like, when the next tour of the Peyton Randolph House will be?"

"Sure. I'll check the schedule and get back to you."

"Perfect. Thanks!"

For some reason, Orlando hesitated before hanging up. He did that a lot, she noticed. It was as if he always wanted to say something else but never did. The idea of him being shy, as Jackey had suggested, seemed preposterous. But was it possible he was shy with women?

They ended their conversation, and Paige did her best to put her romantic notions aside. For now, at least.

Orlando texted her a short while later and told her there was a tour ending at the Peyton Randolph House at 3pm. He said he couldn't guarantee that Anthony was working today, but they could meet at the house just in case.

Paige eagerly headed over there in the afternoon. The idea of speaking with Anthony and trying to convince him to help a ghost made her nervous, but she was excited about the possibilities. Jackey found the man attractive and, despite her initial reluctance, Paige was confident she would come around and actually enjoy talking to him.

"Hey," Orlando said with a grin when he saw her walking toward the house.

"Hey," she said, trying to ignore the familiar flutter in her heart every time she saw him. He was in full costume, powdered wig and all. Seeing him dressed that way reminded her of how incredibly talented he was. She wished she had more time during the day just to stand around and watch him perform.

"Listen, lemme go talk to the guy and see if Anthony's

working," he said, gesturing to the costumed employee who was sitting on the steps of the house, guarding the entryway. "If he's here, I'll ask if you and me can talk to him real quick."

"Oh, right. I don't have a pass to get in," Paige said.

He nodded and headed over to speak to the guy. Paige seized the opportunity to watch him walk away, admiring his ass. After a short discussion with the man, Orlando waved her over. If he noticed her staring, he didn't show it.

Orlando led her through the breezeway entrance of the house.

"Anthony's out back in the courtyard."

Paige's stomach quivered with anxiety. What if Anthony didn't believe their wild story about ghosts? Worse, what if he was offended by their request?

She spotted him right away behind the house, standing with his arms clasped behind his back, watching the tourists mill around. It was the perfect time to speak with him; he was there to answer questions from guests.

Orlando glanced at Paige, and she nodded. This was her idea, and she knew she had to be the one to get things started.

Approaching him cautiously, Paige called out softly, "Uh, Anthony?"

He turned toward her, looking surprised that she knew his name.

He doesn't remember me. Why would he? He sees dozens of tourists every day.

"Hi. Um, we spoke once before. You probably don't remember me."

"My apologies. I don't recall you offhand," he said with a warm smile.

"Oh, it's fine. We spoke after a tour once, but I know you talk to so many people every day. My name's Paige."

"Well, good to see you again," he said kindly.

"I don't believe we've met," Orlando said.

Anthony chuckled. "Not formally, but I know you're Orlando Blake. Your reputation precedes you."

"Uh-oh," he said, eyes wide.

"All good things," Anthony assured him. "I've seen you around town, and I always enjoy your performances."

"Thanks. Appreciate that."

"We were wondering if we could talk to you for a few minutes," Paige said.

"Certainly. How can I help you?"

"Oh, where to begin," Orlando said dryly.

Paige laughed. "Exactly."

It suddenly occurred to Paige that, for all she knew, Jackey was there now. Invisible. Listening. She decided to plow forward anyway and hope she wasn't present. There was nowhere in the historical district Paige could possibly go that Jackey couldn't follow. The ability to walk through walls was useful like that.

"Oh, wait. I do remember you," Anthony said, looking at Paige. "You were asking me about one of the slaves in particular. Was it Charlotte?"

"Jackey."

Eyes lighting up with recognition, he said," Yes, yes. I remember now. We were talking about how people say she haunts the place, and you wanted to know more about her."

"That's right. And that's why we wanted to talk to you today."

"Well, I'm not sure I'll be any help to you. I've heard the rumors about her ghost hanging around here, but I still haven't seen anything myself."

"That's okay. We have," Paige said, and Orlando nodded.

Anthony looked understandably skeptical.

"I first became aware of her presence when she grabbed me by the ankle," Paige said.

"Yeah, I've heard people say she does that," he said with a shrug.

"I wanted to try to talk to her," she continued. "And maybe try to figure out why she was still stuck here as a spirit after all these years."

"I see," Anthony said, his voice filled with polite disbelief.

"I know what we're telling you is hard to swallow but bear with me. Orlando and I waited around the Peyton Randolph House to see if she would appear. And then one day she did."

"Not only did she appear, Jackey spoke to us," Orlando said.

"You're saying you've actually talked to her?"

"Oh, yes," Paige said. "Many times. That's the thing I never knew before about ghosts—they can look just like the living. I know it sounds crazy, and if I were you, I wouldn't believe me. But it's the truth. There are some people here in Colonial Williamsburg who are dressed just like you," Paige said, gesturing at Anthony's costume, "but they're not reenactors. They're people who died back in the 18th century."

Anthony nodded again. He looked back and forth between her and Orlando, apparently interested in what they were saying, but it was hard to tell if he believed their story.

"I know of at least two people who look like reenactors but who are actually ghosts," Orlando said, lowering his voice so tourists wouldn't hear. "In fact ..."

Please don't tell him about Rebekah coming back to life. It's too much right now.

Orlando furrowed his brow. "Just to make sure." He gently poked a finger into Anthony's shoulder. "Whew! Just checking."

Anthony laughed, a rich, sexy sound. He had a pleasantly deep speaking voice, the kind that would make for a great documentary voiceover. Sometimes it was hard to turn off her director's brain.

"I promise if you met Jackey and you tried to touch her, well, you couldn't. Orlando here is pretty fearless, but I was terrified at first. It's tough to wrap your mind around the fact that you're talking to a ghost. But once you get past that part, it's wonderful getting to know her," Paige told Anthony. "Think about it. Wouldn't you love a chance to talk to someone who actually lived here?"

That piqued his interest. His eyes opened wide as he considered her words.

"We've spent a lot of time talking to her because we want to help her cross over. She's so lonely, Anthony. And she's tired. As I'm sure you know, she had a very tough life and she's still suffering in the afterlife. And well, we were hoping ..." Paige felt her face get hot. "I—I'm not sure how to put this delicately."

"It's all right, Paige," he said kindly. "You can just tell me what's on your mind."

His eyes crinkled, a half-smile lifting the right corner of his mouth.

"W—well, it's that ... Well, you're Black and you're a slave reenactor and you can probably help her in a way we can't."

"We've never had to deal with anything like this

ourselves," Orlando said. "Racism, I mean. We know it exists, but we can't possibly know how it feels."

"I appreciate you saying that," Anthony responded thoughtfully. "So you're telling me that a former slave who died hundreds of years ago needs my help."

"That is what we are saying." Paige laughed. "Like I said, I don't blame you if you don't believe us. If I hadn't sat down and spoken with Jackey, not to mention having seen her appear and disappear into thin air, I wouldn't believe it myself. But what we're telling you is true. Jackey is a good woman. She's my friend. And she's suffered long enough. We just want to do everything we can to help her find peace."

"So, what do you say? Would you be willing to help us by coming with us to talk to Jackey?" Orlando asked.

After a brief pause, Anthony said, "I've got nothing to lose, I guess."

"Great!" Paige said excitedly, making Anthony laugh.

"We're supposed to meet with her tonight," Orlando said. "We'll talk to her and find a time where we can all sit and talk."

"Works for me," Anthony said, still a bit hesitant. He was probably wondering what the hell he was getting himself into.

"Can I give you my cell phone number?" Paige asked.

"Sure," Anthony said. "You got something to write it down with? I don't have my phone with me."

"I have a notepad in my purse."

Paige wrote down her phone number as well as Orlando's number and gave it to him. Anthony recited his number for her, and she jotted it down.

"Thank you so much! We'll be in touch as soon as we can," she said.

"I'm still not sure what to think," Anthony admitted. "But if this is real, I sure don't want to miss out on it. It's funny. Sometimes I feel a presence in the house. Not a bad presence, but it feels like someone is here with me. Usually when I'm by myself at the end of the day. I always thought it was my imagination."

"It might be Jackey you're sensing," Paige said.

Most likely, since she finds you quite attractive.

"Or it could be any number of people who once lived here," she said.

"Perhaps," Anthony said, a contemplative look on his face. He might still be unsure, but one thing was certain.

He *wanted* to believe.

18

Jackey was already waiting for them at the Public Gaol by the time they got there. Paige was especially optimistic about helping her since she had come to visit her at the college. Apparently, they'd really bonded during their chat on campus.

"Must be warm out," Jackey said. It was unseasonably warm for an October night. Paige didn't even bring a jacket.

"Yeah, it is," Paige said. "That's Virginia weather for you."

Jackey eyed Orlando up and down, her eyes lingering on his chest. He'd changed out of his costume into jeans and a long-sleeved blue shirt.

"You could stand to undo a few more buttons," she observed.

"On my shirt or my pants?"

That got a big laugh from her. "Your choice."

"Hmm," he said, pretending to think it over. Slowly, sensually, he unbuttoned one of his shirt buttons. He was pleased to see Paige watching him intently.

"One more," Jackey said, and he obliged. "Much better."

"I aim to please."

"You sure do," she said flirtatiously.

Orlando grinned at her, enjoying the attention. Jackey was no slouch in the appearance department, either. With her smooth, dark skin and rich dark eyes, she was lovely to behold.

She certainly did enjoy flirting with men, and Orlando was hopeful she would warm to the idea of talking to Anthony. He seemed to be a really nice guy. Calm and rational. Maybe he could talk to Jackey about everything she'd been through without her completely flipping out.

Orlando and Paige took a seat in the grass near Jackey.

"How's school going?" she asked Paige.

The two women chatted briefly about Paige's classes, and Orlando noticed a difference in the way they spoke to each other. The conversation flowed easier than ever before. They sounded like old friends. Paige had done wonders in breaking through Jackey's hard shell. If anybody could solve the centuries-old riddle of why Jackey was still here, it was Paige.

Once Paige finished talking about school, she shot a glance at Orlando. It was time to move on to the task at hand.

"So, Orlando and I were thinking. Since it seems to help you when you talk to us, and you said it helped when you spoke with Rebekah, we feel like there's someone else you should talk to."

Jackey shook her head but didn't seem upset. "You ain't gonna be happy until this whole town knows about me. Who now?"

"We went over to the Peyton Randolph House and spoke to Anthony about everything. Though I'm not sure he believes what we told him, he seems interested in trying to help you. I know you said you didn't want to talk to him, but I think he could be a huge help for you. I think—"

Jackey's eyes blazed with anger. "That's right. I *did* say I didn't want to talk to him. Pretty sure I made that quite clear."

Paige flinched at Jackey's reaction. Her whole body tensed.

"W—well yes. You did. But when we told Anthony all about you—"

"Wait a minute," she said, trembling as she spoke. "You're saying you told Anthony Alick about me."

Paige nodded, too afraid to speak.

"You told him who I was. My story. My life. And you told him I was dead."

"We only wanted to help you," Orlando said.

"Why do you think he can help me?" she snapped. "Just because he's Black?"

"Yes," he answered honestly. "And because he's an expert on the people who were enslaved there. And because he cares deeply about every last one of them."

Jackey's glare never wavered from him, but she didn't argue. All he could do was hope they could keep her calm enough to talk this thing out rationally.

"Jackey, I'm so sorry," Paige said mournfully. "I didn't mean to upset you."

"You knew damn well this would upset me! I told you I didn't want no part of talking to Anthony."

"I wanted to help you. I just didn't understand why you don't want to talk to him."

Jackey jumped up and charged toward Paige, who scrambled to her feet. Instinctively, Orlando leapt up to protect her. Jackey's demeanor seemed so dangerous, it was easy to forget she couldn't do much, if any, physical harm to

Paige. He tried to stand in the middle with the two women on either side of him, rather than next to Paige, which might make it seem like they were ganging up on her. Jackey had every right to be angry, yet he knew Paige must be utterly devastated by her reaction. His heart ached for both women.

"You don't have to understand why. It's none of your goddamn business! My reasons are my own. I said no, and that's all you needed to know. But that wasn't good enough for you. Because you think you know best. You think you know how to help me, but you ain't got a clue!"

Tears rolled down Paige's face, and Orlando ached to hold her in his arms. But he couldn't. Not yet.

Jackey's ghostly form slumped in defeat.

Staring at Paige, she said softly, "I thought we were friends. You promised me you wouldn't talk to Anthony unless I wanted you to. You *betrayed* me, Paige."

Orlando swallowed hard. It was true. Paige had made that promise, and she shouldn't have gone back on it. But Orlando also knew Paige would rather die than hurt Jackey intentionally. Trouble was, getting Jackey to believe that would be nearly impossible. Especially after everything she'd been through.

"You're just like Hannah," she whispered.

Orlando stood, powerless, watching Paige's heart break right before his eyes.

Jackey turned and, after walking a few steps away, vanished into thin air.

"Oh my God, what have I done," Paige whispered. "I should have respected her wishes. She's right. I did betray her."

Covering her face with her hands, she began to sob.

Orlando rushed to Paige's side and pulled her into his arms. Holding her close, he let her cry for a short while. He figured she needed to release her emotions, so he briefly held his tongue.

After she'd calmed down slightly, he said, "It's all right, Paige. Everything's gonna be all right."

He hoped he sounded more convinced than he felt.

19

Paige wept as Orlando held her close. His comforting touch soothed her, and she hated the idea of letting go. Still, he shouldn't have to stand here all night just because she was a total idiot.

"We'd better get going," she said, wiping her tears after releasing him. Orlando eyed her uncertainly, looking unsure of what to say or do to help. She started walking, and he fell into step next to her. Then he slipped an arm around her shoulder to hold her as they walked. Though she appreciated his kindness, she felt she didn't deserve to be comforted.

Jackey had made it abundantly clear that she did not want to involve Anthony in her situation. And the one thing the woman needed most from Paige and Orlando was honesty. Jackey's trust in them had been a huge leap of faith but she'd done it anyway. And she'd gotten stabbed in the back in return.

Paige berated herself for being so unbelievably arrogant in thinking she knew what was best for Jackey. Even if her heart had been in the right place, what did that matter now? Jackey probably felt worse than she did before they met.

Her tears began to fall again as they walked through the darkened streets of Colonial Williamsburg. She could feel Orlando's eyes on her. Any other time she might have felt embarrassed to appear such a blubbering mess in front of him, but at that moment, she was too distraught to care.

As long as she lived, she would never forget the look of betrayal on Jackey's face.

"Please don't cry, Paige," Orlando said tenderly.

"How could I have done that to her? What the hell was I thinking?"

"You were only trying to help. And it wasn't just you. I'm every bit as responsible as you are for what happened."

"It was my idea. And when I told you about it, the first thing you did was point out that she didn't want us to involve Anthony. But no. I thought I knew everything and charged ahead anyway."

"I admit I wasn't sure about it at first, but the more I thought about it, the more I believed it might actually work." Orlando sighed heavily. "Jackey's issues are so big, you know? So much to unpack there. And I still think you were right about us being limited in what we can do for her. We can support her. We can be her friend. But as far as helping her work through all her trauma? I'm at a total loss."

"Exactly," Paige said. "I promised her I wouldn't give up on her, and I won't. But I'm fresh out of ideas on what to do."

She put her head on Orlando's shoulder as they made their way to the student parking lot. With great effort, she forced herself to disentangle herself from his warm, comforting embrace once they got to her car. She dreaded the idea of going back to her apartment alone, knowing she would likely be up all night, obsessing over the colossal mistake she had made.

"God, I wish there was something I could do. I would give anything if I could go back in time and fix this." Her sorrow was suddenly replaced with a surge of fury at herself. She slammed her fist down on the hood of her car so hard she was lucky it didn't leave a dent. "I am so incredibly stupid!"

Orlando grasped her hand. Looking up into his face, she saw deep compassion in his sweet brown eyes. "You're not stupid, Paige. You made the decision to talk to Anthony with your heart, not with your head. Because you care so much about Jackey."

Her anger eased a little upon hearing his gentle words. She was still furious with herself, but deep down she knew he was right. She had made a terrible mistake, but she would never have done anything to hurt Jackey on purpose.

"I guess that's true, but it doesn't matter now. Oh God, Orlando. What if she vanishes and we never see her again?"

Orlando's face fell slightly. He quickly recovered, but it was too late. Clearly, he feared that was a real possibility.

"That probably won't happen. She has a bad temper, but she always calms down. I didn't know what she was gonna do after talking to Rebekah, but she handled that whole thing a lot better than we thought. As long as she's willing to talk to us again, we can sit down and discuss it rationally with her."

Tenderly stroking her hair, he said, "There's nothing more we can do tonight. So try not to worry."

"What a mess. You must be sorry you ever got involved in this whole thing."

"No, I'm not sorry," he said. "It's been quite an adventure."

Paige scoffed at that.

This poor man. When I think of everything I've dragged him through ...

She knew he felt bad that she was so upset. But it wasn't fair for him to have to waste any more time on her.

Putting on a brave face, she smiled wearily. "Thanks so much for everything, Orlando. I appreciate you putting up with me. Go on home and get some rest."

"I hate the idea of you being alone right now," he said.

Me too. But I've burdened you enough.

"I'll be fine. I just need to get some sleep," she said, knowing there was no way in hell she would sleep tonight. Paige was the queen of overthinking things, and she knew she was in for a long night of tossing and turning, squirming over her own stupidity.

Orlando hesitated for a moment. Then he said, "Would it be okay if I took you somewhere real quick?"

"I don't know. I'm such a mess right now."

"Not any place where you'd have to talk to anyone. Just someplace I go when I need to be alone. To think."

He seemed so earnest that it was impossible for her to say no. Though she didn't want to inconvenience him any further, the temptation of remaining in his comforting presence was too much.

"Okay, sure."

"Let's take my truck. I don't want you to have to drive anywhere right now."

"Oh. Umm, okay," Paige said.

They began walking back toward the Visitor Center parking lot. Her mind spun with the possibilities of where Orlando was taking her. Her emotions still roiled inside her, and she realized that she wanted more than anything to sit and talk with him somewhere private about what was going on. After all, he had been there from the beginning of this "adventure" as he called it. Who else could possibly understand how she was feeling?

As they walked, Paige found herself wishing he would wrap his arm around her again. He only did that when she was upset, though, and right now she was fairly calm. He led her to a red Toyota Tacoma truck. Partially rusted, the thing had seen better days.

"Sorry," he said. "Not exactly a luxury vehicle."

"I like it," she said truthfully. It was a manly kind of truck, and it suited him. He grabbed some papers and other trash from the front passenger seat and stuffed them into a plastic bag to make room for her to sit.

"Sorry it's such a mess. I wasn't expecting company."

"No problem."

"This place isn't too far away. I promise to have you home at a decent hour."

"No rush. I didn't feel like going home anyway."

"That's what I figured," he said, starting the truck.

They didn't talk much on the way, and Orlando seemed slightly nervous. He was taking her someplace that was personal to him, so maybe that was why he was on edge.

He drove her to an open field a few miles away. After parking the truck, he sat there for a few seconds. Like he was second-guessing himself. She wasn't sure, because he was so damned hard to read sometimes.

Orlando got out of the truck and walked around to open her door. Gallantly, he offered his hand and helped her step down. He had a way of making her feel like a princess. Helping her out of the truck like it was a chariot. The way he always protected her. They were good friends and they spent so much time together, and she knew he didn't have a girlfriend. She wished she could determine whether he had any romantic interest in her. Even if the answer was no, at least she could stop obsessing over it.

Still holding her hand, he led her to the back of the truck. There, he let go of her hand so he could flip the tailgate down. Reaching into the truck, he grabbed a rolled up sleeping bag. He untied it, unrolled it, and then spread it in the truck bed like a flat bench.

Anxiety prickled in Paige's stomach. Though she trusted Orlando, she wasn't sure exactly what he had in mind. Here she was, a woman alone with a man in a secluded area in the middle of nowhere.

Orlando turned to look at her. The warmth in his eyes was so sweet, so familiar, that her fears eased immediately.

He's not a stranger. He's Orlando.

"Have a seat," he said, offering his hand again to help her up. She obliged and sat down in the truck, and he climbed up and sat next to her. They sat for a moment, their feet dangling down the back of the truck.

Orlando gazed skyward, and she followed his eyes. Dozens of bright stars were visible in the cloudless October night. The view was breathtaking, and the nearly full moon provided lovely, soft lighting.

"It might sound kinda silly," he said, "but I like to come here when I'm feeling down."

"Not silly at all. It's gorgeous here. So peaceful."

"Exactly. I come here on days when I feel like I'm looking for answers," he said, still gazing at the sky. "Days like my mom's birthday or her death anniversary. Hard days."

Paige nodded, even though he wasn't looking at her.

"Everything feels so vast here. The field is so big, and then looking up at the stars and thinking about the universe and all that. Makes me feel like I'm a part of something so much bigger than myself."

"That's beautiful," Paige said softly. She held still, not wanting to move a muscle for fear of snapping Orlando out of his trance. She'd never heard him say anything personal like this.

"I came here one night after talking with you and Jackey. Hearing her talk can be overwhelming. Like I just can't wrap my mind around what happened to her. How could anybody for one moment think it was okay to own slaves? It's mind-boggling, you know?"

"Yes. Orlando?"

At last, he turned to look at her.

"Yeah?"

Paige's emotions overwhelmed her when she gazed into his eyes. She cared so much for this man she likely couldn't have. She also cared deeply about a friend she had wronged so badly, she might never see her again. It was all too much.

Tearing up, she asked, "Do you ever find any answers when you come out here?"

Orlando smiled gently. "Not exactly. But coming here helps anyway. Feels like maybe it's okay that I don't have all the answers. Maybe there's a reason that terrible things happen in life, even if I don't understand those reasons. Does that make sense?"

Wiping her eyes, she said, "It does, actually. When you look up at all those stars and think, really *think*, about how big the universe is and how small you are in comparison, it helps to know you're a part of something huge. And that it's okay to be confused and overwhelmed, because maybe somehow everything will be okay in the end."

"Yes," Orlando whispered. "That's exactly how I feel."

He gazed into her eyes for a moment, and she could see, even *feel* the affection he had for her. It was so real she could almost taste it. Maybe a handsome, dynamic, talented force of nature like Orlando could fall for a plain Jane like her after all.

Orlando swallowed hard, and she watched his Adam's apple bob up and down as if in slow motion. His eyes drifted down to her lips and then back up to her eyes again.

Then he turned away.

Paige wanted to scream in frustration and nearly did so.

She was physically and emotionally exhausted by her longing for Orlando. It just hurt too damned much, and she couldn't bear it one moment longer.

Enough was enough.

"Orlando," she said, forcing him to turn toward her.

"If you don't kiss me right now, I might actually die."

His eyes flew open wide. That was probably the last thing he'd expected her to say. Paige held her breath and waited.

Orlando let out a short, breathy laugh. "Well, we can't have that, can we?"

Tenderly, he pushed her hair out of her face and gazed into her eyes.

Orlando caressed her lips with his finger, sending shivers of delight down her spine. Then he gently lifted her chin and pressed his lips to hers.

Paige melted into him as his warm, sensual mouth covered hers. Kissing Orlando felt as natural as breathing, with none of the awkwardness of other first kisses. His kiss deepened, and he threaded his fingers through her hair. She could hardly believe this was happening, and she wanted to drink in every second of it.

His large hands massaged her hair while his mouth explored hers. She didn't know what had possessed her to be so brazen as to ask him to kiss her, but thank God she'd found the courage somehow.

Orlando nibbled down her neck, making her moan with desire.

"I've wanted to kiss you for so long," he murmured in her ear. "I just wasn't sure you wanted me to."

"Oh, I wanted you to," she said, tilting her neck to give him better access.

His hands roamed down her shoulders then stopped short. Paige put her hand over his and guided him toward her left breast. Orlando let out a deep, throaty moan as he massaged her breast, making the nipple grow hard as a rock.

That was the precise moment when Paige realized she wanted nothing more than to have Orlando make love to her right there in the back of his pickup truck.

The idea was impulsive, insane, and utterly un-Paige-like. But it was what she wanted. She just wasn't sure how to make it happen. She might have been bold enough to ask for a kiss, but initiating sex was way out of her comfort zone. Besides, what if he rejected her? She couldn't survive that kind of humiliation.

As Orlando rubbed both her breasts with his huge, manly hands, she was tempted to unbutton his shirt. But she couldn't summon the courage to do it. She let out a soft moan to at least let him know how into this she was.

That seemed to be all the motivation he needed.

He gently but firmly pushed her down onto her back. Her head was off the sleeping bag now, and she landed on the hard metal of the truck bed. She didn't care. Orlando pressed his hardness between her legs, making it clear he was hers for the taking if she wanted.

And oh, she *wanted*.

Feeling more confident, Paige began unbuttoning his

shirt. But then he pulled away. She held her breath, horrified that he was going to reject her.

Gazing down at her with worried eyes, he said, "This is so fast. Are you sure this is what you want?"

Here she was, practically throwing herself at him, and he still had the restraint to make sure she was all right. His sweet concern only made her even more certain that she wanted this.

"Yes, I'm sure. I want you to make love to me under the stars, Orlando," she said softly.

It sounded silly to her own ears, and she felt a deep blush creep into her face, afraid Orlando would laugh at her.

"That sounds wonderful, Paige," he said.

His eyes were so full of kindness, she wondered how she could ever have thought he would laugh at her. Besides, he'd brought her here to see the stars and because this place was meaningful to him.

"Do you have protection?" she asked.

"Yeah. I do. First, let's make you more comfortable," he said, offering her his hand to help her up. Pulling the sleeping bag up from under her, he repositioned it. He kissed her again before taking out his wallet and pulling out a condom.

Paige tried not to read too much into the fact that he was prepared for sex. But she couldn't help wondering if he'd carried that condom around in his wallet for months just in case, or if he used them so often that he was always packing them.

He reached for her, kissing her again. He rubbed her breasts, picking up where he left off. She moaned softly as his kisses became more forceful, passionate. Orlando pushed her onto her back on the sleeping bag, and it was at that moment it all became real to her.

Orlando Blake is about to make love to me.

The man she had admired for so long while hiding in the crowds, watching as he gave those scintillating speeches in front of the courthouse. The hero who had carried her to safety when Jackey had frightened her. The sweet guy who spent countless hours after work trying to help a lost soul find her way home.

The man she had fallen in love with.

As hard as she'd tried, Paige could no longer deny the truth. She did love Orlando, and she might be opening herself up to a world of heartbreak by sleeping with him if he didn't feel the same way.

Live in the moment, Paige! You can overthink this later.

Being intimate with Orlando was a dream come true, and she didn't want to miss a single moment. She unbuttoned the rest of his shirt so she could finally see, and feel, that broad chest she found so alluring. Slipping the shirt off his huge shoulders, she indulged in staring at his muscled chest for a moment before allowing herself the pleasure of touching it.

She caught a hint of a sexy smile as she ran her hands across his torso. Orlando clearly enjoyed being admired, and who could blame him? She loved how *big* he was all over. Broad shoulders, big hands, and large biceps. He even smelled masculine, musky with a hint of manly sweat. She hoped to make him sweat a lot more before this was over.

Orlando pulled off her top and unclasped her bra. Both half-naked and intensely aroused, the urgency to be together became desperate. Orlando sucked on her left breast, and she arched her back and cried out with pleasure at the sensation. He gave equal attention to her right breast, licking and stroking her nipple until she was half out of her mind with desire. Her need for him to be inside her was almost painful.

Paige began tugging at his pants, and Orlando quickly unbuckled his jeans and slid them off. She wasted no time in grabbing his underwear and yanking them down. Unabashedly, she looked down at his cock, feeling his eyes on her as she did.

"Wow," she said in a breathy voice. She reached down and stroked him a couple of times, eliciting a delightfully masculine growl from deep in his throat.

Orlando grabbed the waistband of her pants and pulled them and her underwear down in one quick motion. She barely had time to register that she was naked before he thrust two thick fingers inside her. She screamed in both surprise and the intensity of the unexpected burst of pleasure. He hesitated, seemingly unsure of what to make of her sudden cry.

"Don't stop," she whispered. He grinned devilishly as he thrust his fingers in and out of her, making her wetter by the second. Paige arched her back again and whimpered with delight.

"Orlando," she said huskily. "Please. I *need* you."

Acutely aware that it had been more than a year since she had had sex, her body cried out for release.

"I need you too, Paige," Orlando said in a deep, sensual voice. "You have no idea how bad I need you."

He straddled her, pressing his hard cock between her legs, eyes blazing with an almost scary need. Orlando looked like a man possessed, ready to take what he desired. And yet, he swallowed hard, collecting himself first. He gazed down into her eyes, as if giving her one last chance to back out if she wanted to.

"I need you," she whispered again, feeling desperate and vulnerable and so much in love she could hardly breathe.

They locked eyes as he slowly slid himself inside her. She let out a soft whimper as the sweet invasion of his cock sent ripples of pleasure throughout her body. He began thrusting faster, and now she let out a cry so loud, it echoed into the empty field. She realized she had to get some measure of control before she started screaming his name and letting everyone within a two-mile radius know there were people having sex out here.

She wrapped her arms around Orlando's neck and closed her eyes, relishing every second as he gave her what she sorely needed. Paige panted hard and Orlando made all kinds of sexy grunting and growly masculine sounds as he pounded into her. Even the truck bed's rhythmic squeaking was exciting. Their lovemaking was frenzied, like they couldn't get enough of each other and yet they were desperate to make it to the finish line.

Paige had only been with a few other men, and they hadn't really known what they were doing in bed.

Orlando knows what he's doing.

Strong and dominant, he instinctively knew how and where to touch her to drive her completely out of her mind. She couldn't help crying out again once her pleasure came close to its achingly delicious peak.

"Orlando, Orlando," she cried, grabbing fistfuls of his hair. She tried to say his name a third time, but it just came out *Ohhhhh* as she reached orgasm. Throwing her head back, she let go and allowed her climax to consume her. Even as her blissful orgasmic release utterly overwhelmed her, she heard Orlando let out a deep groan and felt him spasm inside her. Paige liked to think watching her have an orgasm was what sent him over the edge.

Orlando was sweating all right, and so was she. He was still inside her, panting and hot despite the rapidly cooling October air.

Coming down from the high of her climax, Paige began to feel vulnerable and shy. She'd made her desire for Orlando so achingly clear, she was embarrassed. Just as her usual obsessive thoughts began to creep in, Orlando cupped her face and tenderly kissed her.

Her body relaxed as he stroked her hair, kissing away all her doubts and fears.

He pulled out of her and found an empty plastic bag where he disposed of the condom. Then he lay down beside her, pulling her close.

Resting her head on his chest, Paige let out a sigh of deep relief. She had never needed to be held by anyone so bad in her life. She didn't know what she would do if Orlando had simply gotten up after having sex with her.

"Wow. We are *really* good together," he said.

"Yes, we sure are," she said lazily, basking in sexual relief and in his tender touch. Staring up at the stars, she said, "I never thought having sex in the back of a pickup truck could be so romantic."

He chuckled softly. "Me neither. This was amazing."

"Mmm hmm."

They lay there until she began to doze off.

"You're exhausted," he said. "I better get you home."

With a heavy sigh, she said, "Yeah, I guess so. I have class in the morning."

She felt vulnerable again when they sat up, seeing as they were both still completely naked. She picked up her bra and put it back on. When she looked up, there was Orlando with a sweet smile, holding her shirt up. He helped her put it on. He gave her her underwear and, after letting her handle those herself, helped her on with her jeans before getting dressed himself.

That was classic Orlando. When she was upset, he reached for her and held her close. When she felt vulnerable, somehow he always knew and did what he could to make her more comfortable.

No wonder she loved him so much.

The question was, did he love her? Was he serious about her at all, or was this just a crazy, impulsive, "just for fun" thing?

She was tempted to flat out ask him, but then she figured she was far enough out of her comfort zone for one night.

The next move needed to be his.

20

Orlando kissed Paige again before taking her hand and helping her into the truck. His head spun with the events of the evening. When he'd brought her out to the field to see the stars, sex was the last thing on his mind.

Well, maybe not the *last* thing on his mind, but he certainly hadn't expected it to happen. Paige didn't strike him as the type to have one-night stands, so he'd taken care to hold and kiss her afterward, to make sure she knew how much he cherished her.

Orlando was ready to go all in with Paige, but he wasn't sure if she felt the same way. The way she looked at him made him hopeful. And sharing her body must have meant something.

He'd been with lots of women and being with them hadn't meant anything. That point was totally clear before anything physical happened. Most times, he came right out and said, "I'm not looking for anything serious." He had a healthy sexual appetite but had no desire to break anybody's heart.

But "casual" was not what he wanted with Paige. Saying stuff like *You're cool with this being a one-night thing, right?* came easy to him. Expressing deeper feelings felt like trying to speak a foreign language. He didn't even know where to start. What could he possibly say?

Oh hey, by the way, I'm in love with you.

He pictured Paige making a face if he said that. Like she thought he was nuts. What if she laughed at him? Worse, what if she *pitied* him? Then she'd have to try to let him down easy, explaining that she appreciated his words, but that she was only looking to blow off some steam by having sex with him in the back of a pickup truck.

God, just imagining her saying that was painful. Funny how he'd always worried about the woman feeling hurt after sex. He hadn't considered it might happen to him.

Paige snuggled up next to him on the drive back, which was a good sign.

"You okay?" he asked.

"Yeah," she said quietly.

Knowing her, she was back to obsessing over Jackey again. Poor thing. She'd worked so hard to gain Jackey's trust, and he knew she must be heartbroken over what had happened tonight.

"It's gonna be okay, Paige. With Jackey, I mean."

"I hope so. I'm not so sure. I just wish I could understand why she was so resistant to talk to Anthony in the first place. I mean, I shouldn't have meddled when it came to him. That much is clear. But if I knew why she didn't want to talk to him, maybe I could fix this somehow."

"I've been thinking about that," Orlando said. "And I do have one idea."

"Really?" Paige said, sitting up to look at him.

He suppressed a smile, not wanting her to think he was

taking this lightly. She was just so damned cute when she got excited.

"Yeah." He forced himself to focus on the road and not Paige's pretty face. "I've been thinking about some stuff Rebekah told me. She was crazy about Gregory back when she was a ghost. Had been for a long time, before he even knew she existed. Like, she used to go to Hay's Cabinetmaker's Shop and watch him work when she was invisible,"

"Just like Jackey said she sometimes watches Anthony," Paige said.

"Gregory had no idea she was there, and she never planned on letting him see her. Rebekah told me she thought he was so handsome, and she hated the idea of him thinking she was some gross, ghoulish thing. And she couldn't stand the idea of having him be afraid of her."

"I can understand that."

"Yeah. Me too."

"So, what changed? How did they end up getting together?" Paige asked.

"Rebekah saved his life, that's what happened. He's diabetic, and she knew all about his medical condition from watching him for so long. One day when he was working by himself, Gregory nearly went into diabetic shock. She was the only one around, so she had no choice but to let him see her so she could help him. Scared him, snapped him out of his shock long enough to help him get the sugar he needed to survive."

"Wow! She actually saved his life. That is so *romantic*," she said.

Orlando chuckled. He reached over and stroked her hair. "You would say that. You're such a girl."

Paige laughed. "I know. But it is an amazing story. Thank God she was there."

"Yeah, that's for sure. It was bad. From what Gregory says, he really might have died if not for her. After that, he knew she was a ghost and they became friends."

"And then they fell in love," Paige said with a dreamy sigh. Orlando chuckled again.

"So I'm thinking, we know Jackey finds Anthony attractive. She might feel the same way Rebekah did about not wanting him to know she's dead. That, and the way she's forced to be dressed as a slave," Orlando said bitterly. "I mean, I think Jackey's a beautiful woman. I really do. And she deserves to feel beautiful. Being forced to be dressed in the clothes of your captors for all eternity is yet another cruelty she has to endure, you know?"

"That is such a good point. I can't believe that never occurred to me. Of course she would want to look beautiful for Anthony. To dress up and feel good about herself, and that's humanly impossible. And she's probably used to people screaming at the sight of her, not to mention scaredy-cats like me nearly passing out in fear of her."

Paige moaned and covered her face for a moment. "No wonder she was so upset!" She lowered her hands and said softly, "I can imagine how she feels. It would break my heart if I thought you were afraid of me, or if you thought I was some kind of ghoul."

"I would never think that. Even if you were dead."

"Thanks," she said with a gentle laugh. She fell silent as they turned down the road near her college. Then she exclaimed, "Oh my God. Oh my *God.*"

"What's the matter?" he asked, alarmed at her tone.

"I think you're even more right than you thought," Paige said. "Oh my *God!*"

Thankfully, they had just arrived at the student parking

lot. Orlando quickly parked the truck so he could turn and look at her.

"What's happening in that pretty brain of yours?" he asked.

"Jackey's in love with Anthony," she said, eyes wide. "It all makes sense now. She said she watches him give tours at the Peyton Randolph House the same way Rebekah used to watch Gregory. Then, when she came to see me on campus and we were talking about our ideal man, she said hers was a nice, kindhearted guy. The kind who was good with kids. That's Anthony all over. And remember that time I asked her if she'd ever been in love, and she said once, but it happened too late? When she was describing the guy, she said when he smiled, it was kind of a half-smile that made the corners of his eyes crinkle up. That's how Anthony smiles!"

Paige's words came out in such a tumbled rush that it took Orlando a few seconds to register everything she had said.

"Oh wow. I think you're right," he said.

"Dammit. If only I'd figured this out sooner! I could have sat down and talked to her about it. It might have taken some time, but I might have been able to convince her to talk with him."

"You might still be able to convince her, Paige."

"Not if she decides to vanish for another hundred years."

She shuddered, and he could see how worried she was.

"I'm telling you, sweetie. I don't think she will. Might take her some time to cool down and talk to us again, but I have a feeling she's not done with us yet."

"I hope to God you're right." Looking around at the dark parking lot, she said, "It's getting late. I better let you go home and get some sleep."

Orlando nodded. He got out of the truck and walked around to her side. After helping her out, he gazed down into her lovely green eyes.

There was so much he wanted to say to her. How brave, strong, and smart he thought she was. How incredible tonight had been.

How much he loved her.

But telling her all that was just too big of a risk. If he came right out and told her he loved her and she didn't feel the same way, he would look like a complete fool. It was best to adopt a wait and see attitude. Follow her lead. If it seemed like she had feelings for him, then he would tell her how he felt.

He tried not to think about how utterly cowardly that was. Instead, he cupped her face, bent down, and pressed his lips to hers. Expressing his feelings through touch was a lot easier than through words. She moaned softly, her body melting into his.

"Thank you for a perfect night, Orlando," she murmured, wrapping her arms around him.

Paige was wonderfully warm and affectionate now, but she might feel different in the light of day.

Wait and see.

WALKING ALONE through the historical district felt strange without Orlando. After all, they'd made love last night, and she hadn't heard a word from him yet. He was off work today so she hadn't expected to see him, but shouldn't he at least have called her? Paige had hoped that last night would be the start of a serious relationship, but maybe it had been nothing but a one-night stand to him.

Between stressing out over Jackey and daydreaming about Orlando, concentrating on her classes had been one hell of a struggle. But she had made it through the day and come straight here. She wasn't optimistic about the odds of Jackey showing up tonight, but she had to at least try to find her. She planned to go to the gaol in the late evening in hopes of seeing her.

She also figured she owed it to Anthony to provide him with an update of the situation, depressing as that might be right now. She'd checked the day's tour schedule and found he was probably working today. With no paid pass and no Orlando by her side, she had no choice but to wait for him to emerge from the Peyton Randolph House at the end of the day. By the time she remembered she had his number and could have called or texted him, she was already there.

Fortunately, Anthony came out of the historical building not long after quitting time. A flicker of attraction rippled pleasantly through Paige's stomach when she saw him. He stood tall and handsome, still wearing his costume. Like Orlando, he was knowledgeable about history, and there was such kindness in his face.

No wonder Jackey fell in love with him.

Anthony's eyes lit up when he saw Paige, and he strode toward her.

"Paige, how are you?" he asked.

"Doing good, thanks."

"How's everything going? With, you know ..." His eyes sparked with interest. Anthony seemed excited about helping Jackey, and Paige hated to disappoint him.

"Well, that's what I came to talk to you about. I talked to Jackey about having you meet with her. And, well, it didn't go so well."

"What happened?"

"As strange as it might seem, some ghosts are sensitive about being seen by the living," Paige began carefully. Though she wished she could explain to Anthony exactly what was going on, she was not about to betray Jackey's trust by telling him how she suspected she felt about him. "Mostly, they just want to be thought of as people. And not —" she lowered her voice, "dead people."

Anthony nodded, looking concerned.

"It can be hard for them to show themselves sometimes. Lots of times people are afraid of them. God, I was terrified at first. I nearly fainted when I first saw her."

He smiled warmly at her confession.

"So there's that. And I think sometimes she's sensitive about the way she looks. Don't get me wrong, she's *beautiful*. But she can only appear dressed in what I guess she wore when she died, which is pretty much rags."

"Slave clothing," he said somberly.

"Exactly. It's incredibly unfair. And another reason she's hesitant to show herself is that people around here mistake her for an employee and ask her lots of questions."

"Oh, wow," he said, wincing a bit. "I can't blame her for hating that."

"I have to say, I'm kind of surprised at how much you seem to believe what I'm telling you," Paige said with a laugh. "I mean, every word I'm telling you is true. It's just I think I would be more skeptical if I were you."

"Yeah," Anthony said, stroking his chin where a sexy five o'clock shadow had sprouted. "Lately, I've felt a strong presence around here. Like I told you last time, I've always felt like maybe something—some*one,* is with me sometimes when I'm working in the house. Paige, I think Jackey might be here with me sometimes."

"Wow," she whispered. "Oh, I just wish so much she

would talk to you. I think it would help her. Maybe if I hadn't made such a mess of this whole thing."

"What do you mean?"

The gentleness in his voice made her eyes water. Anthony was so nice, and she hadn't realized how much she needed that right now.

"It was all my fault. Jackey said no when I asked her if it was okay to get you involved. She, uh, knows who you are because she's seen you around and, like you said, it might have been her presence you felt."

It was definitely her.

"And she said in no uncertain terms she didn't want to involve you in this. Please don't take that personally. I think it's for all the reasons I said before, about ghosts being sensitive and the way she's dressed and all that. But really, it doesn't matter why she didn't want to talk with you. It's none of my damn business what her personal reasons were. I should have respected her wishes."

Paige started to cry as she spoke. She didn't want to make Anthony uncomfortable by getting so upset, but she couldn't hold back her tears.

"I'm sorry," she said, quickly wiping her eyes with the back of her hand. "It's just Jackey has been through so much in her life and in her death. Believe me, it was hard for her to trust ... and ..." She managed to continue without completely breaking down. "She was so angry and sad, and I'm scared she'll never speak to me again."

Paige wiped her eyes with a tissue from her pocket, hoping she hadn't made the situation too awkward for this poor man who barely knew her. She chanced a look into his eyes and saw nothing but compassion. He didn't look uncomfortable. Instead, he looked like he wanted to give her a hug but wasn't sure if he should.

Anthony settled for putting a reassuring hand on her shoulder. "It's gonna be okay, Paige. You were only trying to help. Deep down, she probably knows that."

"I hope so. I may not be much, but I'm the only friend she has. Well, me and Orlando. Hopefully she hasn't given up on me altogether. I hate the idea of her being all alone again."

"Me too," Anthony said thoughtfully.

"Anyway," she said, wiping her eyes again and stuffing the used tissue in her pocket. "I guess talking to Jackey is off the table for now. But if I see her, or if anything changes, I'll let you know."

"Okay," he said, nodding, a thoughtful look on his face. "Sounds good."

After saying their goodbyes, Paige wandered aimlessly around the district for a little while. Since she had planned to visit the gaol after dark, there was no point in going home first. She bought some take-out for dinner from one of the taverns and ate it outside, even though it was getting cold out as the evening progressed. It would have felt awkward to sit in the tavern and eat by herself.

Once again, she wondered *why* she was alone. She told herself maybe Orlando had plans for his day off, but that just made her feel worse. Whatever his plans were, they clearly didn't include her. Even if he was busy, couldn't he have spared a moment to at least text her to see how she was? To tell her he was thinking of her?

Unless he wasn't thinking of her.

After finishing her rather sad and lonely dinner, Paige headed over to the Public Gaol. She sat there for a while, but there was no sign of Jackey. She closed her eyes, hoping to sense her presence the way Anthony clearly could. She felt nothing. But then again she never had, even when it turned out Jackey was nearby. Paige didn't seem to have that natural sensitivity to ghosts. Just in case, she tried calling out to Jackey, but there was no response.

Eventually, she trudged back to the Peyton Randolph House. She stood and watched a ghost tour stop right in front of the house where Jackey had once lived. The tours were always popular, especially in October because of Halloween. Paige hoped to hear the scream of a tourist being grabbed by the ankle. More so, she hoped to experience that herself.

Still nothing.

Paige texted Orlando to let him know that Jackey hadn't shown up. She walked back to her car in the dark, missing Orlando's protective presence. He texted her back a few minutes later.

That's too bad. We can try again tomorrow I guess.

Her heart sank. Without Jackey, Orlando saw no reason to go to the historical district with her tonight.

That was not a good sign.

21

———————

Jackey regretted the day she ever met Paige and Orlando. Especially Paige. She should have known better than to trust her. Apparently, she had learned nothing from her experience with Hannah if she was still making the same stupid mistakes hundreds of years later.

How could Paige betray me like that?

She had thought they were friends. And then she went behind her back and spoke to Anthony against her wishes. How would Paige feel if Jackey went running to Orlando and told him how she felt about him?

Now there was an idea. Jackey could tell Orlando all the gushy, embarrassing things Paige had confided in her about him.

It took merely seconds for Jackey to dismiss that notion. She simply wasn't the kind of person to betray her friends. Not even former friends.

She glided invisibly through the streets of Williamsburg in the late afternoon, her thoughts returning to Anthony. She felt so humiliated knowing that he knew all about her.

That she'd been forced to be a slave and that she still haunted the Peyton Randolph House. There was a reason she chose to be invisible most of the time, goddamnit. Because she didn't want to be seen. Jackey wouldn't ever let Anthony lay eyes on her, so Paige talking to him had been utterly pointless.

Jackey wanted to scream out with anger. Her pain was greater now than before she'd started talking to those two jerks. Sure, she had felt better temporarily. Speaking with Rebekah had helped a bit, and hearing her apology for being a slaveholder had provided a tiny amount of healing.

But befriending Paige had been the most healing part of all. When she sat and talked with her on the school campus, for a short while she actually forgot she was a dead slave. They had been just two friends giggling and gossiping together. For the first time in forever, she hadn't been lonely. And for perhaps the first time ever, she'd felt like she belonged.

But that made the pain all the more devastating when Paige betrayed her.

Jackey wandered around, trying to decide what to do now. The only things she knew for certain were that she never wanted to see Paige or Orlando again, and that she wanted the pain to stop. If she wished, she could vanish for a decade or so. By then, Paige would have graduated from college and Orlando likely would have moved on from his job in Williamsburg. Hell, just to be sure, she could vanish for a hundred years and they would both be gone for good.

Trouble was, vanishing would mean abandoning Anthony. Not that he would know she was gone, but seeing him regularly was the only bright spot in her lonely existence. Why should she have to give him up just to avoid Paige and Orlando? All too soon, Anthony might be gone anyway. He might get another job. Worse, he could get married and move away from Colonial Williamsburg. Surely, her days with him were numbered, and she would not waste them.

She had watched him for a while earlier this afternoon, but it hadn't been the same. Jackey used to be able to watch him work, and he was none the wiser. Now he knew who she was. Worse, Anthony seemed to sense her presence. Several times, he looked right in the direction where she was standing. He might not be able to see her, but he knew someone was near. Sure, he'd done that before, but it could have been any number of ghosts haunting the place. Now, she felt incredibly vulnerable, knowing he probably knew it was her there with him. She hadn't been able to bear it any longer, so she'd left before the tour even finished.

Now the stupid ghost tours were starting. She considered frightening some tourists, which sometimes made her feel better when she was all worked up and angry. But she found she didn't have the energy. She was sick of being dead. Tired of being feared. And Anthony probably thought of her as some disgusting, zombie-like creature. The thought hurt so badly.

Yet, she had been angry enough earlier today when Paige came by looking for her at the gaol. Since Paige didn't have Anthony's sensitivity, she didn't know Jackey was there with her as she called out her name. Jackey had been tempted to grab the girl *hard*. Hard enough to leave bruises, like she'd done to Orlando long ago. Hell, she could have tripped her, too, and laughed when she fell flat on her face. Somehow, Jackey couldn't bring herself to do it. And that just made her angrier.

Forget grabbing Paige. Jackey decided she would ignore her altogether. That girl could search for her forever, and

Jackey wouldn't ever show herself to her again. Let her spend the rest of her life wondering what happened to her.

Jackey wandered around aimlessly for hours until even the ghost tour visitors had left. Her ghostly heart seized in her chest when she saw a man approach the Peyton Randolph House long after dark. She would know that familiar stride anywhere.

Anthony.

What in blazes was he doing here at this late hour? Still invisible, she rushed over to stand in front of the Peyton Randolph House and watched him walk straight up to her.

Anthony paused and looked around. If she'd had breath, she would have been holding it.

"Maybe I'm crazy," he said. "Maybe I'm imagining it, but Jackey, I have a feeling you're here."

He looked around the yard and then back at her. His concentration focused where she was standing—not only did he know she was there, he had a good idea exactly where she was.

Jackey had sworn to herself she wouldn't ever let Anthony see her. But she never dreamed he would actually come looking for her. Panic gripped her.

What should I do?

There was no going back once he saw her. Watching Anthony work wasn't much, but it was all she had to look forward to. What if she ruined it by showing herself?

"If you're here, Jackey, I would really like to talk to you," Anthony said, his brown eyes filled with warmth and kindness. Notably, she saw no fear in them. Maybe he wouldn't scream and run at the sight of her. After all, Orlando never had.

The truth of her situation suddenly dawned on her. She was dead, had been for hundreds of years, and she couldn't touch anything or do much of anything. Nothing she had done in all those years had brought her any closer to escape. Anthony already knew who she was. She didn't have much to lose by letting him see her.

She decided to give him a little warning before she appeared out of thin air. She placed her hand gently across his cheek, and even though she couldn't feel a thing, it was still thrilling to touch him.

Anthony drew in a sharp breath and shivered, which she'd expected. After allowing him a few seconds to recover from that initial shock, she faded into view a few feet away from him.

His eyes grew wide, making her painfully conscious of how she looked. Hair wrapped in a cloth, drab gray skirt, and white blouse. She couldn't possibly compare with those gorgeous Black women she saw visiting Williamsburg. Some of the ladies on Anthony's tours had been quite stunning. Hair done up all fancy in braids or other nice styles. Makeup that brought out their pretty features. Beautiful nail art. My God, she felt ugly in comparison. Two seconds in, and she already regretted her decision.

"Jackey?" he whispered.

She nodded, fighting the urge to look away. To hide herself. Inwardly, she cursed Paige for putting her in this position.

How would she feel if she had to show herself to Orlando dressed in rags?

She wanted to cry and nearly did so. Steeling herself, she vowed to be brave in front of Anthony. She could weep tears of shame all night after he left.

"I can't believe it's really you. And you actually lived in this house?" Anthony glanced at the big brick building and then back at her.

"Yes."

"It's such an honor to meet you."

He stared at her in wonder. It made sense. The man was passionate about history, and she knew how much he cared about the Black people who had inhabited the place where he worked.

"You're not afraid of me?"

"Of course not," he said.

Drinking in the sweet kindness of his eyes and that familiar partial smile that lifted the right corner of his mouth, Jackey could hardly believe she was standing here, talking to this dear man.

"In a strange way, I feel as if I know you a little. I spend so much time here talking about the people who lived here so long ago. I can't help but feel connected to them. Through everything I've learned about them over the years and through our shared heritage."

Jackey was loath to admit it to herself, but Paige might have been right all along. She hadn't spoken directly to another Black person in over a hundred years. From time to time, she'd spoken to other ghosts. Some revolutionary soldiers who'd lingered after their violent deaths. A shopkeeper from the 1700s, a blacksmith—people like that. Plenty of white ghosts ignored her in death just as they had in life, having no use for a ghostly slave they couldn't control for their own use. Until now, she hadn't realized how much she needed to speak with someone who truly understood what it felt like to look like her.

"It's lovely," Jackey said. "What you're doing to keep our memory alive."

"Thank you for saying that. It means a lot."

Anthony's eyes roamed over her ghostly form, and she found herself wanting to run away again.

Damn these horrid clothes.

"If you don't mind my saying so, you're a beautiful woman."

She stared at him as if he had gone mad.

"Like Cinderella," he said with a flirtatious grin that reminded her of Orlando. "You might be in plain clothes, but you're prettier than all the other girls at the ball anyway."

"Oh, go on with you," she said, waving him off. It took an effort to brush off his compliment as if it was unimportant. In reality, it was one of the most meaningful things anyone had said to her since her death. Mostly because it came from him.

"I mean it," he said with enthusiasm. "If I could, I would kiss your hand."

"You're quite the charmer, now aren't you?"

"I have my moments, I suppose."

"Here. Why don't you come sit?" she said, walking toward the benches in the front yard. "You must be tired from working all day and bein' here so late."

Anthony followed her and they sat on separate benches. Though he showed no fear of her, she didn't want to press her luck by sitting too close to him. She needed to avoid his touch. Nothing like having your hand slice right through a ghostly body to drive home the reality that you were speaking with a dead person.

"Did you come back here tonight just to find me?"

"You bet I did," Anthony said with a grin. "I'm so thrilled to finally meet you!"

Scanning his face, Jackey saw no fear or disgust. Rather, he looked like an excited child. She'd never seen him look so giddy, and it was incredibly endearing. All this time she'd been concerned with her feelings about speaking to him, it hadn't dawned on her he might wish to talk to her.

"So, let me ask you a question," Jackey said, some of her usual boldness returning.

"Ask me anything."

"Are you married, handsome?" she asked with a flirty wink.

He laughed heartily. "No, ma'am. I am not."

Jackey laughed too. She already knew, but she figured it would be a good way to break the ice. She knew many things about him, but he didn't need to know that.

"Were you married, Jackey? Way back when? We have some records, but we don't know a whole lot about the personal lives of the enslaved people."

"Because nobody cared."

"That's exactly right," he said with a firm nod.

"No. I never married. Didn't want to marry, knowing I could get separated from my spouse at any time."

"Yeah. I get that," he said sadly. "So often, I think of those parents. Living in terror every day that they could be sold away from their children."

"That was another reason I didn't get married and have babies."

"Jackey, I ..." He faltered for a moment. "I know that happened to you. That you were sold away from your father. I'm so sorry."

A rush of emotions and memories of her father came swirling back. No matter how long ago, there were days when she still felt like that scared little girl who had lost her papa.

She found the depth of sorrow on Anthony's face profoundly moving. Deep in her soul, she felt a spiritual connection to him.

He understands.

"After all this time," she said shakily, "I still miss him."

"I feel so blessed to still have both my parents with me. My dad, though. He's not in the greatest of health. Heart troubles. I do my best to treasure each day with him, because you just don't know what will happen."

"So true."

"Can I ask you something?"

"Of course you can," she said, encouraging him with a smile.

"Will you tell me about Johnny?"

Jackey laughed, charmed by Anthony's enthusiasm. "Certainly. I will say that, while you look awful nice in that costume you wear as John Harris, you look nothin' like him."

"Really?" he said, sounding slightly disappointed.

"Oh no, you're much better looking," she said with a grimace.

Anthony laughed.

"Honestly, he wasn't bad lookin' at all," she said, smiling at the memory of John. "You are more handsome, but he was attractive. Johnny was older than me, and he acted like my big brother. Teasin' him 'bout his looks—that was something I did a lot back in the day. It was all in good fun. He was a kind man. Strong, and I mean physical strong and also emotionally. He looked out for all of us, 'specially the younger ones. And so smart, he was. I often wonder what he might have become had he been a free man. He coulda been a lawyer or a doctor. Or a successful businessman. So witty and smart, John coulda done just about anything if he'd been given the chance."

"That's good to know," Anthony said thoughtfully. "Sounds like he was a good man."

"He was. He truly was."

Anthony smiled, looking relieved. He'd devoted so much time to honoring the memory of John Harris, and it would have broken his heart if he found out the man was a jerk. Jackey had nothing but fond memories of Johnny, and Anthony's portrayal of him made her happy.

"Will you tell me about yourself?" he asked.

"Why?"

"Because Paige told me you're trying to figure out how to cross over. To finally escape this existence. And I want to do everything in my power to help."

Fresh pain stabbed her heart at hearing Paige's name. She wasn't ready to forgive her, and she might never be.

"What do you know 'bout me so far?"

"Very little. From what I understand, you were born at another plantation and sold along with your mother to the Randolphs. I believe you were born around 1750 or so and died in 1784. You were personal servant to one of Betty's nieces. Is that right?"

"It is," she said. "And that's all you know?"

"Yes. So far. But I'm hoping you'll tell me more."

He'd been easy to talk to so far, and Jackey was tempted to tell him everything about her. Somehow, he made her feel valued. Beautiful, even. He genuinely *cared*. She could see it in his eyes and feel it in his gaze.

"Please, let me try to help you," Anthony said after her short silence. "Every day I work hard to keep the memory of people like you alive. In fact, I plan to dedicate my life to it. I hope to work my way up here at Colonial Williamsburg so I can eventually have some real say in the programming about slavery and make sure it keeps moving forward. This is my life's work, Jackey. And I never dreamed I'd ever get the chance to actually meet one of those people I've read so much about. More than anything in the world, I want to help you find peace."

"You're a wonderful man, Anthony," she said softly.

He lowered his head modestly and smiled.

It was much easier to trust him than Paige and Orlando. She felt like she knew Anthony's heart, his intentions, and she knew they were pure. As far as those other two went, well, she wasn't sure what to think anymore.

"Well, I suppose it's best I start at the beginning."

Anthony leaned forward, his eyes filled with concern. Jackey told him the important details of her life. How she and Betty's niece had been the best of friends until the harsh reality of the differences between Black and white people were explained to them. The way her life was forever changed when Hannah gleefully accepted the role of slave owner. She told Anthony about her days working for the Randolphs, the way her mother and other friends and relatives loved and supported her, doing their best to survive their lot in life together. She expressed her passion for drawing, telling him how much she missed it since her death. How she ached for the ability to hold a pen or a paintbrush so she could pour out her feelings on paper again.

All the while, Anthony listened patiently. Truthfully, he did more than listen. He grew angry along with her when she spoke of Hannah's betrayal and was sorrowful when she told of her mother's passing. Even in his silence, she felt more connected to him than she had ever felt with another human being.

"So much suffering," Anthony said. "I guess it's no wonder you're still here. So much to deal with."

"Yes. That's part of it. But there's one reason I'm still trapped here. One I only recently discovered."

"And what's that?" he asked, eyes wide.

"I'm too *angry*." Fresh rage built in her. The injustice of it all was simply too much. She didn't see how she could ever stop being furious about her life.

"What do you mean too angry?"

"After all this time of wanderin' around, trying to figure out why in hell I'm still stuck here, another ghost told me what the problem is." Jackey decided the whole "former ghost coming back to life" thing was a discussion for another time. "A slaveholder, of all people. It's my anger that's keeping me earthbound. So I got to let go of my *anger* about everythin' in order to be set free."

Jackey watched Anthony's face as the truth dawned on him.

"So you're saying because you're outraged that you were enslaved and had your entire life and your family stolen from you, that's why you're trapped here?" he asked, eyes blazing.

That was exactly what Jackey wanted. Somebody to get good and goddamned mad right along with her instead of telling her to calm down.

"Apparently so," she snapped.

"Son of a *bitch*!" Anthony roared, probably louder than he'd meant to. He glanced around in the dark, but there was no one in sight. It must have been well past midnight by now.

"So, all I got to do is cool down and stop being so upset about the whole slavery thing, and I can just march on up to Heaven," she said. Then she added quietly, "How am I supposed to do that, Anthony?"

"Question is, *why* should you have to do that?"

"I don't know."

Shoulders tight and teeth clenched, Anthony let out a sharp breath. She'd never seen him so angry, and she adored him for it. Jackey knew he had a deep, emotional connection to the Black men and women of the Peyton Randolph House. His mission was to honor and protect them. And now he wanted to honor and protect *her*.

"From what I understand," she continued wearily, "I don't have to stop being mad altogether. That would be impossible. I just have to let go of some of it. Enough to break the hold that's keepin' me here. Strong emotion, any strong emotion, is what keeps spirits trapped. The other ghost I told you about was trapped by guilt."

Anthony took a moment to calm himself before speaking.

"Well, if nothing else, at least we know what we're dealing with. If we can somehow help release some of your anger, we can set you free." He shook his head. "My God. Just hearing you speak about your life makes me so mad I can hardly see straight. I can't imagine how you feel."

"That helps, Anthony. Truly it does."

"I'm so glad. Okay, so now we know exactly what the problem is. The next step is figuring out what to do about it."

"Perhaps. But not tonight. You better go home and get some rest," she told him.

"But we're just getting started. Maybe we can—"

"I won't hear of it. Not tonight. There's too much, Anthony. Too much. I've been here hundreds of years with the same problems. We're not gonna solve them all tonight. You *must* go home and rest. We'll talk again soon. I promise."

"How about right here, tomorrow night. Around 10:30? By then the ghost tours will be done."

"Okay. It's a date," she said with a wink.

"Looking forward to it." Anthony stood up, but then he

sat back down again. "There's one more thing. If you don't mind my saying, I hope you'll give Paige a second chance."

"Why should I?" Jackey asked, though she was already finding it hard to stay mad at her.

"Well, for one thing, she was kinda right about having you talk to me. I mean, I assume you found it helpful since you agree to meet with me again."

"Yes. It helped a great deal."

"Good. She might have made a mistake in the way she went about it, going against your wishes, but her heart was in the right place when she came to me. Both she and Orlando seem to really care about you."

"I suppose. I just wonder what they want from me sometimes."

"Nothing, Jackey. They don't want anything from you."

"How can you be so sure?"

"Because you're dead," Anthony said gently. "What could they possibly want from you? Far as I can tell, nobody but me even knows what they're up to. They tell me they come talk to you every night to try to help you. It's not like they're selling ghost tour tickets or trying to get you to make an appearance to show off for their friends. Believe me, I see that a lot. People wandering around at night trying to tease the ghosts. Paige and Orlando would never do that."

"No. They wouldn't. But Paige. She knew all about Hannah and what she did to me. She knew how hard it was for me to trust her. So why would she betray me like that?"

"Because she made a mistake. Because she's human. I know you've been hurt in ways I can't even imagine. I can't begin to understand what you've been through, and I'm sure it took a great deal of strength for you to put your trust in a couple of white people. There's still a lot of racist people in the world, but those two aren't like that. They're trying. They may not get everything right, but they're trying."

Sorrow pierced Jackey's heart. It had only been a few days, but she dearly missed talking to her friends. Especially Paige.

"I want to trust them," Jackey said, her voice quivering. "But I'm scared."

"Of course you are, Jackey," Anthony said, reaching for her hand. Naturally, his hand went right through her ghostly form. Chuckling, he said, "Sorry. Habit."

She smiled, taking it as a compliment. For a brief moment, Anthony had forgotten she was dead.

"It's understandable that you're scared. Putting your trust in anyone after what you've been through is a tremendous leap of faith. But if you ask me, I think it's safe to trust Paige and Orlando. I really do."

Jackey took great comfort in his words. More than anything, she wanted Paige and Orlando as her friends.

"I watch the crowds here, and I get so angry. That's why I'm still here," she said, gesturing at her ghostly body. "I see white tourists and all I see is the people who hurt me and my family. So, sometimes I grab people by the ankles when I'm mad."

Anthony laughed, a deep, rich sound. "Yeah, that's what I've heard."

Jackey smiled. "Orlando, he was surprised at first, but I don't think I ever actually scared him. But Paige ... Dear God, she was petrified when I grabbed her. Poor little lamb. And yet, she kept comin' back to see me once she found out who I was. Scared half to death, but she kept comin' back."

"Paige was crying when she came to see me today. Or yesterday, I guess it is now. She was so upset. Said she was afraid you'd never speak to her again."

"I thought about it, believe me."

"They just want to help you, Jackey. That's all."

"I haven't made it easy on 'em, have I?"

Anthony shook his head and smiled. "Does that mean you'll give them another chance?"

"Yes. If they'll still have me."

"I know they will. So I gotta ask. What's the deal with them? Are they, you know, together?"

Jackey grinned. "No. Not yet. But Paige, well, she'd like them to be."

That was all she would say. To say any more would be a betrayal to her friend.

"I see," he said. "Well, I hope it works out for them."

"So do I. Now go home and get some rest."

"I will," Anthony said, standing up. "We're gonna figure this out, Jackey. I promise. We're gonna get you home."

22

———

Paige figured it was a waste of time, but she decided to visit the Peyton Randolph House the next evening anyway. She feared she had seen the last of Jackey. It was just after dark and the ghost tours were out in force, yet none of them were currently stopped in front of the house. From a distance, the front yard looked empty. As she got closer, she saw someone sitting on one of the benches. It was a woman. Dressed as a slave.

Oh please, oh please, oh please don't be a reenactor.

Paige jogged toward the house. The woman lifted her head, revealing her face.

Jackey.

Breathless from running and from nerves, Paige rushed toward her. For all she knew, Jackey might disappear the moment she saw her approach.

Instead, Jackey smiled.

Maybe she doesn't hate me anymore.

"Jackey, it's so good to see you," Paige said.

"It's good to see you too. Where's the other one?"

"Orlando? I'm not sure."

She hadn't seen him since they'd slept together, but right now Paige was focused on repairing her friendship with Jackey.

"I want to see him, too."

"Okay. Okay! I'm sure that can be arranged." Paige took out her phone and sent Orlando an all-caps message telling him Jackey had shown up and wanted to see him.

Jackey made a face at the Peyton Randolph House. "Can we talk at the gaol instead?"

"Yes. Anything you want," Paige responded, sending Orlando another text asking him to meet them there. Jackey got up and started walking, and Paige fell into step beside her. She wanted to apologize again, but she was afraid to say the wrong thing and set the woman off. It felt like their friendship was hanging by a thread.

"Orlando should be here in a minute. He just got off work."

They walked the rest of the way to the Public Gaol in silence. She hadn't realized how long this stretch of road was before. Paige hoped Orlando would hurry. She was nervous about facing Jackey alone.

Once they reached their usual spot in the grassy area, Jackey sat down and Paige tentatively sat next to her.

Paige saw Orlando's familiar confident stride in the distance. She wished she could control her heartbeat when she saw him, but it sped up involuntarily. It had been two days since she'd slept with him, and all she'd gotten from him was a few scattered texts about Jackey. The silence had been deafening. And painful.

She fought to keep her expression neutral, not wanting Orlando to know how utterly insecure she felt.

"Hey," he said when he reached them. At first, he looked directly into Paige's eyes, not even acknowledging Jackey.

"Hey," she responded, feeling heat creep into her face. She hadn't been so nervous around him since they'd first met.

Turning toward Jackey, he said, "It's wonderful to see you."

Orlando sat down beside Paige and kept sneaking side glances at her, raising her blood pressure every time.

"It's good to see you too. Both of you," Jackey said.

Paige let out an audible sigh of relief, and Jackey smiled at her warmly.

"I want to tell you," Jackey began. "Well, I owe you both an apology."

"No you don't," Paige said emphatically. "Not at all. Jackey, I'm the one who—"

"Please. Just let me finish," she said softly, and Paige nodded. "Right from the beginnin', I was scared to death to trust you because you're white."

Paige bit her lip to keep from interrupting the poor woman again. It was hard to hold her tongue and not cry out *Of course you had trouble trusting us!*

"At first, I hated you because of the color of your skin, and I'm sorry for that. Wasn't right when that happened to me, and it wasn't right that I did it to you."

Paige and Orlando exchanged shocked looks, hardly believing what they were hearing.

"All this time, you two have been tryin' so hard to help me, and I been fightin' you every step of the way. I might disagree with the way you go about it sometimes, but I know everythin' you done was out of concern for me."

Jackey turned to Paige and looked her in the eyes. Her voice breaking, she said, "Oh Paige, I'm so sorry I said you were just like Hannah. You ain't *nothin'* like her."

"Thank you for saying that," Paige whispered, fighting back tears.

"You're a *true* friend," she said. "Not like her at all. And I just want to thank you both for everythin' you done for me."

"Why does that sound like goodbye?" Orlando asked warily. Paige's breath caught in her throat. She'd been thinking the same thing.

Please don't give up now, Jackey.

"Oh, no. Not at all. I'm just tellin' you I'm sorry for making things so hard on you. I promise to do better." She smiled ruefully. "Maybe if I wasn't so damn difficult all the time, I might make more progress."

"You have every right to be difficult," Paige said.

"Maybe so, but it ain't helping matters. Anyway, there's somethin' else important I want to tell you."

Orlando placed a hand on Paige's back as he leaned in to listen. Her face grew hot again. She was acutely aware they'd seen each other naked, and now a little touch from him felt explosive. The small gesture of placing his hand on her back also felt like a "boyfriend" move. At least, she hoped it was.

"Anthony came to see me last night," Jackey said with a smile.

Paige gasped. "He did?"

"Oh, yes. Came 'round the Peyton Randolph House looking for me."

Orlando raised his eyebrow. "And you didn't grab his ankles? Or, you know, any other body part?"

Jackey and Paige both laughed.

"I didn't, though maybe I should have when I had the chance. Was so shocked to see him that I didn't think of it."

"What happened?" Paige asked, eyes wide. "Did you talk to him?"

"I certainly did. For quite some time. Poor soul, I kept

him out later than I normally keep you two. He must be so tired today."

"What did you talk about?" Paige asked. "I mean, you don't have to tell me if you don't want to."

"It's all right. Mostly we talked about stuff you two already know. My life, what happened, things like that."

"Did it help? Did it make you feel better?" Paige was pretty sure she knew the answer, judging by the relaxed manner in which Jackey spoke.

"It did. It truly did. I don't know if it's 'cause he's Black or 'cause of what he does for a living, or maybe just because of the kind of person he is, but it helped a great deal to talk to Anthony."

"Oh, I'm so glad!" Paige said happily.

"You were right to get him involved, Paige."

"I took a gamble and was lucky enough to win, that's all," she said, relief coursing through her.

"For all I knew, this risk could have ended badly. I'm glad it worked out, but I swear to you, I won't ever do anything like that again. If I had it to do over again, I would have worked harder to convince you to talk to him instead of going behind your back."

"What good would that have done? I would have just hollered at you some more until you quit asking," Jackey said soberly.

It was the truth, but Paige saw no reason to rub it in. Instead, she just smiled.

"Anthony's a wonderful man. He was so eager to help you. I'm not surprised he wouldn't give up on you."

"You three are 'bout the best friends a lady could ask for."

Paige turned to Orlando and he smiled, his eyes filled with wonder. Jackey had come a long way already in this fight. If she held true to her word and stopped battling them so much, she just might make it to the other side.

"We made plans to meet again tonight," Jackey said with uncharacteristic shyness.

She does love him. Can't believe I never realized it before when she spoke about him.

"That's great," Paige said. She almost wished Orlando wasn't here so she and Jackey could gossip about Anthony.

"You look so tired, honey," Jackey said to her.

"I am. Didn't sleep much last night."

Worry over her relationships with both Orlando and Jackey had kept her awake.

"Ugh, and I have so much homework to do. I just don't have the energy."

"You go on home then."

"No, Jackey. I didn't mean—"

"I know, but you need your rest. I'm meeting with Anthony later, so I'll be just fine. I promise to give you a full report."

She and Paige exchanged a knowing glance. They would have much to discuss when Orlando wasn't around.

"Okay. Sounds good," Paige said.

Orlando stood and offered his hand to help her to her feet, which reminded her of the way he'd helped her into the front seat of the truck after they'd had sex. That just made her blush again.

"You can walk with us if you want," Orlando said to Jackey.

"That's okay, baby. I just like watchin' you walk away," she responded, turning her attention to his cute butt.

"Ooh, I like that," he said, blowing her a kiss. Then he wiggled his butt for her as he turned to walk away.

The sound of Jackey's laughter warmed Paige's heart.

"You've done wonders with her," Orlando said once they were out of Jackey's earshot. "And you were totally right about Anthony. Spending time with him might be the thing that helps her make it to the other side. Can you imagine that? All this time she's been wandering around and you might be the one to help her."

Though she loved hearing his words of praise and she was immensely relieved to be friends with Jackey again, she wondered if "this Jackey project," as he'd once called it, was all there was to their relationship. Except for that one perfect night under the stars, they hadn't hung out together without discussing Jackey. Even then, the evening had started and ended with talking about her.

Though she didn't regret that night with Orlando, she was getting tired of ruminating over what it all meant. Was he serious about her, or was he just fooling around? She felt so off-balance with him. The way he looked at her sometimes made her believe he had real feelings for her, but he never said anything or made any kind of commitment. Technically, they hadn't even been out on a real date yet. Paige was tempted to ask him what his deal was, but she was sick of making all the moves with him. Despite being in love with him, she refused to make a fool of herself. If it turned out he just wanted to be friends, he wouldn't ever know how she really felt.

They didn't talk much on the way back to her car, and it was a struggle for Paige not to read all sorts of things into the silence.

Just tell me what this is between us already. Are we together now? Are we friends with benefits?

No. She wouldn't settle for that. Paige didn't judge anyone, male or female, for having casual sex. But it wasn't for her.

Orlando turned to face her once they got to the parking lot.

Caressing her hair, he said, "I know you have a lot of schoolwork to do, but try to get some rest. Don't work too hard. I worry about you, you know."

"No, I didn't know."

"Well, I do," he said with a smile. Then he dipped his head and kissed her tenderly.

Paige wrapped her arms around him, suddenly desperate for his touch. She needed him so much more than she wanted to. She felt his body relax at her touch, and he held on to her as they kissed.

Orlando broke off the kiss but seemed reluctant about it.

"Get some rest, Paige."

"I will," she said softly.

Still no commitment, still no answers.

As sweet and affectionate as this kiss was, it hardly made up for the fact that he hadn't contacted her in any way after being intimate with her.

The uneasy feeling in her stomach grew stronger during the drive home. Was this what it was going to be like with Orlando? He expected to be able to kiss her, or worse, sleep with her, when it was convenient and ignore her when he wasn't around?

Paige had never been the type to have a casual fling, and she wasn't about to start now.

But that was the problem. It was far too late for "casual" for her. She was in love with Orlando. If he didn't feel the same way, she was headed for serious heartbreak.

23

———

Jackey arrived early in front of the Peyton Randolph House. She didn't want to miss Anthony or have him think for a moment that she wouldn't show up.

It was late enough that there were no tourists around as she sat on the bench in the yard. She stood to greet him when she saw him approaching.

If she'd had breath, the sight of Anthony would have taken it away. He wore a black leather jacket and tight blue jeans.

"My, my, don't you look handsome in that jacket," she said.

"Thanks," Anthony said with a deliciously sexy grin.

"I wish I could dress up for you."

"No need. You're perfectly lovely just as you are."

The way his eyes lingered on her made her almost believe he was sincere. As she admired his sexy leather jacket, a thought suddenly occurred to her.

"Oh dear. It's cold out tonight, isn't it?"

Anthony shrugged. "A little, I guess."

"I shouldn't keep you here outside so late. Bad enough

for Paige and Orlando, but at least I meet with them earlier in the evenin'. It must be awful chilly now."

"It doesn't bother me, Jackey."

A delicious quiver went through her, and she hoped she would always feel that special thrill when he said her name. As much as she adored being with him, she couldn't abide having him freezing outside.

"I think it's too cold tonight. Let's meet again durin' the day or somethin'."

"No way! I've been counting the hours 'til I got to see you again," he said, flashing that irresistible grin.

"I do love hearin' you say that." Jackey was never shy around men, and she saw no reason to behave differently with Anthony just because she was in love with him. She'd flirt with him the same way she did with Orlando, and Anthony likely wouldn't realize she felt different with him. "But I still think we should—"

"You know," he said thoughtfully. "We could always go inside."

"Inside the Peyton Randolph House?"

"Sure, why not? I'm an employee. I got a key, and I know the alarm code."

"I suppose we could do that," Jackey said, forcing a smile. She knew she could tell Anthony how much she hated that place and he would understand. But it made sense—going inside would keep him warm and safe, and it was really the only option. He probably didn't have access to any of the other buildings. It would do for tonight, anyway.

Though she'd been inside many times over the years, lately to watch Anthony work, she still felt sick to her ghostly stomach when she walked into the house. Jackey grimaced at the strangeness of stepping inside instead of floating through the door, but she managed to straighten her face when Anthony turned around.

With the alarm disarmed, they walked down the hall. Anthony picked up a small electric lantern from a table and flicked it on to light the way. Jackey walked ahead, not realizing where she was going until Anthony spoke up.

"Jackey," he said gently. "You're not a slave anymore."

She glanced toward the slave quarters where she had been headed.

"You can go anywhere you want now."

"You're right."

Naturally, she'd been in all the rooms before, but then it felt different. She typically just followed Anthony around during his tours but never stayed long in any of the rooms.

"Where shall we go?"

"The parlor," was Jackey's immediate response. "The idea of two Black people loungin' in Miss Betty's parlor would be enough to set her spinnin' in her grave."

"Good," Anthony said forcefully. Damn, but that man was especially attractive when he spoke like that.

To get to the parlor, they had to pass through Betty's office.

"See? I can even mess up Betty's perfect paperwork," Anthony said, roughly shuffling the papers on the desk.

Jackey laughed, and Anthony's sexy half-smile turned into a full one. It wasn't really Betty's paperwork, just props for the tour, but it still held great satisfaction for her.

"I been locked up overnight for less than that," she said.

"Betty was known to do that," Anthony said, shaking his head.

"She sure did. Most of the time I did what I was told," Jackey said, feeling shameful at that admission. "But sometimes I just couldn't bear it no more, and I'd mouth off to her. Might not sound so bad, bein' locked up in a dark room all night. But I'm ... What was that word Orlando taught me? It means being afraid of small spaces?"

"Claustrophobic?"

"Yes! That's it. I'm claustrophobic, and that made it so much worse."

"I'm sure it did," he said, pursing his lips tightly in anger.

Jackey followed him into the parlor, noticing Anthony's brief glance of distaste at the paintings of the Randolphs hanging on the wall. She'd never seen him make that face in here before, and she felt flattered that it was likely on her behalf. The parlor had two cushioned, light blue chairs that were either genuine 18th century furniture or they were simply fashioned to look that way. Anthony gestured for Jackey to sit in one chair and then he took the other.

"Are you okay? Are you ... comfortable?" he asked, eying her uncertainly.

"Oh yes, I'm fine. Sitting, standing, it doesn't make a difference since I don't feel anythin' anyhow."

He still looked concerned, and she understood why. She was a nervous wreck, and he'd noticed.

"I know it's silly, but I can't help it. I'm nervous. I'm actually *nervous*, sitting here in this fancy parlor. Like I'm expectin' Betty to walk in here any minute now and catch me."

Jackey scanned the familiar room, with its fireplace, the mirror with the gold-plated trim, and the fancy china vases displayed on the mantle.

"She can't hurt you anymore," Anthony said.

"Sure she can. You don't live inside my head, Anthony. You better believe she can still hurt me. So can Hannah. So can all of them. That's why I'm still here."

"That's fair. But that's why we're doing this. So you can take your power back."

"I never thought of it that way. I like that," she said. "Most of the time it feels like I still have to bow to them. Since I'm suppose to let go of my anger 'bout what they did, it still feels like they're in control."

"But they're not," he said firmly, brown eyes blazing in the most attractive, masculine manner. "You remember that. You're running the show now."

Jackey mulled over his words. Such a thought had never occurred to her. That she had the power to decide things now. To change things.

"I always imagined what it would feel like to be in charge of my own life. So many days I dreamed about runnin' away and leaving it all behind. Just up and runnin' away as fast as my legs could carry me. Lots of brave souls ran from their masters."

"Yes. Many ran and many stayed. Couldn't have been an easy choice either way. My God, I'd have been terrified to run." Anthony shook his head. "I've read about what they did to runaway slaves who were recaptured. Some they lynched by hanging. Others were burned alive. I read about one who had a nail driven into his earlobe and then ripped off."

"Horrifyin'," Jackey said. "But yes, that's what happened. I had an awful lot of time to think since my death. Makes you second-guess everything you ever did, believe me. Sometimes I think I was weak. I should have been braver. Feel like I let them beat me."

"Whether you ran or you didn't run, you did what you had to do to survive," Anthony said firmly. "It's not right to call somebody weak for doing what they're told to do to keep from being murdered, for God's sake. It's like handing over your money when you're being held up at gunpoint."

Jackey's heart was filled with renewed love for Anthony as she listened to him speak with such passion.

"I see what you mean," Jackey said.

"I definitely think John Harris was brave. The way he made the best of his life as Peyton Randolph's manservant."

"Johnny ran, Anthony. You must know that."

"Yes, I know. He ran. But not from Peyton. He stayed with him until his death in 1775. Johnny ran from his new master, Peyton's nephew Edmund. Right?"

Jackey nodded. "That's right. I heard Edmund and his wife were no better than Peyton and Betty. Must have been worse, since John ran from them. And they never caught him, far as I know. Dear Lord, I hope he made it. I hope he was okay."

Anthony's expression softened as he watched Jackey struggle to keep her emotions under control.

"I hope so too," Anthony said. She could see the admiration in his eyes, and it warmed her heart to share how much they both loved Johnny. "I'm just saying there's no shame in how you dealt with being enslaved. No right or wrong answer, and it's nobody's place to judge."

Gathering her courage, Jackey said quietly, "There's something I never told Paige and Orlando. I don't want them to know. I don't like talking 'bout it. But I feel like I can tell you."

"Of course you can, Jackey. You're safe with me. You can tell me anything."

She nodded but fell silent for a bit.

Anthony said gently, "When you're ready. And only then."

He relaxed in the chair, looking around the room and giving her space.

"I did run," Jackey said at last. He leaned in to listen.

"Back in 1781."

"Ah, you must have run away when Eve and her son, George, did. I know several people went with them."

"Yes," she responded. It helped that he was already familiar with some of the history. She found it hard to continue, so he helped her.

"You ran away to follow the British during the war." Anthony paused to see if he had gotten the facts right. When she nodded, he went on. "It was when General Cornwallis occupied Williamsburg. The British promised you all freedom if you joined them."

"Yes."

"Then he surrendered at the Battle of Yorktown."

Jackey closed her eyes. It was her only defense against the onslaught of painful memories. The devastation of having her dreams of freedom dashed. The deep shame at what happened next.

"It's okay, Jackey," Anthony whispered. Lost in her agony, she had nearly forgotten he was there. His voice soothed her.

Opening her eyes, she found Anthony watching her carefully. There was such sorrow in his expression.

"He surrendered, and we were recaptured. After all that time, I finally got up the courage to run, and I failed."

"But Jackey, you didn't—"

"*But that's what it felt like,*" Jackey yelled, startling Anthony. "I was a failure. Betty won. She always won. You can't imagine what something like that does to a person's spirit."

"No, I can't imagine. I know the facts, Jackey. I know what happened. But I cannot begin to know how it felt."

"I died three years later. But really, it felt like I died when I had to come back here," she said, glancing distastefully around the parlor room. "My God. If you thought Betty was bad before. You wouldn't believe how she treated us after that."

"She sold Eve after that. But you had to stay."

"Yes."

"Thank you for trusting me with this," Anthony said. "I hate hearing about your suffering, but I'm honored that you told me about it."

"I hate this house. When I talk with Paige and Orlando, it's usually not here. We meet at the Public Gaol so I don't have to be near this place. You suggested we come inside, and I was about to say no. But now?" She scanned the room in reflection. "Now, I'm glad we're in here. I think ... I think facing this place is somethin' I need to do."

"We can talk anywhere you want. You're in control, Jackey."

Throughout her life and long afterlife, Jackey hadn't ever felt in control. But Anthony had a point. She wasn't under anybody's thumb any more. She was free to roam anywhere in the house she wanted, and she was free to leave at any time. Usually she felt helpless being dead, but between Paige and Orlando helping her determine why she was still here and Anthony aiding her in the next steps, Jackey finally felt some measure of choice. Of control. Of power over her own destiny.

"I am startin' to feel more powerful, Anthony, and I can't tell you how much that helps. Still, it's hard to know what to do next."

Anthony rubbed his head wearily. He looked exhausted,

but she wasn't sure if it was emotionally or physically or both. Either way, he needed rest.

"Maybe if you can find some level of forgiveness for the sins committed against you."

"Forgiveness," Jackey snapped angrily.

"I know," Anthony said. "I'm struggling with the notion just sitting here listening to all you've been through. Saying out loud that you have to forgive them is like poison in my mouth."

Paige and Orlando always listened patiently, lovingly to her, but they rarely got angry along with her. Jackey was starting to see how both audiences were helpful. Right now, though, it felt good to watch the anger blaze in Anthony's eyes.

"So I'm just supposed to forgive and forget?"

"Oh no," Anthony said sharply. "You forgive and *remember*. It's not fair to expect anyone to forget the damage done by someone who wronged you. The pain is real. You can't forget it, but you can work to release the hold it has on you. And I'm hoping that just some measure of forgiveness will be enough. Like perhaps you don't have to forgive Betty and Peyton and Hannah for everything they've done to you. That would be too much. But maybe some small bit of forgiveness. As long as it's sincere, might be enough."

Jackey nodded as she listened. When Rebekah first said that it was Jackey's anger holding her back, she thought she would never be set free from this existence. Naturally, being told such a thing only added fuel to her fiery anger. But Anthony had a way of speaking, of understanding, that made her feel something she hadn't in a very long time.

Hope.

"Anger isn't a bad thing, Jackey. Though things are one hell of a lot better than they used to be in this country, there's still so much injustice. It can be exhausting at times. Blatant racism runs rampant, right in front of your eyes, so you need that anger. You need it to fight."

His eyes flashed with rage at the injustice and with the passion to fight it.

"But you can't let that anger consume you."

Jackey nodded, drinking in his words. How good it felt to be told she wasn't crazy or unreasonable for being so filled with rage. How healing it was to be told that she held some control over her destiny.

"I understand," she said softly.

Gazing at her, he smiled. Seeing the weariness in his eyes, Jackey knew it was time to send him home.

She stood up and announced, "It's late. Time for you to go home and rest."

"I hate to go, but you're probably right. Gettin' tired." Eying her with concern, he asked, "Where do you go all night? What do you do?"

"Don't you worry about me. I can vanish anytime I want. It's almost like sleepin', because I'm still here but I'm not conscious. The same way you go to sleep and the next thing you know, it's morning."

"Good. I hate to think of you wandering around alone all night."

"Sometimes I do, but at least it's my choice."

Anthony nodded, and then picked up the electric lantern to light the way out. After setting the alarm and locking the door behind them, he stood at the front door of the house and faced her.

Sighing wearily, he said, "I wish I could touch you."

"Is that so?" Jackey asked in a teasing tone. "What would you do if you could touch me?"

Anthony's lips formed that sexy, half-curved smile. "If

you don't mind my saying, I would kiss you. That is, if you would let me."

"Oh, I'd let you," she said flirtatiously. Then she grew serious. "Would you? Really?"

"Yes," he said in a deep voice and without hesitation.

24

———

Paige was surprised and delighted to see Jackey on the college campus. She couldn't wait to hear how last night's talk with Anthony went. Judging by the lovely smile on Jackey's face, it had gone well. Her heart fluttered with joy at having her friend back.

"Hey, girl, I wanna talk to you," Jackey said, eyes sparkling. "You're between classes now, right?"

Paige nodded. Jackey had arrived around the same time she had on her last visit, so she must have remembered Paige's schedule. Out of the corner of her eye, she noticed some of her fellow students looking at Jackey curiously. It was so damned unfair that she was forced to appear dressed as a slave for all eternity. Paige hoped the sideways glances didn't bother her too much. If they did, she didn't show it.

Hands on her ghostly hips, she asked, "So, how was the sex?"

"What?"

"You and Orlando. The way you were blushin' every time you looked his way, I figure you had sex. Or at least fooled around some. Which is it?"

"We had sex," Paige admitted, thrilled to finally be able to talk about it.

Jackey's eyes flew open wide. "How was he in bed?"

"In wasn't in bed. It was in the back of his pickup truck."

"You shut your damn mouth!" Jackey said, and they both dissolved into giggles. "Come over here, girl."

Jackey rushed over to a nearby tree where they could have some privacy.

"Tell me everything," she said the moment they were both seated.

"Okay. Well, it happened that night I told you about Anthony and you were upset. Rightfully so, I mean—"

"Yeah, yeah, yeah," Jackey said with a dismissive wave.

"I felt so bad about what happened between you and me, and I guess Orlando wanted to comfort me."

"By having his way with you in the back of his truck," she said wryly.

Paige laughed. "Sort of. But I don't think that was his plan starting out. He always walks me back to my car after we're done talking to you because it's dark and he wants to make sure I get there safely."

Paige noted the fondness on Jackey's face while she talked about Orlando.

"By the time we got back to my car I was still all upset, so he asked if he could take me somewhere. We went to this beautiful open field where you could see so many stars," Paige said, voice dreamy at the memory. "It was so lovely. We sat and talked, and he made me feel a little better."

"And then he made you feel a *lot* better," Jackey said. "If he was any good."

"Oh, he was good all right."

"I knew it! I had a feeling a guy like him would know how to please a woman."

"He sure did. But it wasn't just that. He was so sweet about it, you know? It happened so fast, but he stopped and asked me if I was sure this was what I wanted."

"That's nice," Jackey said with a smile. "He talks a good game, but when you come down to it, he's a gentleman."

"Yes." She had summed Orlando up perfectly. Paige wrapped her arms around herself, feeling warm and happy at the memory of being with the man she loved. "It was so wonderful. After all this time, I loved being able to touch him. And to be touched by him."

All too soon, Paige's warm and fuzzy feelings faded, and familiar doubts crept back in.

"What's the matter?" Jackey asked, eying her suspiciously.

"I'm afraid it meant a lot more to me than it did to him. I don't know what any of it means, really. Are we together now? I'm not sure. He hasn't said anything about making our relationship official. Hasn't said much at all. I don't know what to think, because when he touches me ..." Paige struggled to explain what she was feeling. "When he walked me back to my car last time, he kissed me and held me and it felt real, you know?"

Jackey nodded.

"But then again, the day after we slept together, he didn't call me or anything. So that was kind of weird. In fact, I was the one to contact him to tell him there was still no sign of you around. And that's kind of all we talked about that day."

Jackey nodded again, looking concerned, which put Paige more on edge. She tried to convince herself things were okay with Orlando, but she remained uncertain.

"Thing about Orlando is he doesn't seem to talk about his feelings much either way," Jackey observed. "He won't ever come out and say he likes me, as a friend of course, but when he teases and flirts with me? That's his way of telling me."

"That's true."

"And that day he talked about his mama. That was the most personal he ever got with me. I'll never forget that. Meant a lot because I think that was his way of sayin' he trusted me."

"That's a good point. I guess he's that way with everybody."

"But you wish he was different with you," she said gently.

"Yes. We slept together. Doesn't that mean anything to him?"

"I'm sure it does, Paige. I'm sure it does."

The uneasy feeling in her stomach grew stronger, and she tried to ignore it. She decided it was best to change the subject.

"So tell me how things are going with Anthony."

Jackey's face brightened at the mention of his name.

"Mmm, the things that man does to me with just the sound of his voice," she said.

"Can I ask you something?"

"Sure."

Hesitating, Paige said, "I don't want to mess things up between us again."

"I understand. Like I told you, I promised I wasn't gonna fight you on everythin' anymore. And I want us to be able to talk about anything, me and you."

"Me too."

"So ask already."

"Anthony. He's the one you love, isn't he? You told me you'd been in love only one time, but it was too late."

Paige tensed up, fearing Jackey would get mad despite

her promise not to. Instead, her face turned sad and mournful.

"Yes."

"And that's why you didn't want to meet with him."

"I was afraid."

"I understand."

"I was scared to talk to him. Didn't want him fearin' me, and I hate the way I look."

"You're beautiful, Jackey."

"He said that too," she said, her eyes brimming with a joy Paige had never seen in her before. "Though I still wish you'd have told me first, there's a chance I wouldn't ever have agreed to talk to him unless you forced me. Anyhow, it all worked out for the best."

"Oh, I'm so glad."

"Do you know we actually sat inside the Peyton Randolph House and talked for hours?"

"Oh, no. You hate that place."

"I do, but I think it actually helped me. We sat in the parlor, which was a place I didn't dare sit when I was alive. And it made me feel better. At first, it scared me."

"Why?"

"Because I'd have been beaten and locked in the closet had I dared sit there when I was living."

"Of course," Paige said softly.

"Made me a nervous wreck at first. Was hard to shake the feelin' that Betty might show up any minute. But sittin' and talkin' with Anthony for a while made the feelin' go away. He's so kind, Paige. So kind."

"I know he is," Paige said, picturing Anthony's warm expression and easy smile. How happy he must be to have finally gotten a chance to spend time with Jackey.

"He kept saying that I was in control now. I never

thought of it that way, but I suppose he's right. Now, I get to decide when and how to let go of my anger. And if I decide to forgive."

"Forgiveness." Paige blew out a breath. "That's a tall order."

"You said it. But Anthony makes me feel like it may be possible after all. And Paige," Jackey said, casting her eyes downward shyly, "he said he wished he was able to touch me so he could kiss me."

"He said that?"

"Yes," Jackey said, eyes shining.

"That's amazing!" Paige exclaimed. Her heart nearly exploded with joy for her friend.

Jackey laughed, pleased with her reaction to the news.

"See that? Not only is Anthony not afraid of you, I bet he'd like to have his way with you in the back of a truck."

That comment got a second, louder burst of laughter from Jackey.

"Mmmm, can you imagine?"

"No, but I bet you have."

"You know it, girl. You *know* it! Hey, what time is it?"

Paige picked up her cellphone. "12:40. Why?"

"I saw the schedule, and your boyfriend's doing a courthouse presentation at one o'clock. You wanna go watch?"

She wasn't sure if Orlando was her boyfriend exactly, but she loved the way it sounded. And she rather liked the idea of watching him perform with Jackey by her side. They could both check out Orlando's cute butt while he strutted around. Not to mention that watching him perform was in incredible turn-on.

"Why not? My next class isn't until three. Let's go."

They arrived at the courthouse just in time for Orlando's entrance in front of the building. He was working with another actor, and it was fun to watch them play off one another. Orlando was arguing against British rule, while the other guy was defending it.

At first, only a few tourists were in attendance, but as the show progressed, more people stopped to watch. Despite the autumn temperature, Orlando sweated as he shouted about freedom.

"He is so *sexy* when he performs," Paige muttered.

Jackey chuckled beside her. "He sure is."

A couple of women stood nearby, talking loudly. Paige was tempted to shush them, but she didn't want to be rude.

"Hush now. We're trying to hear!" Jackey said, shooting them an annoyed look.

"Sorry," said one of the women—the blonde one—but she didn't look sorry. She did lower her voice, though.

The women prattled on about their jobs in one of the gift shops over in Merchants Square. Paige did her best to block out their chatter.

But she perked up when she heard Orlando's name.

"Damn, he looks so sexy all sweaty up there," one of them said as she watched the show.

"Yeah, the same way he was all sexy and sweaty when he was on top of you," the other woman said.

They both giggled, earning them some "*shhh*"s from the crowd.

"God, he is so good in bed." That comment came from the brunette.

Orlando slept with both of them.

Paige felt like someone had sucker-punched her in the stomach. Jackey's mouth opened wide.

"Last I heard, he was bangin' some girl who works at the Raleigh Tavern bakery," said one of the women. It didn't matter which one. They were interchangeable. At least to Orlando, they apparently were.

The pain in Paige's chest was so bad, she felt she might pass out.

"I—I better get back to class," she mumbled to Jackey as she turned to go.

"The hell you will," she said, her voice tight. "Follow me."

Paige stumbled as she blindly followed Jackey's lead. The crowd laughed at something Orlando said. It felt like they were laughing at her. Jackey walked to a grassy area behind the Chowning's Tavern building and sat down. Trembling, Paige managed to sit across from her. Her stomach felt queasy, and the ache in her chest grew worse by the second. She was still too stunned to cry, but she knew the tears would come soon enough.

In Jackey's eyes, Paige saw a mixture of anger and sadness.

"Paige, honey, I'm so sorry."

"I am so *stupid*."

"You're not stupid. You're in love."

With tears now forming in her eyes, she nodded. She was grateful that Jackey had figured that out without her having to say the words out loud.

"Same thing."

Jackey chuckled softly. "Feels that way sometimes, don't it?"

"Fell for the wrong guy, that's for damn sure." Paige's voice quivered as she spoke. "I knew it. I knew it!" The shock was beginning to wear off, and now the reality was sinking in. "This whole time, I've been thinking he's too good to be true. That he wouldn't go for a girl like me."

"Because *you're* too good for *him*," Jackey snapped angrily.

"Maybe," she said, not really believing it. Still, she didn't deserve to be used like this. "He's just not the type to settle down with anybody."

"Well, if you're stupid, then so am I. Orlando had me fooled too. The way he looks at you..." Jackey shook her head sadly. "Can't say I'm surprised to hear he gets around. But I thought it was different with you. I truly did."

"I should have known I was just another conquest to him."

They were close enough to the courthouse that they could still hear Orlando's voice when he got especially loud.

"Bastard," Jackey muttered when she heard him yelling.

"I don't even know if I should be mad at him."

"What?" Jackey yelled, making her jump. "Sorry."

Paige laughed as she wiped her eyes, "It's okay. It makes me feel better that you're pissed off too. But the thing is, it's not like he cheated on me. We're not exclusive. We're not anything. He didn't even call me the next day."

Jackey's nostrils flared.

"Okay, maybe he is kind of a bastard. Jackey, I didn't tell you before, but sleeping with him was my idea." Paige closed her eyes as a fresh wave of shame washed over her. Opening her eyes, she winced as she finished her thought. "I initiated it. Just got caught up in the moment. I wonder now if he ever would have touched me if I hadn't asked him to. I love him, and I guess I just wanted to be with him."

"Nothin' wrong with that, Paige. Nothin' at all."

"I admire you so much, Jackey. The way you took charge of your sexuality when you were alive. Sometimes I wish I could be like that."

"But that just ain't your way," she said gently. "And that's okay too."

"Orlando's a grown man. He didn't make a commitment to me. He's allowed to sleep with anybody he wants. I'm not angry, I guess. I'm just ..."

"Hurt."

"Yes," Paige managed to say before she started crying. Covering her face, she wept silently into her hands.

Jackey waited patiently as she tried to get everything out of her system. She was such a good friend.

"I'm sorry, Jackey. This is all so stupid. Me whining about man troubles. This is nothing compared to what you've been through."

"It's not a contest, honey. Oh, I hate seeing you so upset. Can't even hug you," she said wearily.

Wiping her tears, Paige thought about how much that would help. To be able to literally cry on her friend's shoulder. You just didn't realize how important the sense of touch was until you lost it.

Glancing over in the direction of the courthouse, Paige said, "It's funny, you know? Even now, I'm not sorry I did it. As much as this hurts, part of me is still glad I got to be with him. To have him touch me. To be intimate with him. I feel lucky in a way. Not everyone gets that chance."

"I got a feelin' all you gotta do is ask."

Paige burst out laughing, and Jackey did too.

"You're right," she said, wiping her eyes again. "You're so right."

"We don't have to meet up with him anymore, honey."

"No way. I'm not jeopardizing your progress. I don't know what to think of Orlando right now, but I do know he really cares about you, Jackey. As one of the few people who knows about you and your situation, we can't afford to lose him."

Jackey nodded wearily. Paige could see she was conflicted too.

"Want me to trip him for you?" she asked.

Paige laughed. "Maybe so. Maybe so."

25

———

Orlando texted Paige to see what she was up to. She was over at the gaol talking to Jackey.

That's weird. Why didn't she tell me about them meeting?

He chalked it up to needing some girl time. Hopefully they'd had enough time to gossip, because he had texted Paige that he would be right over. His finger hovered over his phone as he debated what else to type. As always, his mind filled with lots of things he wanted to say. How much he missed her when she wasn't around. How beautiful she was. How he couldn't get enough of her pretty flower-like scent, and how he wanted to run his fingers through those luscious brown curls of hers.

Orlando knew how idiotic it would sound if he actually dared to say those things out loud, and yet texting them seemed an even worse idea. Like she would have a written record of him saying silly, lovey-dovey crap like that. He was frustrated with himself, since he always seemed tongue-tied when it came to her. She hadn't given much indication that she wanted to date him seriously, so that made him even more hesitant.

He sensed something was wrong the moment he saw the two women waiting for him. Jackey looked pissed, which wasn't good.

Damn. And she's been doing so well lately.

Worse, there was a deep sadness in Paige's eyes.

"What's the matter?" Orlando asked, alarmed.

She shook her head quickly as if shaking off her thoughts. She did that when she was upset. That, and she bit her lip. Like she was doing now.

"Nothing. I'm fine."

Neither of them were fine, but it was clear to Orlando that they weren't going to tell him what was up. Jackey's expression softened a bit, but he felt that was an act. She was still angry about something. Orlando wracked his brain, trying to figure out what he might have done wrong.

Maybe they're not mad at me. Maybe something else happened to upset them.

"We were just wrapping up here," Paige said abruptly. Then, in a much kinder voice, she said to Jackey, "We'll talk soon, okay?"

"Sounds good," Jackey said with a smile. Her smiled faded when she looked at him.

Without another word, Jackey walked off into the distance, leaving him alone with Paige.

Paige shivered from the cold, wrapping her arms around herself.

"Here, take my jacket," Orlando said, starting to take it off.

"No, I'm fine."

"But you're shiver—"

"I'm fine," she snapped.

Paige began walking in the direction of her car, and Orlando fell into step next to her. He had to walk quickly, as even her pace seemed angry.

It suddenly occurred to him that Jackey and Paige had become pretty close friends. No doubt, Paige had told her they had slept together. But why would she be mad about that? It wasn't like Orlando had coerced her into doing it. It had been Paige's idea from the start. Maybe they had moved too fast for her comfort after all. As much as he hated the idea of Paige hurting, he still didn't understand why she was angry with him. He'd done his best that night to make sure having sex with him was what she wanted.

He and Paige walked back to her car mostly in silence.

When they reached Paige's car, he finally spoke, "Are you ... Are *we* okay?"

"Sure, why wouldn't we be?" she answered in a clipped tone.

"I don't know. I honestly don't know."

The urge to put his arms around her was overwhelming. He longed for the way things were the last time. When he'd kissed her and held her and everything felt right with his world.

Paige unlocked the car, and Orlando placed his hand over hers on the door handle to stop her. She turned to face him, her sadness more pronounced than ever.

"Are you mad at me?"

"No, I'm mad at *me.*"

Her eyes welled up with tears, making his chest ache.

God, just tell me what to do, what to say, to get that look off your face and those tears out of your eyes.

He took a chance and caressed her cheek. "Paige, if I somehow pressured you into doing something you weren't ready to do, I'm so sorry."

As incredible as having sex with Paige was the other night, being able to hold her and kiss her and physically love her like that, it wasn't worth hurting her. As dear as that memory always would be to him, he'd take it back in a heartbeat if it could heal her pain.

"I'm an adult, Orlando. I can make my own decisions. It's just ... Sometimes I make the wrong ones."

With that, she yanked open the car door and disappeared inside.

26

———

The next day, Orlando trudged across the little bridge outside Hay's Cabinetmaker's Shop. Lost in thought, he barely noticed the chilly wind whipping around him. Orlando walked in the back door of the shop. He was relieved to find his friend alone, quietly working on a woodworking project.

"Hey, man," Gregory said, briefly glancing up from his work.

"Hey," Orlando responded. "Could I talk to you for a minute?"

"Sure, what's up?" Gregory asked, carefully inspecting his intricate work.

Orlando glanced at the entrance door down the hall, where tourists could enter at any moment. The buildings had only just opened up for the morning, so hopefully nobody would come in for a while.

"What are you working on?" Orlando asked, stalling.

"An end table," he said, etching a small detail onto a thin piece of wood.

"Looks great."

"Thanks. But you didn't come in here to talk about the end table. What's going on? Everything okay?"

"No," Orlando said with a sigh. "So I think I really screwed up with Paige."

"That's too bad. I can tell how much you like her."

Orlando nodded.

"So what happened?"

"We slept together, for one thing."

"You did?" Gregory asked. He set down his woodworking tool and gave Orlando his full attention. "Last I heard you were just friends."

"It happened fast. Maybe too fast. I don't know. She's acting weird around me lately. Like she's upset. Mad, even. I feel terrible because I get the feeling she might regret having sex with me."

"Well, did you ..." Gregory began hesitantly.

"Did I what?"

"I'm trying to figure out a tactful way to put it."

"Just say it, dude. I need all the help I can get here."

"Did you kind of push her into it? I'm not saying you forced yourself on her. I know you'd never do a thing like that. I just mean, did you kind of coerce her, or..."

"No. Not at all."

"That's good. That's what I thought. Just had to ask."

"But it was Paige's idea to do it. I swear. I was surprised because it wasn't like her. We haven't even been out on a date or anything. It was after she told Jackey that we'd talked to Anthony, and Jackey got mad at Paige. So Paige was all upset about it, and I took her somewhere to try to calm her down."

"Where'd you take her?"

Orlando hesitated. He didn't like talking about his private spot and why he went there, because it was personal.

But Gregory was cool. He wouldn't make fun of him, and he needed to know all the facts.

"It's this big open field where you can see the stars and stuff. I go there when I need to think."

"Nice," Gregory said casually, turning over the end table on his work bench and picking up his tool again.

"Yeah, so I thought it might make her feel better to get away from it all for a while."

"Sounds like a good idea. It's relaxing, looking at the stars," he said as he etched.

"Exactly. We got to talking. And then before I knew it, we were making out. We got carried away, I guess, and we ended up doing it in the back of my truck."

"It was in your truck?" Gregory exclaimed, eyes wide.

"Yeah," Orlando said, laughing self-consciously. "It was crazy, the way it all happened. But she was the one who initiated it. I even stopped to ask her if this was what she wanted. I tried to slow down, you know? Give her a chance to back out if she wasn't ready."

"That's good. Sounds like you did everything right so far. Then what?"

"I don't know. Now, a few days later, she's distant. Won't say much to me, and she won't tell me what's wrong."

A terrible thought suddenly occurred to him. "You don't think it was her first time, do you?" Orlando clasped his hands behind his head. "Oh my God, if I took her virginity in the back of a dirty pickup truck, I will never forgive myself."

"I guess it's possible, but I doubt it. If she's been saving herself all this time, it's pretty unlikely she would suddenly give in like that. You're not *that* irresistible."

He laughed with relief.

"Yeah. You're probably right. So why is she so pissed at me then?"

"What happened afterwards?"

"I kissed her and held her, and then I drove her back to her car at the college a while later."

Gregory nodded. "Okay, that's good. I thought you might have rolled over and fallen asleep or something. Then what happened?"

"I don't know. Saw her around here a few days later." He said with a shrug.

"Did you call her the day after you slept with her?"

"No."

Gregory winced.

"That's bad, huh?"

"Well, kind of. So you still haven't taken her out on a date or anything?"

Orlando slowly shook his head.

"And you haven't told her anything about how you feel about her?"

"Okay, now that I hear it out loud, it sounds pretty bad."

Gregory smiled sympathetically. "Since it was her idea to have sex, she might be kind of embarrassed now. Like she threw herself at you, and she might be feeling like it didn't mean anything to you."

"But it did mean something. It really did! Damn, I screwed this up big time."

"Maybe, but it's not too late to fix it."

Orlando groaned, burying his face in his hands. Gregory chuckled.

"Wow. I've never seen you like this over a woman before. How *do* you feel about her?"

Orlando knew exactly how he felt about her. He was absolutely crazy, in every sense of the word, over her. His heart beat faster every time he caught a glimpse of her. That sensual voice of hers did things to him other women couldn't with their entire bodies. From the depths of his soul, he admired her bravery, her determination, and that sweet, loving heart of hers. How could he possibly find the right words to say all of that?

"You love her, don't you?"

Orlando nodded, grateful he didn't have to say the words out loud.

"Then why can't you at least give her a clue about how you feel?"

He groaned. "Look, I know it sounds dumb, and I know it's no excuse, but I grew up in a house where we didn't say 'I love you' all the time. And by not 'all the time,' I mean never."

"You were just raised by your dad, right?" Gregory ventured carefully.

"Yeah. He's not the touchy-feely type. He taught me how to get laid, but didn't tell me what to do if you fell in love with one of the women you … took to bed."

Gregory nodded. "I know you've been, um, *friendly* with your share of women around here. Have you been with others since you've been with Paige?"

"No. No way. I haven't even thought of another woman since I met Paige."

"Wow. That's saying a lot," Gregory said with a laugh.

"Tell me about it. Love sucks," Orlando said with annoyance.

Gregory laughed again. "No it doesn't. Not if you do it right. I remember some advice you gave me once. It was before you knew Rebekah was dead. I told you I would have to move Heaven and Earth to be with her. Do you remember what you said?"

"No," he said with a scowl. But he did remember.

"You said, 'Then do it.' Dude, the woman I love was dead at the time. Talk about star-crossed lovers. We managed to work *that* one out, so I'm sure you can fix this situation."

"It's so annoying when you make sense," he grumbled. "I'm no good at this kind of thing. I don't know how to tell her or what to say."

"Look, you don't have to get down on one knee and pledge your undying love, but you gotta let her know you care about her."

"What if she doesn't feel the same way?"

"There's no guarantee she does. That's how life is sometimes. But think about it. She wouldn't be this upset if she didn't have feelings for you, right?"

"I guess."

"Do it for her, Orlando," Gregory said. "Sounds like she's really hurting. I can imagine how devastated Rebekah would have been if I'd had sex with her and she didn't know how much I loved her."

"Bet you didn't call her the next day," Orlando muttered.

"Rebekah was from the 18th century and didn't have a cell phone. Besides, she was still in bed with me the next morning," Gregory said and then stuck his tongue out at him.

Orlando laughed. "Fair enough."

"Just go find Paige and tell her you care about her and you're sorry you didn't say anything sooner."

His stomach quivered with nervousness.

"You got this, Orlando. I promise. Paige is worth it, right?"

"Absolutely," he said.

That much he was sure about.

HE DOES LOVE HER. Thank God.

Jackey had planned to hunt Orlando down and give him hell for hurting Paige. Invisible, she followed him down Nicholson Street. An elderly couple out for a stroll deprived her of a chance to fade into view.

Instead of being able to confront Orlando straight away, she had followed him into Hay's Cabinetmaker's Shop where she overheard his entire conversation with Gregory. Everything made sense now. Orlando might be a devil with the ladies sometimes, but he hadn't been playing around with Paige after all.

Her heart went out to Orlando. The man was out of his element. Paige had brought out emotions he probably didn't even know he had. He might be a pro at charming women in general, but he was an amateur when it came to love. It was rather endearing.

But Orlando didn't need to know that Jackey knew the truth. She decided to carry on with her plan, the only difference being she wasn't genuinely mad at Orlando anymore. He still seemed unsure of himself, and he might very well lose courage before he could tell Paige how he felt about her. If he knew how bad Paige was hurting, he might push past his discomfort and do the right thing. Besides, she could fake it. After all, she was an expert on being angry.

Luckily, the side street where the cabinetmaker's shop was located was mostly empty, so she seized her chance.

"There you are," she said, using the harshest voice she could muster. Orlando whirled around, looking lost and alone. It might be harder than she thought to pretend to be angry.

That dear boy loves her so much.

She reminded herself that the sooner she spoke to him, the sooner he could clean up this mess with Paige, and then everyone would be happy.

"I've got something to say to you, young man."

"Uh-oh. Am I in trouble?"

"You could say that." She narrowed her eyes at him. "I'm worried about Paige and I won't have you hurtin' her."

"I would never hurt her!"

"I want to believe that, but I ain't so sure. We both heard a bunch of women talking 'bout how they enjoyed your," she gestured toward his groin, "male company."

Orlando's eyes flew open wide with shock and then understanding.

Yes, that's why she's so upset, you silly fool.

"My God, man, are you trying to have your way with every woman in town? We heard two shop girls talking 'bout bein' with you, and they mentioned some hussy at the Raleigh Tavern. And those are the ones we know about!"

She felt slightly guilty about calling another woman a hussy, but she had gotten carried away in the moment.

"So you were just using Paige for her body. How could you do a thing like that to her?"

"But I wasn't, Jackey. I swear. I wouldn't do that to her."

"She ain't like those other girls, Orlando. Hell, she ain't like you or me. I never had any problem enjoyin' the company of more than one man, but that's just not her way."

"I know that," he said softly. "I really do."

"Do you have any idea how violated she feels?" Jackey knew she was laying it on a little thick, but she figured it was necessary to get this oaf to do the right thing.

Rubbing his forehead wearily, he said, "That's the last thing I wanted. God, I hate that I made her feel that way. She deserves so much better."

"I'll say."

"I promise you, Jackey," Orlando said pleadingly, "I was never just playing around with Paige. I love her."

See, that wasn't so hard to say, now was it?

"Tell her, not me. You better do it before you lose her forever."

"I will." His face held a look of determination.

"You better, because if you cause that girl any more pain, I will haunt your sorry ass 'til hell won't have it again!"

With that, she stormed off, fighting the urge to giggle.

You're not the only good actor 'round here, honey.

27

Paige groaned as she shut off the morning alarm on her phone. It had taken her forever to fall asleep, and now she was groggy. She wasn't ever motivated to attend her morning algebra class, and having her heart crushed into a million pieces by Orlando didn't help matters. It was so unfair to have to suffer through the heartache of a breakup when she hadn't even gotten to date the guy. No romantic dinners, no late-night cuddle sessions on the couch, no movie nights with shared popcorn. Nothing. Just cheap sex in the back of a pickup truck.

Except it hadn't been cheap sex to her. In her mind then, and even now, it felt like she had been making love with her soulmate under the stars.

Paige angrily wiped the tears from her eyes. How on earth could she have been so utterly wrong about what she thought was a real relationship? She'd never thought of herself as naïve, but she'd really been suckered this time.

When she got out of the shower, she was stunned to see a missed call from Orlando. Her heart lurched in her chest. The man rarely called her. He only texted, and it was usually about when and where to meet up with Jackey. He hadn't left a voice mail, and it took all of Paige's restraint not to call him back. She was determined to hold onto at least a shred of her dignity. He had used her for her body and had utterly broken her heart, but she had no intention of ever letting him know how much he had hurt her.

When he called again, she let it ring five times before picking it up.

"Hello?" she answered as casually as she could.

"Hey, it's me," Orlando said. The familiarity of the phrase "it's me" stung. His words made her think of the relationship with him that she desperately wanted but couldn't have. Calling just to check on each other, quick "I love you" texts during the day, sharing a kiss every time they met. Clearly, that wasn't what Orlando wanted. He was not the boyfriend type.

"You got a break after your algebra class, right?"

Paige was surprised he'd paid that much attention to her schedule.

"Yeah? So?" Her response came as harsh. She wasn't sorry.

"Can you meet me at the Governor's Palace after class this morning? There's something I want to talk to you about."

"Sure. I guess. See you then."

Paige hung up before he had a chance to say another word, but she soon regretted that decision. She'd been so eager to hide how much he had wounded her that she hadn't stopped to consider she would have the whole morning to stress out over what he wanted to talk about. If she'd had the conversation to do over again, she would have demanded to know why he wanted to see her.

There was a time when Paige would have given anything

to be alone with Orlando, but not anymore. The more she thought about that night in his truck, the more humiliated she felt. Letting her emotions get the best of her had been an awful mistake. Since she wasn't the type who could separate sex and love, she now knew it would have been better to see how Orlando felt about her before making such a dumb move. She'd given her body and her heart to a man who went through women like tissues, and there was no undoing that.

Paige trudged over to the Governor's Palace Garden after her morning class, her stomach filled with dread. She'd come up with a bunch of potential reasons why Orlando asked to see her and none of them were good. He wanted to stop seeing her and Jackey since they were clearly mad at him. Now that he'd had sex with her and she'd made it abundantly clear it wasn't going to happen again, he'd probably make some excuse about being busy with work so he could continue banging his way through the historical district. That theory was most painful— it made Paige feel like she didn't even know who this man was. She'd fallen in love with a charming, handsome, talented man who had seemed to care about her and Jackey, but was it all an act?

Perhaps the most cringeworthy guess about why he wanted to meet was so he could let her down gently. Tell her in the nicest way he could they were just friends.

Paige groaned out loud just thinking about that.

I get it. I was an idiot to think that night was anything more than mindless sex for you. Do we really have to discuss it?

The Governor's Palace Garden was a beautiful spot, at least. With a large wrought iron gate at the entrance, red brick pathways, and green shrubs and flowers lining the path, it was lovely. Such a romantic place, in fact, that it made Paige wonder how many other women Orlando had brought here so he could charm the pants off them.

And how many women has he brought to the field to "see the stars"?

Paige's nerves began to calm slightly when she entered the garden. Drawing in a breath of crisp November air and being surrounded by the beauty of the garden was therapeutic.

All those good vibes went out the window when she saw Orlando sitting alone on an ornate cement bench toward the back of the garden. Instantly, her muscles hardened and her defenses went up. She was determined to hold her head high, no matter what that man had to say.

As much as she tried to fight it, she let out a soft sigh as she approached him, looking resplendent in his 18th century costume. It was impossible not to care about him. Remembering that look of deep regret in his eyes when he'd apologized if he'd pressured her into sex, she knew he hadn't meant to hurt her. And the truth was, he hadn't pressured her one bit.

"Hey," Orlando said with a smile. "Thanks for coming. Have a seat."

Reluctantly, she sat beside him on the bench, but not too close.

"I hope I'm not keeping you from your schoolwork or anything," he said, wiping his hands on his wool pants.

Was he *nervous*?

He hesitated a moment, which he always did. It made her crazy sometimes. Sick of being an emotional wreck over him, she wanted this over with so she could get on with her life.

"Orlando, what is this all about? Please just say what you've got to say."

"Right," he said, shifting uncomfortably. "Look, Jackey told me you overheard some girls talking about, you know, being with me, and—"

Paige moaned loudly, burying her face in her hands. A fresh wave of humiliation washed over her.

Forcing herself to face him again, she said, "Why would she tell you that? Was this revenge for me talking to Anthony without her permission?"

"Of course not," Orlando said. "She was worried about you, and that's why she came to me. And I'm so glad she did. Now I understand why you're so mad at me. I wanna explain—"

Paige jumped up from the bench. "You don't owe me any explanations. You're allowed to sleep with whomever you want. We're not exclusive. We're not even dating. We're not anything."

"But I wanted to explain—"

"Orlando, this makes me feel even more embarrassed and stupid. Look, it was silly of me to make this out to be more than it was. I get that now. Can we just drop it?"

"Paige, I'm trying to tell you how I feel about you." Orlando swallowed hard and wiped his hands on his trousers again. "Please let me."

Paige eased herself back down on the bench, heart seizing in her chest. She was afraid to let herself have any hope for a future with him.

He paused again, but this time she gave him space. Whatever he was trying to say, it wasn't easy.

"It's true that I've been with my share of women around here. I'm not gonna lie about that. But what happened between you and me that night, it wasn't like that."

"What do you mean?"

"I just mean I've never been serious about any woman. Until you."

"I want to believe that. I really do."

"I should have said something to you much sooner, Paige."

"So what *are* you saying?"

"That I ... I guess I'm saying. I'm sorry, Paige. I'm not very good at expressing my emotions through words."

"You expect me to believe that? Orlando, you're an *actor*."

"Exactly! That's just it. Give me a character and some words on the page, and I can nail it. I can express a whole range of emotions publicly because it's not me. It's the character. When I'm laughing or crying or yelling or expressing undying love on stage, hopefully people will be either thinking, 'Damn, that guy's a good actor,' or they'll be so caught up in the performance, they'll forget what they're seeing isn't real. Acting gives me a chance to express all those pent-up emotions without feeling exposed, you know what I mean?"

"Yes, I think so," Paige said, gazing at him. This was the Orlando she knew. And loved.

"I was in *Romeo and Juliet* once." Leaning in close to her and gazing intensely into her eyes, Orlando quoted, "'Love is a smoke raised with the fume of sighs; being purged, a fire sparkling in lovers' eyes; being vexed, a sea nourished with loving tears. What is it else? A madness most discreet, a choking gall, and preserving sweet.'"

Her breath caught in her throat as Orlando's eyes bored into her soul. His eyes seemed filled with a desperate love for her. Sitting here in this luscious garden with this dashingly handsome man expressing his devotion with such poetic language, Paige felt she could literally swoon.

Then he turned away, laughing softly.

"Ugh!" Paige cried. "That's ... That's *terrifying*."

Orlando whipped his head around. "What is?"

"The way you can just turn it on and off like that. How am I supposed to know what's real?"

"Paige," he said gently. "I would never use my acting skills to manipulate people. I'm not that kind of man. You know me better than that. Believe me, you'll know when I'm speaking from the heart and using my own words, because I'll sound like an idiot."

Orlando looked at her plaintively, his expression similar to the way he gazed at her as Romeo a moment ago.

"I'm sorry, Paige. I've never been in love before, so I don't know how to do it."

"What?" she asked, trying to process what Orlando was telling her.

"I love you, Paige. That's all I'm trying to say."

"Oh," she whispered.

She reached for him and pulled him close. Breathing him in, she relished being able to touch him again. They remained locked in a sweet embrace until Paige released him. Orlando needed to know she loved him too, but something was weighing on her mind.

"Can I ask you something?"

"Of course," he said.

"Have you, you know, *been* with any other women since we slept together?"

Orlando grinned. "Sweetie, I haven't been with anybody else since the day we met. Since the day I first held you in my arms when I carried you away from the Peyton Randolph House, I haven't even been tempted to touch another woman. I was quite taken with you right away."

"That's good to know." Gently stroking his chin, she said, "I love you too, Orlando."

"Thank God," he said with a sigh of relief. "I didn't mean to mess this up so badly. I should've told you how I felt, especially after we had sex. I was too chicken to tell you I loved you, but that doesn't mean I wasn't thinking of you every second of the day."

"Well, it's not all your fault. I didn't speak up either. I was waiting for you to say something."

"And I was waiting for you."

"We suck at this relationship stuff," Paige said with a laugh.

"Pretty much. But we'll get better at it."

"Does this mean we're ... official?"

"I dunno," Orlando said, affecting a voice like an impish child. "You tell me first." Laughing, he said, "Yes. I definitely want to be *o-fficial* and *ex-clusive*. That is, if you'll have me."

"Oh, I'll have you," she said huskily.

Orlando cupped her face and kissed her, and soon they were going at it in a way that was entirely inappropriate for a family tourist spot. Paige was so turned on, she felt like lying down on the bench and giving herself to him right there and then.

Suddenly, Paige broke off the kiss and started laughing. Orlando looked horrified at her reaction.

"No, no. It's not ... She just grabbed my ankle."

Orlando chuckled.

"Does this mean you approve?" Paige asked the seemingly empty air around her.

Since no one else was nearby, Jackey made herself visible.

"Yes, I approve," she said, eying them both. "And I promise, I wasn't listenin' in on your whole conversation. I just showed up for the grand finale."

"I see," Orlando said with a grin.

"By all means, go on back to what you were doin'. But maybe try a real bed this time? I mean, a *truck* of all things, boy. You need to take better care of that girl."

"You told her?" Orlando said to Paige with a smirk of amusement and not a little pride.

"Of course. She's my best friend. I tell her everything. I also told her what an amazing lover you are."

"She sure did," Jackey said. "Good job."

Orlando laughed. "Thanks."

"I best take my leave. Have fun, you two," she said. She walked a short way down the garden before disappearing.

"I do like the idea of taking you to a real bed," Orlando said in a voice so deep and sensual that it triggered an almost primal urge in Paige to get him inside her as soon as possible.

"Me too," she managed to say.

"You got class this afternoon?"

"Yes, but I could skip it."

"No, don't do that. Your schooling is important." He traced her face with his finger. "Tonight."

That single word was loaded with delicious, sensual possibilities.

"Yes," she said hungrily.

"My place is kind of a mess. Wasn't expecting company. Your place okay?"

Paige nodded.

Orlando stood and offered his hand to help her up.

He kissed her again and nuzzled her neck.

"Gonna be torture for me to wait until then," he muttered. "*Torture.*"

28

———

Orlando had been so worried Paige wouldn't feel the same way about him, that he hadn't thought about how it would feel to hear she loved him back.

The answer was, incredible, exhilarating, *amazing.* He couldn't believe Paige loved him. If he hadn't been such a wuss all this time, she could have been his girlfriend long ago.

Orlando shuffled awkwardly down the street. Paige had gotten him so hot, he was overrun with sexual fantasies of her. He imagined having sex with her right there in the Governor's Palace Garden. Now that would have scandalized the founding fathers.

Tonight, he wanted to be sure to show Paige how much he wanted her. He realized how brave she had been to put herself out there with him. She had asked to kiss him, and she had initiated sex. This time, he would take charge.

After changing out of his work clothes in record time at the stroke of five, Orlando sped over to her apartment. She answered the door in the same jeans and long-sleeved blue shirt she'd had on earlier, but somehow, she looked even more beautiful than she had this morning.

Six hours of intense lust will do that to a person.

It was like being served your favorite meal on an empty stomach. And good God, he couldn't wait to taste her.

"Hey," she said with a smile.

"Hey, gorgeous," he said, pulling her in for a kiss.

Paige wrapped her arms around him, and their bodies molded together easily. No more waiting for an opportunity to rub her back when she was upset or hoping to graze her hand when he offered her his coat. Now he could touch her whenever he wanted. It was glorious.

"Come on in before we upset the neighbors," Paige said, though there was no one in the apartment hallway. Pulling him inside her place, she said, "It's not much to look at, but it's all mine."

"It's about the size of my place, only much cleaner," Orlando said.

He scanned the tiny kitchen to his left, then his gaze landed on her living room, which had several glossy photos of film stills on the walls.

"Wow, these are great," he said, heading toward them. "Oh, man. I love this one."

On the wall near the window was a black and white photo of Andy Dufresne and Ellis "Red" Redding from *The Shawshank Redemption.*

"Isn't that beautiful?" Paige said.

"I remember you saying it was one of your favorite movies," Orlando said, and she smiled. He scanned the other photos; images from *Pirates of the Caribbean, Jurassic Park* and *The Avengers.*

"You like Marvel movies?" he asked incredulously.

"Oh yeah. Dr. Strange is my favorite."

This woman gets sexier by the minute.

"Wait 'til you see my place. I've got nerdy action figures all over the joint."

"Nice," she said, stroking his back as she stood next to him.

"You've got good taste," he said, admiring the pictures.

"Thanks. Sometimes I feel bad for liking popular movies so much. As a wannabe director, I feel like I'm supposed to like snooty, under-appreciated flicks nobody's ever heard of. But the truth is, I want to make *movies* not *films,* if you know what I mean."

"I definitely know what you mean. As much as I'd like to tackle complex, meaty acting roles, I also want to be *seen* in stuff. Like I'd love to be in a franchise like this," he said, pointing to the *Pirates of the Caribbean* photo featuring Captain Jack Sparrow.

"I love movies like those. Ones where you just feel good after you watch 'em, you know?"

"I remember you saying you wanted to make movies that make you feel something," he said, turning to look at her.

"Wow."

"Wow, what?"

"It's cool that you remember things like that. Most guys don't listen to what I have to say."

Paige kissed him on the cheek and then led him through the rest of her tiny apartment. He felt giddy just being near her. Being her boyfriend was new and exciting, and he relished every second he got to spend with her.

"Not much else to see. Bathroom there, small closet there," she said, gesturing. Then she opened a door just past the living room. "And in here is the bedr—"

"Finally!" Orlando swept her off her feet, causing her to yelp in surprise and then laugh. He kicked the door shut behind them and gazed at her, lust gathering like a storm inside him. The intensity of his expression stopped her laughter.

Tightening her grip around his neck, Paige pressed her lips to his.

Orlando carried her to the bed and laid her down.

"I don't think I can wait another second to have you," he growled.

"Then don't," she said breathlessly.

He grabbed his wallet, pulled out a condom, and set it on the bed.

Orlando straddled her, kissing her deeply. Already rock hard, it would be an effort to take his time, but he was determined to satisfy her every need, no matter how much restraint it required. He'd get his rocks off eventually, but not before he had her screaming his name.

"Orlando," she said softly between kisses. "Will you do something for me?"

"Baby, I will do *anything* for you."

"Will you quote from *Romeo and Juliet* again?"

Orlando chuckled. "Hmmm, you liked that, did you?"

She nodded, biting her lip in anticipation.

Not only was he willing to do anything to make her happy, he was honored she had been so taken with his acting that she wanted a repeat performance. He pondered for a moment, trying to recall another romantic passage from the play besides the obvious, "But soft! What light from yonder window breaks? It is the east, and Juliet is the sun."

Stroking her hair, he affected his most adoring look. It was barely even acting, because he loved Paige intensely. "'One fairer than my love? The all-seeing sun ne'er saw her match since first the world begun.'"

Romeo was talking about Rosaline and not Juliet in that line, but Paige didn't need to know that.

"'See how she leans her cheek upon her hand. O, that I were a glove upon that hand that I might touch that cheek,'" Orlando continued in the deepest, manliest voice he could muster. That time, Romeo was speaking about Juliet. And Orlando was speaking from the heart about how much he craved Paige's touch. Once again, little acting required.

Paige sighed dreamily, and then she favored him with a look of such hungry lust, he thanked his lucky stars she was a fan of his acting. Orlando kissed her again, feeling the need in her touch. She'd been aroused but now she seemed positively desperate for him.

Still straddling her, Orlando quickly unbuttoned her shirt, planting kisses on her chest as he did so. She arched her back, giving him more access to her small yet perfect breasts. He pulled off her shirt and reached behind her, expertly unclasping and then whipping off her bra.

Paige let out a deep, sensual moan as he suckled her breasts. Good God, that sound drove him crazy.

Half out of their minds with need, they ridded themselves of their clothing in record time. As much as he longed to plunge himself inside her, he forced himself to slow down. He kissed her lips and down her neck.

"Orlando," she moaned. "*Please.*"

Okay, baby. I won't torture you any longer.

In one quick motion, he slid to the end of the bed, spread her legs, and began to stroke her with his tongue.

Paige screamed. And then she screamed his name, which was the biggest turn-on of all for him. His desire for her and his desperate need for sexual release was so strong, he knew he couldn't possibly last long once he got inside her beautiful body. He needed to pleasure her first.

She reached behind her to grab the headboard, and her screams soon turned to whimpers as he continued to stroke her with his tongue.

"Orlando, Orlando, oh God," she cried. "Oh, God, I'm so close ..."

The only disadvantage of going down on Paige was he couldn't watch her face when she came. How he would have loved to watch her lose control like that. Still, her husky cries of erotic bliss were more than enough reward for him.

Arching her back, her body spasmed and she cried out his name again when she reached her peak. He kept tonguing her until she finally fell back against the bed, panting.

Orlando might not have seen her come, but her post-orgasm face was nearly as good. Her green eyes shone with exhaustion and relief, and he knew he had taken good care of his girl.

"Paige," he said, his voice gripped with intensity. "I've never needed any woman as badly as I need you right now."

"Then take me," she said, staring into his eyes.

Hands trembling with need and anticipation, he ripped open the condom package and rolled the condom on.

Orlando fought the urge to ram into her as hard as he could. She had taken his cock once before, but still. She was so much smaller than he was. No amount of pleasure on his part was worth causing her discomfort.

He slid inside her, the sensation of sharp delight so strong, he was afraid he might humiliate himself by pumping twice and blowing his wad. Concentrating hard, he was able to hang on long enough to get the headboard banging against the wall.

"Ohhhh," she cried, that sensual moan of hers pushing

him over the edge into Heavenly bliss. At least he could watch her face when *he* came.

"God, Paige," he grunted through gritted teeth as he came so hard, he thought he might burst through the condom. Collapsing with sexual relief, he lay on top of her for several seconds before forcing himself to roll off so he wouldn't crush her.

Paige moaned again and sensually ran her fingers through her hair. Still breathing heavily, she looked like a woman who had been well and thoroughly bedded. Pride surged in him. And then she made it even better.

"No man has ever satisfied me the way you do," she said huskily, her eyes heavy-lidded.

He dispensed with the condom and rolled back over and kissed her. "You are one sexy woman, Paige Bratton."

"I never think of myself that way. But you make me feel sexy."

"Good," he said with a grin.

After gazing at him lovingly for a moment, Paige asked, "Are you hungry?"

"*So* hungry! But I didn't want to complain and ruin the mood. You feel like going out?"

"Not really," she said lazily.

"Because you can't walk, right?"

She laughed. "Yes, Orlando. That's why."

He rolled onto his back, dramatically putting a hand on his forehead. "I am positively famished! I did expend a lot of energy, you know."

"That you did."

"Watcha want? Pizza? Chinese?"

"Ooh, I haven't had Chinese in a while."

"Done," Orlando said, getting out of bed and reaching for his phone.

Paige put her hands behind her head as she watched him. "Damn, look at that butt."

He rubbed his naked ass for her, making her giggle.

"And you, sprawled out all *nekkid* like that. I could put you on a calendar and hang you up in my garage."

"You don't have a garage. You live in an apartment."

"Baby, I would build a garage just to display your beauty."

Paige laughed again, and then she got up to get dressed.

After the food arrived, they sat in her living room for a while and talked. It felt so good to have Paige all to himself for once. Orlando really did want to help Jackey. It wasn't just a ploy to get with Paige, but now that she was officially his girlfriend, they weren't confined to only meeting up when Jackey was there. Now he could see Paige, or call or text her, whenever he wanted to.

As much as Orlando hated to leave, he had work in the morning. He didn't have his costume with him and all that, so staying over wasn't an option. Fortunately, Paige understood.

Lingering at her door, it was hard to say good night, though.

He kissed her, then he pulled her into a warm embrace.

"Tonight was amazing," he said.

"Yes, it was," she said with a happy sigh.

"Want to meet for lunch tomorrow?"

"That would be great."

"Cool. Paige, I … uh, you know …"

Laughing softly, she said, "I love you too."

He grinned and nodded.

"Yeah. That."

29

———

Paige's heart began to race the moment she caught sight of Orlando, standing tall and proud in his work uniform in the front yard of the Peyton Randolph House.

He's so handsome.

She loved how she could stare and admire him all she wished now. No more having to hide her feelings or protect her heart. It was much too late for that. Her heart was his now, and she couldn't be happier about it.

Orlando's brown eyes lit up when he saw her. Smiling, she walked up to him and wrapped her arms around him.

He kissed her and then murmured in her ear, "Hey, Juliet."

She laughed and hugged him tighter.

With that proper greeting, Orlando released her. Standing up straight, he said, "Okay, tell me the truth, woman. Do you still find me attractive, even in this flamboyant getup and wig?"

"Of course I do," she answered honestly. "This is not an easy look to pull off, but you do. I swear. I never told you this, but before I knew you personally, I used to go out of my way to watch you perform all the time. I would check the schedules just to find out where you would be."

"You did?"

"Oh, yeah. I'd come through the historical district during breaks in my classes and go to the courthouse or wherever you were working. I loved to watch your amazing performances. I always thought you were cute, but seeing you in action was what really attracted me to you."

"That's so cool. I had no idea."

"You were the most handsome man I'd ever seen, not to mention the most talented. Anyone can be born good-looking, but talent like that is what makes you irresistibly attractive. So you can imagine how I felt when you, of all people, came to my rescue that day."

Orlando stared at her for a moment.

"What?"

"Nothing. I just like hearing you talk."

"Why?"

"You've got this husky, sexy voice thing going. I could just sit and listen to you talk all day."

"No way," Paige said, touching her throat self-consciously. "I hate my voice."

"I *love* your voice," Orlando insisted. "It's like, I don't know. Deep and sensual. Womanly."

He pulled her close and nuzzled up near her ear, and said, "I especially love the way you moan during sex."

"Well, you do put the *ohhhh* in Orlando."

"I swear to God, I could take you right here and now," he said lustily.

Someone cleared his throat nearby. Paige and Orlando looked up to see Anthony attempting to keep a respectable distance from them as they pawed at one another like teenagers.

Orlando took an exaggerated step back, straightening out his woolen coat and patting down his wig.

Anthony laughed. "How's it going, you two?"

"Good," Paige said, blushing.

"Glad I ran into you. I was gonna text you later anyway. Jackey wants to see you guys."

"Everything okay?" Paige asked.

"Oh, sure. Everything's fine. She just thought it would be nice to all meet together instead of you two talking to her first and then her coming to see me. Can you guys come back here around nine o'clock tonight?"

"Works for me," Orlando said, and Paige nodded.

"You've done wonders with her, Anthony. She's always saying how much better she feels after talking to you and how you help her see things with a new perspective."

"Believe me, it's no chore on my part. I love talking with her. She's fascinating. Not to mention headstrong and hilarious."

"Don't we know it," Orlando said with a laugh.

"Gotta run for now. Next tour starts soon. See you tonight," Anthony said, heading off with a wave.

"I think he likes her," Orlando said in a sing-song voice.

Paige nodded. "Sure sounds like it to me."

"It's kind of creepy in here at night," Paige said as Anthony guided her and Orlando through the Peyton Randolph House using only an electric lantern for light.

"What, you afraid it's haunted?" he asked.

Paige laughed. "Good point."

"We usually sit in the parlor, but Jackey thought the dining room might be better since there's more chairs."

They entered the room to find Jackey sitting at the head of the table. She smiled when they entered, her eyes lingering on Anthony before she looked at Paige and Orlando.

"Have a seat," Anthony said, gesturing at the dining room table, complete with linen tablecloth and set with fancy china and silverware.

He placed the lantern in the middle of the table, but it was still fairly dark in the room. Before he sat, he flipped a hidden light switch which discreetly illuminated the room with soft, unobtrusive electric lighting.

Orlando pulled out a chair for Paige and got her seated before taking the chair next to her. They sat across from the two large, gold-plated windows that looked out into the dark streets of Williamsburg. With the fireplace, the room was quite elegant.

"Hope our waiter gets here soon. I'm starved," Orlando joked.

Anthony sat at the opposite end of the table facing Jackey.

"It's nice to see the two of you sitting there," Paige said. "It's like you're taking the house back from its previous owners."

"Exactly," Jackey said, eyes flashing. "Those two would have died—again—if they'd known two Black people would be sat at the head of their table. Took me a while to get comfortable being in this place again, but I'm glad he brought me back in here."

"And I can't thank you two enough for introducing this incredible woman to me. Her strength constantly amazes me. I never met anyone so courageous before."

Paige and Jackey locked eyes briefly.

He is totally into you, Jackey. You must see that.

She could hardly wait to giggle and gossip with Jackey over that later.

Orlando glanced over at Jackey, who was seated to his left. Inspecting her closely, he said, "You're lookin' fine this evening, Jackey."

"I look the same as I always do."

"Which is finnnnne," he said, leaning back in his chair to admire her.

Anthony chuckled and said, "I have to agree."

"You ain't so bad there yourself, stud," she said. She was looking at Anthony when she said it, but she quickly turned back to Orlando. "Them tight jeans show off that sweet backside of yours."

"Madam, you make me blush!" Orlando exclaimed, fanning his face.

Jackey chuckled, but then grew serious.

"Strange, you know? When we get to teasin' each other, and I say things like that to you. There's still this part of me that's afraid you gonna reach over and slap me 'cross the face."

Her powerful words and the heavy fear with which she said them stunned everyone into silence.

"Even though it's not even physically possible. You can't touch me. And yet, sometimes it's still hard to shake that old notion."

"Jackey," Orlando said, looking stricken. "I would *never*—"

"Oh, honey," she said softly. "I know you wouldn't. But back in my day, what do you think would happen if a woman dressed like me and with brown skin ever said something so impertinent to a man like you? Especially dressed like you do durin' the day."

Orlando nodded. "I see what you mean."

"But I suppose it's good for me to be 'round you like that."

"I hope so. I hope it helps," he said. Then, leaning over the table to face her, he said somberly, "Jackey, I swear to you. If you were alive—if it were physically possible—I would *totally* let you grab my ass."

Orlando held that solemn look for a beat while the rest of them burst into laughter. Then he sat back in his seat and grinned, shooting Jackey a wink.

"Starting to regret asking you to join us, dear sir," Anthony quipped.

"Oh, am I horning in on your girl, here?"

"Yeah, ya are," he said, looking across the table at Jackey. It warmed Paige's heart to see the way he gazed at her.

He clearly sees her as a woman and not a ghost. How wonderful.

"Orlando honey, if I was alive, your ass wouldn't be the first one I would grab," she said, staring seductively at Anthony.

"Good," Anthony replied. "I feel much better now."

"Anthony has been an incredible help to me. It's been healing, spendin' time together."

He nodded, still gazing at her from across the table.

"We've been talking a lot about forgiveness. What it means. How to give it. *Why* you give it," she said.

"I really believe forgiveness is both a gift you give someone else, and a gift you give yourself," Anthony said. "When you forgive someone, it helps you let go of some of that pain the person has caused."

"You can forgive," Jackey said. "But not forgive and forget."

"No. You never forget. But you can move on."

"That makes a lot of sense," Paige observed. "You don't forget how you've been wronged, but you can release some of your own anger by forgiving them. Like they say, holding on to anger is like poisoning yourself and waiting for the other person to die."

"Interestin'," Jackey said.

"Trouble is," Anthony said, "I think one of the biggest hurdles is how to go about forgiving someone else who's been dead for hundreds of years. There's no slave owners around anymore, thank God, so it's not like you can talk to any of them."

The room went silent.

"Did I say something wrong?"

"No, no. Not at all," Paige said. Turning to Jackey, she said "He doesn't know about ...?"

She shook her head. "It's not a secret. Just didn't come up. 'Til now. Anthony, I did get the chance to speak with a slave owner. Rebekah Jennings. Her family owned the Jennings Tavern. I met with her. Paige and Orlando set it up."

"Oh wow! I can't believe it never crossed my mind that there could be ghost slave owners around here."

"You ever hear of the Weeping Woman?" Orlando asked.

"Yeah, I have. One of the ghost legends of Williamsburg."

"That's her. That's Rebekah," he said. Paige noted the gentleness in Orlando's voice when he spoke of his friend. "She's not crazy about being called the Weeping Woman, but I figure that's the best way to explain who she is."

"She's actually a very sweet girl," Jackey said.

"Really," Anthony said, leaning forward.

"It was helpful to speak with her. To hear her side."

"Her side?" Anthony asked, bitterness creeping into his voice.

Orlando tensed beside Paige, and she knew how much he wanted to defend his friend. Yet, he kept silent. After all, there was no defense for slavery. Ever.

"She was wrong to own slaves," Jackey said. "But like so many people back then, she was taught to believe there was nothin' wrong with it. Her parents raised her to believe it was the natural order of things. You know your history, Anthony, and how common that was."

Gritting his teeth, he nodded.

"Most importantly, she knows the truth now. She's remorseful. Very much so. I like to think havin' her talk to me helped her heal too, by makin' amends."

"I guess so," Anthony said, his grim expression easing. "Maybe that will help her cross over."

Jackey glanced over at Paige and Orlando.

"You know we wouldn't lie to you, right?" Jackey asked Anthony.

"Yes," he said, looking confused.

"Rebekah died long ago, just like I did. And, like me, she had a lot of emotional things to work through. But she finally did. Anthony, when her time came to cross over, well, she didn't. She came back instead."

"Came back?" he asked, brow furrowed.

"To life. She came back to life."

Anthony stared at Jackey for a moment and then turned toward Paige and Orlando.

"It's true, Anthony. I knew Rebekah when she was dead. Passed my hand right through her, just like with Jackey. And now I can go give her a hug anytime I want," Orlando said with a smile.

"You mean … you mean … You can just come back?" he asked incredulously.

"Rebekah did. That's all we know," Jackey said. "It was because, well, somethin' happened in her life. I'm not sure it's my place to say it."

"I think it's okay," Orlando said. "It will help explain better. Anthony, Rebekah took her own life."

Anthony nodded sadly. "I see."

"And when she worked through the things that were keeping her here," Orlando continued, "her little brother came to see her from the other side and told her she needed to live again, to do the things she didn't do the first time around. Normally, she would be born as a baby and start over that way."

"But she was in love," Paige said. "Rebekah fell in love with a man who works here in Colonial Williamsburg. Gregory, over at Hay's Cabinetmaker's Shop. Because of him, Rebekah was allowed to come back now instead."

"Wow," Anthony said, looking thoughtful as he processed everything he had just been told.

"Maybe we should meet with her again," Jackey said. Glancing down at Anthony, she said, "All of us."

"Sure. We can do that," Paige said.

"That would be incredible!" Anthony exclaimed.

"And Paige, you be sure and tell Rebekah it won't be like last time," Jackey said. Addressing Anthony, she added, "That girl really bared her soul last time. We talked it all out, and she's apologized. There's no need for her to do it again."

"I understand," he said, though he looked a bit unsure.

"As slave owners go, it sounds like her family weren't as

bad as some of the others. You know what I mean by that," she said to him.

"I do."

"She wasn't allowed to treat the enslaved men and women the way Hannah was allowed, and probably encouraged, to treat me. Most important, she knows better now. She truly does."

Anthony nodded and turned to Paige and Orlando. "If Jackey wants to meet up with her, count me in."

"We could all meet at the cabinetmaker's shop," Orlando said. "Maybe we could get Gregory to play the harpsichord for us."

"That would be lovely," Jackey said.

"She came back to *life*?" Anthony marveled.

"She sure did," Orlando said.

"Incredible. Simply incredible," he said, looking at Jackey.

Paige saw a glimmer of hope in his eyes.

30

———

Paige rubbed Orlando's back, doing her best to ease his tension as they headed toward the cabinetmaker's shop. Still, worry lines creased his forehead. Orlando had discussed his fears privately with Paige about Anthony and Jackey's meeting with Rebekah. According to Orlando, Rebekah was quite nervous about the idea. Though they'd assured her that Anthony was a perfectly nice guy, Rebekah knew he and Jackey were good friends. She worried that the two of them might gang up on her when they all met together. And yet, like last time, Rebekah was willing to dive right into the fray if it meant she could potentially help Jackey.

But a lot could go wrong in a meeting between a former slave owner, a formerly enslaved woman, and a current slave reenactor. Orlando was close with both Rebekah and Jackey, and he'd confessed he was concerned about getting caught in the middle.

With a nervous glance at Paige, Orlando opened the back door of the shop. Rebekah had been standing near the door and was badly startled. She gasped and pressed her hand against her chest, her gray eyes darting anxiously from Anthony to Jackey as they walked in the door.

Anthony's face radiated compassion when he saw Rebekah, who was physically trembling. Gregory jumped up from his seat at the harpsichord and stood next to her, placing his hand on her back for support.

Everyone held their breath as Jackey stepped forward.

"Rebekah, it's very nice to see you again."

"Nice to see you again too," Rebekah said in a small voice.

"I would like you to meet Anthony Alick." Jackey gestured to him.

Anthony eyed Rebekah curiously as he shook her hand. After all, it wasn't every day you met someone who had risen from the dead.

"How are things with you?" Jackey asked Rebekah warmly and with confidence.

It occurred to Paige that she was taking charge of her situation the way Anthony had taught her. Clearly, Jackey had chosen to forgive Rebekah for her past transgressions, and it did seem to empower her.

"Good. Things are good. H—h—how are you doing these days?" Rebekah asked.

"I'm doing well. Going slow, but I feel like I'm makin' some progress. One day at a time."

"I'm very glad to hear it."

Jackey turned to Anthony and the other two men. "You boys go on. We women wanna talk." Gesturing to Rebekah and Paige, she said, "Here, come with me."

With that, she charged down the hallway toward the main entrance of the building. Paige followed, unsure what she had in mind, her stomach fluttering with nervousness. She heard Gregory draw in a deep breath as he watched

Rebekah go with them. Like the last time, Paige knew it must be tough for him not to rush to Rebekah's rescue.

Jackey led them to the front door and turned to face them. There was no danger of tourists coming in since it was late in the evening and the cabinetmaker's shop had shut down hours ago.

"So," Jackey began, addressing Rebekah.

Paige's heart caught in her throat. She couldn't imagine how distressed Rebekah must be.

"You got yourself a fine man, that Gregory," Jackey said without a trace of animosity. "Tell me, do you plan on marryin' him?"

Rebekah's smile was tentative, as if she wasn't sure if this was some kind of trick. Paige, however, wasn't worried any longer. Jackey wasn't one to play games, and now Paige understood she was simply trying to put them at ease. Jackey's compassion and concern for Rebekah's discomfort was truly a testament to her strength.

"Oh, yes. We hope to marry someday. Trouble is, I don't legally exist yet. We're trying to get all the paperwork sorted out so we can somehow make me official."

"I see," Jackey said thoughtfully. "Do you live with him?"

"Yes. Yes, I do."

"Tell me this," Jackey said, a sparkle of mischief in her eye. "How is he in bed?"

"Jackey!" Rebekah said, blushing deeply.

Paige laughed. It was such a *Jackey* question. Jackey laughed, too, but not unkindly.

"Sorry about her. She can be a tad blunt sometimes."

"I sure can," Jackey said with a wicked grin. "So? Tell me. What kind of lover is Gregory?"

"It's best just to answer her, Rebekah," Paige said with a smile. "She's not gonna let it go."

"I'm not used to talking about such things," Rebekah said, fanning herself a bit. "But then again, I haven't had any female friends around here to talk with."

"Now you do," Jackey said, as if her words didn't carry tremendous significance. "Now spill it."

With a shy glance down the hall in Gregory's direction, she said, "Wonderful. Just wonderful. Not that I have anything to compare him to. He was my first. My only." Rebekah's dreamy voice clearly showed she had no regrets about being with only one man.

"If he's good enough, you don't need anything to compare him to," Jackey said. "If he satisfies you good, that's all you need to know."

"Exactly," Rebekah said, blushing and giggling adorably. Then she turned to Paige. "What I want to know is, how did you ever manage to tame *that* one?" She looked down the hall where Orlando was making Gregory laugh.

"Believe me when I tell you, I have no idea," Paige said, shaking her head.

"Gregory and I both said we've never seen him so crazy about a woman before. We knew he had feelings for you even before he told us. We could tell because he never stopped talking about you."

"Really?"

"Oh yes. Talked about you all the time. How smart you were, how beautiful, and how sexy he thought your voice was. And then there's the way he lit up every time he said your name."

Paige was rendered speechless for a moment. To think, all the lovely things Orlando had said to her recently, he had said to others as well. For a man who had trouble expressing his emotions, that was a huge deal.

"Wow," she said softly. "Thank you for telling me that."

"And Jackey," Rebekah ventured carefully. "If you don't mind my saying so, Anthony seems quite taken with you."

"See!" Paige exclaimed. "Orlando and I both told her that, and she didn't believe us. Anthony is really into you, Jackey. It's so obvious."

"You all are crazy," Jackey said with a wave of her hand.

"Jackey," Rebekah said firmly. "He's been watching you the entire time we've been talking."

All three women glanced quickly yet discreetly toward the men. It was true.

"He has," Paige said. "He's not listening to a word Orlando and Gregory have been saying. He's too busy staring at you."

"I just," Jackey began. She took a moment to gather her thoughts. Her thoughts and perhaps, her courage. "I've been in love with him for so long. I guess I just never dreamed ..."

"I know," Rebekah said. "Believe me, *I know.* You feel like he won't feel the same way about you. You think, because you're dead, he can't see you as a woman."

Jackey nodded slowly.

"But he does, Jackey. The look in his eyes. He sees you as a woman. One he's attracted to. A woman he cares deeply for," Rebekah told her.

"Rebekah," Paige said, "you should have seen the look on Anthony's face when we told him you came back to life. You know what I saw, Jackey?"

She shook her head.

"Hope."

Jackey glanced down the hallway. Anthony's gaze still hadn't wavered.

She seemed lost in thought for a moment. "Well, I suppose we should get back to our men. Come along, ladies." Jackey led the charge back down the hallway.

Paige noted the look on each man's face as the women approached. Anthony gazed at Jackey with a combination of admiration and downright lust. Gregory looked relieved to see Rebekah was happy. Orlando smiled lovingly at Paige.

"I do believe I was promised some harpsichord music this evenin'," Jackey said.

"Coming right up." Gregory headed toward the wooden bench. "You know, Rebekah has a beautiful singing voice. Maybe—"

"Bring her on, then!" Jackey said with a smile.

As Paige scanned the room of people she adored, her heart was filled with joy. Thanks to Jackey, the atmosphere was one of friendship, laughter, and love. She had never admired Jackey's strength more than she did in this moment.

Of course, her incredible demonstration of love and forgiveness could mean that her days on Earth were numbered.

Gregory and Rebekah performed several songs. Though she'd been aware of Gregory's musical talent, Paige had no idea Rebekah could sing so beautifully. At the end of each song, Jackey whooped her approval while the living people in the room clapped their hands.

"What about you, Jackey?" Anthony asked. "How 'bout you favor us with a song?"

"Oh, I can't sing like that," she said, gesturing at Rebekah.

"I know music was very important to the enslaved men and women back in those days," he said, sounding like a tour guide.

"Thanks, Professor," she said dryly, making everyone laugh.

Chuckling, he said, "You know what I mean. Come on. Do one of the songs you know."

Mulling it over a moment, Jackey said, "You know, one of the most frustratin' things 'bout being dead is you can't touch anything. I mean, besides grabbin' an ankle now and again. Since I can't touch nothin', I can't keep a beat. We didn't use musical instruments. At least not professionally made ones. We used whatever we had handy. Buckets, barrels, you know."

Anthony jumped up, quickly locating a small wooden barrel.

"Like this?"

"Yeah, that'll work," Jackey said, eyes flashing with excitement.

"Okay, show me the beat," he said. Jackey obliged, gesturing with her hand. In no time, Anthony had the rhythm down.

"This one was always my favorite," she said. "It's Jamaican. Not all of us were African. Slave owners were what you'd call nowadays 'equal opportunity' folks. Kidnapped people from Africa, Jamaica, the Caribbean, you name it."

Rebekah swallowed and nodded, and Jackey smiled at her.

Anthony continued the beat, and Jackey began to sing. The words were in another language, but the tune was quite catchy. Fascinating how the words flowed, and how she clearly recalled the song well, after all this time. The lyrics went so fast that the song resembled rap music in a way. The only phrase Paige could catch clearly was "Ya Ya Dempo," which was often repeated.

Anthony soon caught onto that as well and started chiming in on that part. It was thrilling to see and hear.

"Everybody now!" Jackey hollered, and they all joined in singing, "Ya Ya Dempo."

At the song's end, everyone cheered and applauded wildly. The moment felt transformative. Beautiful. Healing.

"All right, now," Jackey said once everyone had quieted down. "Gregory, Rebekah, and me did our part performin'. Now I want to hear you sing."

She looked directly at Anthony.

"Hey, what about me?" Orlando said, acting wounded. Everyone turned to look at him. "Forget it. You don't wanna hear me sing. *Believe* me."

"I do believe you," Jackey said. "Besides, we watch you perform all the time, ya damn showoff."

"Guilty!" he said with a grin.

"How 'bout it, sir?" Jackey said to Anthony.

"Sure, why not? I'll do one of my favorites," he said.

The room grew quiet as they waited for him to begin. He walked toward Jackey, stood before her, and launched directly into a stunning *a capella* version of Stevie Wonder's *Isn't She Lovely?*

They all listened, spellbound as he serenaded Jackey with a famous song that she most likely had never heard before. His performance was lively, energetic, and passionate. And wow, that man could *sing.*

No one was more stunned than Jackey, whose shocked expression soon faded into a warm, loving smile as he sang to her. When the final note was sung, everyone burst into applause.

"I told you," Paige murmured to Jackey in a sing-song voice while Rebekah nodded.

Still think Anthony's not into you?

After they finished heaping praise onto Anthony for his

stellar performance, Jackey said, "It's getting' so late. All you livin' folks need to head on home now and rest."

Making eye contact with each smiling face in the room, she said, "I want you all to know ... I haven't known such wonderful friends, and *family*, since I was alive. I promise you, if I ever get to where I'm supposed to go, I'll be watching over you." Her voiced cracked slightly. "*Always.*"

31

———

"Break it up, you two. I don't see no mistletoe 'round here," Jackey said.

Orlando and Paige looked up from where they'd been kissing under a tree on the Palace Green. Jackey grinned at them. They'd been together for more than a month, and it still warmed her heart to see them so much in love.

"Must be warm weather since you're out and about."

"It is," Paige said. "Almost sixty degrees."

Tourists were milling about all over the place, taking advantage of such a warm day in late December. Temperatures were usually closer to forties or fifties this time of year. It probably felt like springtime. Jackey could barely remember how it felt to be cold or hot. For so long she'd felt nothing.

"Come sit with us," Orlando said. "Or are you too good for us now that you have Anthony?"

Guilt coursed through her. He was only joking, but he wasn't wrong.

Jackey sat down across from the couple.

"I am sorry I haven't seen you much lately. Feel like I've abandoned you sometimes."

"Oh no, don't you worry about us," Orlando sniffed. "You just found somebody sexier and more fun to be with, that's all."

"Well, can you blame me?" she teased.

"I cannot. If I had a hot guy like Anthony, I'd do the same," he said, fanning himself with his hand. "He is fine, that man."

Paige and Jackey laughed.

"Anthony's gone home to see his family for a few days."

"Oh, I guess he's spending Christmas in Pennsylvania?" Paige asked.

"Yes. Gone to see his parents and his brother."

"So that's why you came to see us. Your boy toy's out of town."

"I suppose that's kind of true. I'm sorry," she said to Paige.

"You don't have to be sorry. He's just kidding."

Orlando folded his arms and huffed like a child.

Jackey laughed. "Maybe so, but I have been scarce lately. You're my best friend, Paige. I owe you better than that."

Orlando cleared his throat.

"And I missed that cute ass of yours too, Orlando."

"*Thank* you," he said, uncrossing his arms and winking at her.

"It's okay, Jackey," Paige said with a reassuring smile. "But I have missed you. Problem is, it's not like I can call or text you. Sometimes you're hard to track down around here."

"I know," Jackey said. "You can always ask Anthony to text you and help us coordinate a time to meet. That, or I can come see you on campus. I miss our talks."

"Me too. We'll be away for a short while too. Orlando and his father are coming to Maryland to meet my family."

"Is that right?" Jackey exclaimed. "That's a big deal, meetin' the family. You nervous?"

Simultaneously, Orlando answered, "No," and Paige said, "Yes."

"You're nervous?" Orlando asked. "Why, you don't think your family will like me?"

"Oh, they'll love you. I just hope your dad likes me."

"Of course he will," he said, giving her a peck on the cheek.

"I'm worried you'll be lonely with everyone gone," Paige said, looking concerned.

"Oh, don't you worry 'bout me. I can just vanish for a week. It'll seem like no time at all." Jackey stood up. "Go back to what you were doin'. I know you probably don't have much time on your lunch break. Maybe I'll come back to your campus later today since it's so nice out."

"Please do," Paige said, her green eyes lighting up.

Jackey smiled, offering a wave before she headed off.

In her wildest dreams, Jackey couldn't have imagined she could love a white woman as much as she did Paige. She was a true and loyal friend.

I'm really goin' to miss her.

Turning back, she saw Orlando put his arm around Paige and pull her close.

I'll miss them both.

Jackey vanished for the entire time her friends were gone for the holiday. Though Colonial Williamsburg remained open, even on Christmas day, she saw no reason to hang around. She'd seen it all before, and she took little pleasure in watching tourists celebrate the holidays with their loved ones while she remained alone.

It was hard to imagine enjoying Christmas the way normal people did. When she was alive, she had celebrated the holiday with her friends and family, but it had been a far cry from what the white folks enjoyed: a huge feast, fancy decorations, and warmth and comfort by the fire.

Christmas was just another thing she felt cheated out of in her existence as both a living woman and as a dead one.

No sense in dwelling on such unpleasantness. The holiday was over now, and Anthony had returned to Williamsburg.

They met outside the Peyton Randolph House late in the evening, as per their usual.

"Hello there, gorgeous," Anthony said when he saw her. He greeted her the same way every night, and she never tired of it.

"Hello, handsome."

"We're going somewhere different tonight."

"Is that right?" she asked curiously.

"You know what tonight is, don't you?"

"Of course I don't. You know I don't even know the day of the week most of the time."

"It's New Year's Eve."

Jackey laughed. "Oh, I see. I don't even know what *year* it is anymore."

Anthony chuckled. Oh, how she loved that deep, sexy sound.

"Come along with me," he said.

Jackey followed him as they headed down North England Street.

"I had to call in some major favors on this one," Anthony said.

She was tempted to ask where they were going, but it seemed he wanted it to be a surprise, so she held her tongue.

Anthony led her to the Governor's Palace, then up the steps to the back of the building. This back entrance, she knew, led straight into the palace ballroom.

"What in the world are you up to, Anthony Alick?"

Anthony unlocked the door and they went inside. No security alarm sounded, so it must have already been turned off.

Shutting the door behind them, he said, "I wanted to celebrate New Year's Eve in style with you."

Anthony turned on the electric lights that were hidden inside the chandelier that also held wax candles just for show.

Her gaze swept across the ballroom with its turquoise walls, ornately carved doorway painted white, and bright-colored carpet with a fancy circular design. She'd been in the room countless times, but it felt as if she was seeing it for the first time.

In that moment, Jackey didn't feel like an enslaved woman forced to dress in rags for all eternity. She felt like she was a guest invited to a fancy ball on New Year's Eve.

Christmas wasn't the only holiday she'd been cheated out of in the past.

Anthony pulled out his cell phone and cued up some romantic music.

"Would you care to dance?" He walked to the middle of the dance floor and held out his hand.

She couldn't even touch him. How could she dance with him? He stood there waiting. How could she *not*?

Jackey stepped forward to join him. The way he gazed at her, that look of desire in his eyes, made her forget the way she was dressed. Somehow, he made her feel glamorous.

Holding their hands and their bodies close together, they swayed to the lovely music.

"You may have figured this out already," Anthony said. "But I'm in love with you."

Jackey was too overwhelmed to speak.

Yes, she had figured that out. Or at least she'd been desperately hoping with all her heart that she wasn't wrong. Paige and Rebekah had insisted that Anthony was falling for her. He had shown his devotion for some time now. He had told her he loved her with the tender way he spoke to her. The way he watched her admiringly each time she approached. Their endless conversations about love and life and loss that went deep into the night.

"Unless I'm crazy, I think you might love me too."

"You are crazy," she said. "And I do love you."

They danced together, lost in the beauty of the moment. Jackey ached to be able to touch him, yet she felt the depth of a love that transcended physical sensation. At its core, true love was utter devotion to a soul and not a body.

"You're not makin' it easy to want to cross over, you know," she said softly.

"I don't want to make it any harder for you, but the future is uncertain to say the least. I just had to make sure you knew how I felt while there was still time."

"Do you think it's possible I could stay? Like Rebekah did?"

"I don't know. I just don't know," Anthony said, fear and sorrow in his eyes.

Jackey pulled away. "Even if I could. I just don't know ... I don't know if I could—"

"I would never ask you to stay behind for me," he said firmly. "Even if you had a choice." Anthony swallowed hard. "You're doing well, Jackey. I can see the change in you. All the hard work you've put in to overcome the pain of your past. It's working. You're almost ready to go, aren't you? I can feel it."

Jackey nodded sadly.

"That's why I wanted to bring you here tonight. So no matter what happens—"

"I know. I know," she said as she started to cry.

"It'll never be goodbye, Jackey. Only goodbye for now."

She nodded, weeping tearlessly.

"So tonight, my love, we dance."

Jackey smiled, moving closer as another sweet song began to play.

32

———————

"Baby, your phone's going off."

Paige awoke to find Orlando gently shaking her and her phone buzzing on her nightstand. She picked up her phone to see it was 10:30pm. She'd been going to bed earlier these days, since she was taking two accelerated winter classes that were wearing her out.

"It's Anthony," she said, checking the caller ID. He'd never called her at this hour before.

Orlando sat up in Paige's bed, looking concerned.

"Hello?"

"Sorry to call so late. I need you to get to the Peyton Randolph House right away."

"What's the matter? Are you okay?"

"Yes. It's just ... I don't think Jackey has much time, and she really wants to see you guys."

"Okay. We'll be right there."

Heart pounding, Paige told Orlando what was going on. Tears formed in her eyes as she and Orlando jumped up and got dressed as fast as they could.

It's going to be so hard to say goodbye.

They rushed to the historical district to find Anthony waiting outside the Peyton Randolph House in the frigid January air.

"Is she still here?" Paige asked in a panicked voice.

"Yes. She's here."

Oh, thank God.

Anthony led them into the building, to the parlor where Jackey was waiting for them.

"Are you all right?" Paige asked, rushing toward her.

"Yes. I'm okay."

Jackey didn't look okay. Paige had expected her to look calm and serene, like an angel on her way to Heaven.

"Do you think you're ready?"

"I think it's gonna happen soon whether I'm ready or not."

"Are you afraid?" Orlando asked.

"No."

Perhaps not, but she wasn't happy. That much was clear.

"What's wrong?" Paige asked.

"Come and sit with me," Jackey said. She sat on the floor, and Paige, Orlando, and Anthony did the same, forgoing chairs so they could be near her.

"I'm fairly certain it's all up to me now," she said. "As if I can go at any time. I feel I've done what I needed to do. Sharin' my story and my thoughts and emotions with all of you has helped me work through the trauma I suffered."

Turning her attention to Paige, she said, "Meetin' with you and Rebekah helped me see what Hannah could have been if she hadn't been poisoned by such hate. When we were children, she was a good person. Lovin' and generous. But she was told to hate people like me. She was brought up to believe she was superior, and that was the way of it. Don't hear me wrong, though. She's responsible for her own actions. Being taught to do wrong isn't an excuse. But it did contribute to what she did. Lots of people were taught it was all right to own slaves, so many did own them. Some beat them. Some were kind. Some ended up bein' abolitionists. Anthony, what was that phrase you used? Talkin' about how people were brought up?"

"Nature versus nurture," he responded with a smile.

"Yeah! That was it. Hard to know why people turn out the way they do. Was Hannah just an evil person? Or was she like that because of what Betty taught her?"

Everyone listened intently as Jackey posed questions that had no answers. At least, not in this life.

"Hannah wasn't a happy woman. I see that now. You can't go through life with such hate in your heart and be happy. Might make you feel powerful at times. Like the way she enjoyed tryin' to control me. But she was miserable most of the time. For one thing, the man she loved married somebody else."

Looking at Paige again, she said, "I thought a lot about her that day when you were upset and cryin' because you thought Orlando didn't care for you."

Orlando winced, placing his hand on Paige's back. Paige smiled softly at him before turning back to listen to Jackey.

"That must have been how Hannah felt when Frederick married another woman. Thinkin' about that, I can dig down deep and muster up some sympathy for her. Maybe sometimes she took her heartbreak out on me. Mind you, it doesn't excuse it. But it does explain it a little."

"My God, you're so strong, Jackey," Paige said.

Jackey shrugged as if these powerful revelations were no big deal.

"For so long I thought of Hannah as a monster, but she

wasn't. She was mean. She was cruel. She did terrible things. But in the end, she was human. And I can finally forg—"

Jackey's spirit form and her voice began to tremble. "I'm scared to say it. Because if I do, I might …"

"You're not ready to go, are you?" Orlando asked.

"I feel like my heart is torn in two," she cried out in an agonized voice. She jumped up and started pacing. "I want to go. I want to stay. I don't know."

Paige, Orlando, and Anthony all stood, ready to support Jackey in any way they possibly could.

"I don't want to leave you, my dear friends," Jackey said to Paige and Orlando.

"And Anthony, I—" She broke down, sobbing. "But I miss my mama and my daddy. And I'm tired. Oh God, I'm so *tired.*"

Shaking, tears falling, Paige whispered, "I don't know what to do to help her."

Orlando put his arm around her and said tenderly, "Just be her friend."

Anthony looked at Paige and nodded, giving her the strength to pull herself together for Jackey's sake.

He walked over to Jackey and stood by her side. "Jackey darling, everything's going to be all right now."

She gazed at him hopefully.

"I remember when my grandfather passed away in the hospital. We got the call that he didn't have much time, so we all rushed to go see him before it was too late."

Just like Anthony had called Paige and Orlando tonight. The finality of that thought crashed into her. They were really saying goodbye.

"My grandad held on for us. Kept holding on while we were there. It was only after my grandmother leaned down to his hospital bed, kissed him, and told him it was okay to let go that he finally passed. Jackey, it's okay to let go."

Paige covered her mouth, stifling a sob. Orlando gripped her tighter.

"Go, my love. Go to your rest."

Then Anthony began to sing to her. A lovely, haunting melody that sounded like the spirituals Paige had heard while visiting the exhibit on slavery.

"Sit down servant, sit down. Sit down servant, sit down."

Anthony beckoned Paige and Orlando as he sang, and they walked over. The three of them formed a circle around Jackey as Anthony sang.

"Sit and rest a little while. Sit down servant, sit down. I know you're mighty tired. Sit down servant, sit down."

Paige's tears flowed silently as Jackey's sobs began to ebb.

Anthony finished his stirring rendition of the powerful song.

"Whether you are in this world or the next," he said. "I want you to remember that this circle of love surrounds you. Always."

Jackey gazed into his eyes and nodded.

Turning to Paige and Orlando, she said, "Thank you so much for rushin' down here in the middle of the night. I'm so grateful I got to see you before ... You two go on home now, and get yourself warm and get some sleep."

Paige knew Jackey needed a private farewell with Anthony, and she understood.

Placing her hand near her ghostly heart, she said, "Know that I will always love you."

Paige nodded, fresh tears falling. Orlando blew Jackey a kiss, and she could see the pain in his eyes. It nearly broke her.

"Thank you both," Jackey said. "For everything. Until we meet again, my friends."

33

———

"That was lovely," Jackey said to Anthony. "Thank you for makin' this easier for me."

He smiled at her. "The hard part is over now, Jackey. It really is."

It didn't feel that way. She began to cry softly.

"Darling, remember. It's only goodbye for now. I know you're hurting, but where you're going there will be no more pain. I truly believe that. All you have to do is let go, and let God do the rest."

Gazing into his eyes, Jackey was unable to find the words to express her love. Yet, she understood there was no need for words. His heart knew what was in hers, and that was all that mattered.

A sudden, strange sensation overcame her.

"I need to ... I'm supposed to ..."

"What?" he asked.

"The backyard. Where I drew my last breath. I'm supposed to go there."

As if drawn by an unseen force, Jackey drifted through the house and out the locked back door, leaving Anthony to race out the front door and run behind the house to be with her.

Barely aware of Anthony's presence, she closed her eyes as she stood in the backyard. A tidal wave of love, peace, and forgiveness flooded over her as if washing away the pain and suffering of the past. It was gone, just like that. She had intended to say the words *I choose to forgive* aloud, but she found it unnecessary. The Almighty knew what was in her heart and knew she had forgiven those who had sinned against her.

Jackey opened her eyes to find three people standing before her.

"Mama! Papa!" She wasn't sure if she had actually said the words out loud or if they had exploded silently from her heart. It didn't matter. The words had been heard.

She felt as if her heart and soul were glowing. Strangely, she didn't feel the urge to run into the arms of her parents, although she had longed for physical touch all the time she'd been dead. So often, she'd wished she could hug Paige and kiss Anthony. Now, it was as if she had transcended the need to touch. Standing with her parents right in front of her, she felt the warmth of their love wrap around her in ways she couldn't have experienced, even if they were holding her in their arms.

"You've done so well, baby," her mother said out loud, though it was unnecessary to speak.

Anthony gasped, and Jackey understood that her mother spoke for his benefit. He couldn't understand the language of Heavenly love yet.

"Thank you, Mama," she said, basking in the glory of love emanating from her parents.

Then her mother did communicate a message silently to her.

"Yes!" Jackey said in response.

Walking toward the other man who had appeared with her parents, Jackey greeted him silently with her heart and he did the same. Then she turned around and beckoned to Anthony. On shaky legs, he walked over.

"Anthony, I would like you to meet John Harris."

Anthony's mouth dropped open. Jackey could feel the amusement and love from her parents and from John as they enjoyed surprising Anthony this way.

"You've done me proud, Anthony," John said. "You've done all of us proud with the work you've done here."

"Thank you, sir," he said, still awed by his presence.

"Thank *you*," John said in that familiar, friendly voice Jackey had loved so dearly in life.

And with that, it was time to go.

Jackey had never felt so light and carefree in all of her existence. The huge weight of trauma and anger and suffering was gone, just like that. Her mental, physical, and emotional exhaustion had simply vanished. She felt renewed and energized in a way she hadn't ever felt in life.

For the first time, she knew what it was like to be a free woman.

Her mother's heart spoke silently to her again. This time it was a question.

A choice.

Jackey was suddenly overwhelmed with the knowledge that Rebekah's situation wasn't as rare as she had thought. People came back from the dead more frequently than anyone could imagine. Rebekah had had no choice to come back. There were life lessons she still needed to complete.

Jackey had finished her life lessons and could go home. She had the choice to go to her eternal reward or remain on Earth as a living woman.

Silently, her papa reassured her she would never be an earthbound spirit again. Should she choose to live again, when she eventually died a second time, her spirit would immediately be at peace. Forever.

It felt as if a fire had been lit inside of her.

She wasn't done. Oh, hell no. She was just beginning.

Jackey's heart ached to remain with sweet Anthony, her soulmate. She wanted to laugh and gossip with Paige again, and she wanted to flirt shamelessly with Orlando.

But even more than that, she wanted to use her newfound freedom to change the world.

Oh, she wanted to live again.

And this time she was going to do it on her terms.

Look out, world. Jackey is BACK.

34

After Jackey's heart finished speaking words of love and "goodbye for now" messages to her mama, papa, and John, the three Heavenly visitors disappeared. Standing in the yard where she had lived, died, and then returned once again, Jackey's body began to register the bitter cold of the winter air.

Shivering, she wrapped her arms around herself.

"Jackey!" Anthony rushed to her side. "What ... Why?"

"It's all right, darlin'," she said with a warm smile. "Everythin' is just fine now."

"What happened?"

"I was given a choice to go or to stay. I chose to stay."

Sadness and worry lined his face. "Oh, Jackey. I hope I didn't—"

"No, no. It wasn't you. I mean, it *was* you, but not *only* you. I want to be with you, Anthony, but I also realized I want to live again. I didn't think that was what I wanted, but it is. It really is!" Another surge of renewed energy coursed through her veins. She shook with excitement. Her emotions now had a physical part to them again, and that would take some getting used to. "I'm so excited, Anthony! I'm back and I'm alive and I'm *free*!"

Anthony stood, dazed, for a moment.

"Well, what are you waitin' for? Kiss me, you idiot!"

"Oh, right. Y—yes. Of course."

It amused her to see him so flustered. He was usually the calm, cool one who had all the answers.

Anthony wrapped his arms around her and pulled her close to him.

"I thought I was gonna lose you," he whispered.

Resting her head on his shoulder, she relished the warmth and love and comfort of his gentle touch. It was the first physical human contact she'd had in centuries.

"Well, you're stuck with me now," she said.

"Thank God," he said. "Thank *God.*"

Jackey lifted her head to face him, and he caressed her cheek. He kissed her softly, yet urgently. His loving, tender touch overwhelmed her in every way. Body, soul, mind, and heart. Tears streamed from her eyes.

"Are you all right?" he asked, gently wiping her tears with his thumb.

"First time 'round, I wouldn't let myself fall in love with any man. Too risky."

Anthony nodded in understanding.

"That, and I never knew a man who was dear as you before. Not in more than two hundred years. I love you so much, Anthony. I couldn't have made it this far without you."

"I love you too. I've never known a woman as strong and beautiful as you. You made it, baby. You made it."

Drawing in a breath of cool air, she said, "I did, didn't I?

It all feels so strange. To be alive. Breathin'. To feel cold. Even stranger than being alive again is that ... It's so hard to grasp that I'm really free. I've *never* been free. Trapped here after death after livin' my whole life havin' people tell me what to do. I feel a bit lost."

It was a daunting prospect, not only living all over again but doing it in a completely different way than the first time.

"If it helps, I can order you around."

Eyes flashing, Jackey said, "You go on and try it. See what happens."

Anthony laughed heartily. "You're gonna be just fine, Jackey."

Confidence sparkled in his eyes, and the feeling was contagious. He was right. She would be just fine.

"You're a survivor. After what you've been through, you can do just about anything."

Anthony took off his coat and wrapped it around her the same way Orlando always did for Paige. It was romantic, chivalrous. It made her feel like a lady.

"Come on," he said. "Let's get you home."

Anthony took the next three days off from work to help Jackey get acclimated to life again. She felt terrible about not telling Paige and Orlando straight away that she was back, but she had plans to surprise them. The next time they saw her, she would no longer look like an enslaved woman.

She would look like herself.

Anthony pampered her endlessly with new clothes, a new hairstyle, new everything. Having spent years watching beautiful Black women walk through the historical district, Jackey already had a clear vision in mind of how she wanted to look—: to keep her hair natural, with only minimal styling to keep her curls looking nice. Her hair had been covered up for so long, she hardly remembered what it looked like.

Everything made her cry these days, but in the most wonderful way. Anthony took her to a salon filled with photographs of gorgeous Black women on the walls, their hair styled every which way. Jackey couldn't help tearing up. She could never have envisioned a place like this in her wildest fantasies. What a gift it was to be alive in this day and age. Things were far from perfect, but vastly improved from the first time she'd been alive.

Anthony took her to get her nails done and even got her ears pierced so she could wear the dangling earrings she'd always longed for. He bought her lovely colorful outfits and several pairs of shoes. She felt bad that he had to spend so much money on her, but he assured her he was happy to do it. It all felt so decadent, but Anthony seemed to genuinely enjoy spoiling her.

He took his time with her, making sure she didn't get overwhelmed with too much newness at once. Lots of choices, many things to do, and many things she still didn't know. He had to teach her how to use the shower, how to use a modern oven and microwave, and how to wash clothes. Everything was so scary and yet so easy compared to her day. There was a lot to think about, and Anthony had to remind her to take everything one step at a time. One moment she was excited and the next moment she would panic, like when she realized she had no idea how to use modern female products to deal with her monthlies. Rather than acting squeamish as he might have, Anthony told her Paige would surely be happy to help her.

Where she was excitable, he was calm. They were good together like that.

Anthony didn't say a word about having sex with her, but she knew he wanted to. His perfect, gorgeous body betrayed his arousal whenever she got close to him. She relished being desired by the man she loved. Jackey was just as eager to make love, but she had a very specific idea on how that was to happen.

"I CANNOT BELIEVE I let you talk me into this," Anthony said, nervously looking around the room.

It was late at night, and he and Jackey were standing in the bedroom of Betty and Peyton Randolph.

"You have to admit," she said seductively, "it's just too perfect. And we said they would roll in their graves just knowin' we were sittin' in their parlor."

Jackey threw her head back and laughed devilishly, and Anthony tried his best to suppress a smile.

"You love this idea, and you know it," she said.

"It does add an element of danger and excitement," he admitted.

"I can see your *excitement* from here," Jackey said, eying the impressive bulge in the front of his pants.

Sex was such a distant memory, she could barely remember what it felt like. She could hardly wait for Anthony to remind her.

"We can't get too out of hand," Anthony said apprehensively. "The bed's not an original, of course, but I'm not sure how sturdy it is. If we break it, it'll come out of my paycheck."

"No promises," she said in a husky voice.

The hunger in his eyes told her he no longer cared if they broke the damn bed.

Jackey stood in the bedroom, pulse pounding, feeling more powerful and in control than she ever had in her long existence. Now that the spell had been broken, she could be as angry as she damn well pleased.

Eyes flashing, pulse racing, Jackey wanted nothing more than to defile the bedroom with sheer defiance. Taking charge, she strutted over to the bed and plopped down on it. She whipped off her blouse and bra and sat, breasts exposed, leaving Anthony no choice but to have sex with her now or explode with painful, pent-up desire.

He charged toward her with a growl in his throat. One hand on her bare breast and the other behind her head, he kissed her passionately. She quickly relieved him of his shirt, and Anthony got rid of his pants and underwear himself and in record time. Jackey lay back on the bed, giving him access to the rest of her clothes so he could make short work of them.

Straddling her, his eyes flashing desire so intense it was almost dangerous, Anthony gritted his teeth and said, "I need you."

Her own desire was extreme, bordering on madness, but she needed something even more than sexual relief.

Control.

Jackey pushed against his huge, masculine chest with her palms. "On your back. I need you on your back."

Anthony seemed perplexed for a moment but did as he was told. Gripping her shoulders, he rolled over and pulled her on top of him. The bed groaned precariously. It was uncomfortable compared to Anthony's bed, which they'd only slept in at home, yet better than anything she'd rested her head on in life.

Fresh rage surged in her, recalling all the years she'd spent down below in the slave quarters while Betty and Peyton rested in luxurious comfort up in this very bedroom.

Sitting astride him, Jackey lifted herself up, easing Anthony's manhood inside her. He let out the most delicious, masculine groan as she cried out with both pleasure and the high of being utterly in control. Closing her eyes, she rode him, lost in utterly physical delight.

In her rage, Jackey found herself wishing Betty were alive to see this. The look of horror on her face would be too satisfying for words.

She looked down into Anthony's perfect, sweet, loving brown eyes and the realization of what she was doing struck her full force.

Revenge sex. That's what this is. My first time being intimate with the man I love, and I'm turnin' it into something angry and vindictive.

Tears sprung to her eyes, and she slowed the motion of her hips.

She was horrified. How could she have thought of having sex with Anthony as an act of defilement. She loved him far too much to use him like that. And she respected herself too much for that.

"Darling, what's the matter?" Anthony asked, gazing at her with concern.

"I don't want to be angry no more," she said softly.

Jackey lifted herself off him and lay down on the bed.

"Anthony, I need you so much," she said. "Make love to me."

Relief washed over his face, and he bent to kiss her.

Jackey had no regrets about having sex in this room, but she'd been going about it all wrong. She wasn't going to fill this space with revenge and anger and hate. Without letting go of control, she was choosing to take this room of hate and oppression and fill it with love and light and pleasure and joy.

Anthony and Jackey were not defiling this room. They were *sanctifying* it.

She let out a cry of delight as Anthony slid inside her. He groaned in her ear as he began to move, filling their bodies and souls with love and delicious pleasure. The bed squeaked with the sweet rhythm of their joining, slow at first, then gaining speed and intensity.

He reached down between her legs and stroked her most intimate spot. She gripped the back of his head as he pleasured her with his fingers. He quickly found the perfect rhythm of motion to bring her to the brink of ecstasy. She let her head fall back, her mouth open wide, as her orgasm soon took hold. In that perfect moment, her body quaking with sexual gratification and her arms wrapped tight around the man she loved, there was nothing left in the world but the two of them. Crying out, she rode wave after wave of sheer sexual and emotional bliss.

Having thoroughly satisfied her, Anthony began pounding into her over and over and over until he found his own release. Only after he had spent his seed inside her did she realize they had used no birth control.

The thought caused her no worry, however. Assuming her body was as it had been in her first life, she was barren, in all likelihood. Even if she wasn't, bearing Anthony's child might not be so terrible. As an enslaved woman, she hadn't wanted children. As a free woman? She wasn't sure.

Going forward, though, they would need to use protection. At least until they figured out their future plans.

Groaning with relief, Anthony rolled off Jackey and settled down next to her in the bed that was too small for them.

"I've been dying to make love to you pretty much since the day we met," he said, panting heavily. "Can't believe I finally got the chance."

"You are one hell of a lover, Anthony Alick," Jackey said, enjoying the afterglow of complete sexual satisfaction. "And we didn't even break the bed."

Anthony chuckled.

Jackey stared up at the ceiling for a moment and then glanced around the room.

"I want this to be the last time I ever set foot in this house. I want this perfect moment to be my last memory here."

"I love that," he said gently. "And I love you."

"I love you too." She took a deep breath and let it out. "I'm not angry anymore. At least, I'm not angry right this minute. I'm sure I will be again. There will be days ..."

"Sure there will be bad days. Days when you have flashbacks of what happened. There will be moments where you get totally pissed off, and that's okay and normal, and that's the way it should be," he told her, tenderly stroking her hair. "Like I told you, you need that anger to fight for change, but you can't let your anger get the best of you. You are more than your anger, Jackey. You are more than what happened to you. You are a survivor."

"Thank you," she said, pulling him close for a kiss. She never dreamed she would ever meet someone who truly understood her struggles the way he did. "I want to go home."

"Then I want to take you home." He climbed out of bed and they helped each other get dressed.

Once they were ready to go, they stood in the doorway of the Randolph bedroom.

Softly, he said, "Forgive. Forgive and *remember*."

Jackey nodded.

After taking one last look, she grasped Anthony's hand as she walked out of the Peyton Randolph House, knowing she would never return.

35

Paige held hands with Orlando as they walked down Duke of Gloucester Street. They had just finished lunch and were chatting as snow flurries drifted down around them, making the historical district picturesque.

Their relationship had been progressing wonderfully. And quickly. She was learning how to speak fluent "Orlando," understanding that just because he wasn't speaking up about something didn't mean he wasn't overthinking things like she did. Paige had learned to simply ask him what was on his mind, and it didn't take long for him to open up. Best of all, they were already making *forever* plans, talking about moving to Los Angeles after she graduated. Since they both dreamed of careers in the film and/or television business, the move made sense.

Currently, Orlando was telling her about his preparation for a local audition, and he sounded quite excited. She smiled, enjoying his enthusiasm and hoping he would get the part.

Paige's eye seized on something in the distance. A

woman. A beautiful Black woman whose stride was unmistakably familiar.

"Are you even listening to me, dear?" he asked, amusement in his voice.

"No," she whispered honestly, staring straight ahead. Orlando turned to follow her gaze.

"Oh my God," he said. "It can't be."

Paige broke into a run toward the woman. The hope that had bloomed in Paige's heart burst into full-fledged joy when she heard Jackey's laughter. She would have known that sound anywhere.

She stopped short when she reached her, hardly believing what she was seeing. Jackey held out her hands dramatically as if to say *Ta-Da!* as she showed off her new look.

Her hair was styled beautifully, highlighting either her natural curls or a perm. She wore dangling earrings, and her nails were professionally painted the way she always said she wanted. Her clothes burst with color, with a flowing green blouse and snazzy scarf. Jackey wore no coat, probably to show off her new look better.

Paige's mind still struggled to process what she was seeing. Jackey *needed* a coat now because she was probably cold ... Because she was *alive.*

"Oh my God," Paige cried.

"I know," Jackey shouted.

Paige flung her arms around her dear friend, hugging her tightly. Jackey's embrace was warm and firm and *real.* Jackey even *smelled* divine. She could only assume Anthony must have bankrolled this makeover, and it made Paige smile to think how happy that must have made him. To be able to pamper his girl like that.

Finally letting go, Paige asked, "Jackey, what happened? I thought you crossed over."

"I know. I'm sorry I didn't tell you right away, but I swore Anthony to secrecy."

"You're still here," Paige said, her voice tinged with sadness. "Is that okay? Is this what you wanted?"

"Yes. Don't you worry, Paige. Comin' back, it was all up to me. I saw my mama and papa," she said, eyes glowing with joy.

Paige gasped, knowing how much that must have meant to her.

"It was wonderful to see them again. They told me they loved me, and they told me I could go or I could stay. It was my choice. And they promised me I would never be a ghost again." Glancing around to make sure no one else was listening, she said, "The next time I die, I get a one-way ticket to Heaven." She laughed joyously. "I decided I wasn't done yet. I chose to live again. As a free woman this time."

"That's incredible," Paige said. Relief swept through her entire body. She had never seen Jackey so happy. "Anthony must be so excited!"

"I'll say," Orlando said approvingly, eying Jackey up and down.

Jackey grinned at him. He opened his arms wide, and she ran into them. Orlando swallowed hard and closed his eyes as they embraced. Watching him, Paige could feel how much he had missed Jackey. He might have trouble expressing his emotions sometimes, but that didn't mean he didn't feel things deeply.

Before Jackey let go of him, she reached behind him and grabbed his ass.

"Oh *baby*," Orlando said. "Do that again."

Laughing, Jackey obliged. Orlando squeezed her once

more and then let her go. He stood back and looked her up and down again. "So, did you let Anthony hit that or what?"

Paige laughed. Had it been anyone else, the question might have been inappropriate. But this was *Jackey*.

"Now what do you think?" she said.

"Lucky bastard," Orlando muttered.

Eyes wide, Paige said to Jackey, "We have *so* much to talk about."

"Shall I get lost, ladies?"

"Would you?" Paige asked, batting her eyes at him.

Orlando smiled. "I gotta get back to work anyway. I'll let you two gossip in peace."

He turned back to Jackey and pulled her into another hug.

"I love you, lady," he said quietly. "You know that, right?"

"I love you too, honey," she said, holding him close.

Releasing Jackey so he could face her, he said, "Anything you need, you just ask. Okay?"

"Thank you," she said warmly.

"Don't forget, Rebekah can help too. Nobody knows better about what you're dealing with, you know. Coming back like this."

"You're right! I'll go talk to her soon."

"Welcome back," Orlando said, gazing at her with fondness.

As he turned to go, she pinched his ass once more for good measure.

"Oh, *baby*," he said, wiggling his butt as he walked away.

Paige turned back to Jackey. "This is so strange. We can go anywhere together now. Come on. I'll buy you a cup of coffee and we can catch up."

"I'd like that," Jackey said, her lovely brown eyes tearing up. "I'd like that very much."

36

---

ive years later

    Kendrick Banner often knew when ghosts were nearby. She could usually feel the weight of their presence in the air around her. An avid ghost hunter, spirits didn't scare her. Though she sensed ghosts all over the Colonial Williamsburg historical district, she had never felt any spiritual presence here at her workplace.

Until a moment ago.

Kendrick worked as a part-time cashier at Milligan's Wine and Cheese Shop, a store located in the modern shopping area just outside of the historical district. It was late afternoon on a Sunday, and the small shop had only one customer inside. The attractive Black woman was clearly alive and well, considering she was physically picking up specialty spice bottles and adding them to her plastic shopping basket. And yet, Kendrick had the strangest feeling there was an otherworldly spirit close by. She walked over to the back wall of spices and condiments to get closer to the woman, pretending to straighten out the hot sauce bottles. The feeling grew stronger.

How odd.

Goosebumps prickled Kendrick's skin and the vibe of death grew stronger still. She'd only ever experienced this type of sensation late at night when visiting buildings that were reputed to be haunted, or on battlefields where many people had died. Had she been on one of her ghost-hunting adventures, she would have pulled out her thermal imaging camera to check the air temperature, to try to confirm the presence of a spirit. Every time she'd gotten the feeling there was an entity nearby, her camera seemed to confirm it by detecting a cold spot in the air. However, despite spending endless hours tracking down ghosts, she had yet to actually see one.

The door swung open and a few more customers came in. With more people nearby, that odd feeling of death in the air faded a bit. But it was still there.

"Kendrick!" Her coworker Sallie emerged from the back room and called her to the register, indicating that a customer was ready to check out.

"Sorry," Kendrick said, rushing over to ring up one of her favorite customers. She smiled at the woman, who had light brown hair and pretty blue eyes. Though she came in at least once a week, Kendrick didn't know the woman's name. She always used a company credit card. Kendrick just thought of her as Sweet Lady.

"You okay?" Sweet Lady asked, noticing she was distracted.

"Oh yeah. I'm fine," she said with a glance over at the Black woman. "It's just ... That lady looks familiar, but I can't place her."

Kendrick figured the small lie would at least explain why she was staring at a stranger.

"I don't know her personally," Sweet Lady said. "But I know who she is."

"You do?"

"Yeah. She's a local artist. She's done some stunning work. Drawings of the enslaved people in Colonial Williamsburg. You can get prints of her work in some of the shops around here, but I've been thinking about saving up to get an original. I am totally blanking on her name, though. Jamie something? Jacqueline, maybe?"

Kendrick nodded.

"Anyway, you've probably seen her around here."

"That must be it," she said.

Perhaps, but that still didn't explain why she got the essence of a dead person sensation from her.

After ringing up Sweet Lady's usual purchase of Brie, Irish cheddar, crackers, sourdough bread, and garlic olive oil, she stepped aside. The Black lady was next in line.

The vibe of death was a strong as ever with the woman standing in front of her. Sweet Lady almost got her name right. According to her credit card, she was Jackey Alick. She had a warm smile and a keen fashion sense, judging by her pretty nails and colorful outfit. She even looked like an artist.

Dead people can't draw. And they don't eat cheese.

Kendrick shook her head slightly as she watched the artist woman open the door and walk out. She was usually sure of herself when it came to sensing spirits, but the encounter with Jackey made her question herself. Did this mean her senses were wrong when she thought a ghost was present?

Feeling unsettled after the weird encounter, Kendrick decided tonight would be a good time to go ghost hunting. It wasn't just that she found haunted locations fascinating, she had a deep need to believe there was something beyond the earthly existence.

It was time to pay another visit to the Yorktown battlefield.

SILAS MURPHY DRIFTED INVISIBLY through the battlefield where he had drawn his last breath more than two hundred years ago. The historic park grounds closed hours ago at dusk, so there was no one around. No one living, anyway.

At least that's what he had assumed.

He heard footsteps crunching in the dry grass. Ghosts never bothered making noise when there was nobody alive nearby to haunt. If a spirit was heard, it was because he or she wanted to be heard.

Whoever was out there switched on an electric lantern. Silas floated over to see the person.

He was pleasantly surprised to see a lovely young woman with reddish-blonde hair. He watched with amusement as she set up all kinds of new-fangled ghost-hunting equipment. He chuckled, knowing all that junk was unnecessary to have a ghostly encounter.

The woman couldn't have heard his laughter because he was still invisible, but she sure did sense his presence. Lifting her head, her light blue eyes opened wide as she froze in place.

He hoped he hadn't scared her. Lots of people tried hard to search for ghosts, but they could get pretty upset once they finally found one.

"There's someone here, isn't there?" the pretty girl asked. Silas didn't hear a trace of fear in her voice. Instead, he heard curiosity. And hope.

He could see that the lovely young woman truly wanted a ghostly encounter, and it wouldn't be right to disappoint her.

Silas grinned, and then he faded into view.

CHECK out the third and final installment of The Williamsburg Ghost series – ETERNAL GLORY!

SERIES ORDER

The Gettysburg Ghost Series

Somebody's Darling
Darling Soldiers
Forever, Darling

The Williamsburg Ghost Series

Eternal Love
Eternal Hope
Eternal Glory